THE
NOWHERE
GIRLS

BOOKS BY DANA PERRY

JESSIE TUCKER MYSTERY SERIES
The Silent Victim
The Golden Girl

DETECTIVE ABBY PEARCE SERIES
Her Ocean Grave
Silent Island

DETECTIVE NIKKI CASSIDY BOOK 1

THE NOWHERE GIRLS

DANA PERRY

bookouture

Published by Bookouture in 2024

An imprint of Storyfire Ltd.
Carmelite House
50 Victoria Embankment
London EC4Y 0DZ

www.bookouture.com

ISBN: 978-1-80314-794-9
eBook ISBN: 978-1-80314-793-2

PROLOGUE

I still dream about her, even after all these years.

She is always frozen in time—her face perpetually that of a twelve-year-old—in the dreams.

Watching me as I board the ride at the carnival.

Smiling at me.

Looking so full of life.

My little sister.

In the dream, she is still there when I get off the ride a few minutes later. I run to her, and I hug her, and I tell her never to disappear on me like that again. She laughs, that infectious laugh I still remember so well, and promises me she'll always be there for me. I squeeze her tightly and think about how glad I am to have her back. I'll never lose her again. We'll be together forever.

But it never happens that way.

Not in the dream.

Or in real life.

And, when I wake up from the dream, she is still gone...

ONE

A cheer went up in the FBI office.

My face was on the TV screen hanging from a wall. Another interview on how I broke the Mattheu case. Below my face, a crawl moved across the screen identifying me as: "Nikki Cassidy, the star FBI agent who rescued Julie Mattheu and delivered a dramatic message to her kidnapper!"

I stood up from my desk and acknowledged the applause from everyone, holding up a bottle of seltzer water in a mock salute.

"Thank you, thank you," I said. "It was nothing really. Any dogged, determined, brilliant FBI investigator cut from the same cloth as J. Edgar Hoover like I am could have done it."

Alex Del Vecchio, the woman agent sitting at the next desk, leaned over to me as I sat down. Alex was dark-haired, Italian—about the same age as me in her thirties. Alex and I had worked a number of cases together, and we'd become friends as well as partners.

"J. Edgar Hoover?" she asked.

"Too much?"

"I can't believe that you're actually comparing yourself to J. Edgar Hoover, Nikki."

"Why not?"

"History has shown us that J. Edgar Hoover was a pretty mean, petty and despicable person."

"Yeah, but we both liked to wear dresses."

I'm riding pretty high in my career at the FBI right now. I was doing well before the Mattheu case, but that one really pushed me over the top and put me on everyone's radar. Of course, that's not the reason why I did what I did. I did it because I was determined to find Julie Mattheu.

Julie is a thirteen-year-old girl who disappeared from her school in a suburb of Denver four months earlier. One minute she was walking down the hall to class, the next she was gone. After weeks of futile searching by police, my unit—the Crimes Against Children Squad of the FBI—was called in to assist the local authorities.

I spent long hours interviewing everyone who knew Julie Mattheu—her family, her friends, teachers and others at her school, even her minister where she went to Sunday school every week. It was all a dead end. Everyone just assumed the girl had been abducted and murdered, and that her remains would be found. Everyone except me.

I operated on the theory that Julie was still alive, and I had to save her. Finally, after days of interviews and record checking and knocking on doors, I discovered that a school employee—a janitor—had quit his job not long before Julie's disappearance. That was why I'd never talked to him when I was interviewing school personnel. Then, when I went to his home, I learned he had moved away from there too.

I'm still not sure if that was the red flag that motivated me to find him. Or that I had no other potential leads, so I chased this one because there was no other choice. But I eventually tracked him down to a small town in Oregon where he had moved.

The minute he opened his door, I knew he was the one. Maybe it was the look of shock on his face when I showed him my FBI credentials, maybe it was his nervousness in talking to me, maybe it was the way he kept looking around the house like he had something to hide. I got a search warrant, and that's when I found Julie Mattheu. He'd kept her chained up in a small, locked room off the basement. She was scared, she was emaciated, but she was alive.

That by itself would have probably been enough to get me a lot of media attention.

But then something else happened.

Just before we found Julie Mattheu in the basement and arrested him, the guy made a break for it. He knew we'd find her downstairs, so he broke away from the officer that was guarding him. He ran out the front door, but I was right behind him. I chased him down, got him on the ground and pinned him there while I cuffed him and read him his rights.

But I did a bit more than that too. I launched into a tirade against him. Promising him he'd never have another day of freedom in his life.

Of course, someone watching the whole thing had a cell phone and got it all on video.

That video quickly went viral with millions of hits on YouTube and Instagram and all the rest of social media. Usually, that kind of viral video is bad for a law enforcement officer. But this time the opposite happened, and public sentiment was overwhelmingly on my side. I was a hero. And, even more importantly, I'd saved a young girl's life.

On the personal front, I'm in a relationship these days. A real relationship. The most serious relationship of my life. His name is Greg Ellroy, and he's an attorney with a prominent Washington, D.C. law firm.

I met Greg about six months ago. It was a totally chance encounter. I was standing in line at a Starbucks next to the FBI offices to get my usual black coffee, which I needed to get started every morning.

Except when I took the lid off the cup I'd gotten, it wasn't black coffee. It had whipped cream and specks of green and other stuff I didn't recognize.

"Are you looking for a black coffee?" I heard a voice behind me say.

I turned around and saw a guy—good-looking, well dressed, smiling—next to me.

"I am."

"I'm looking for a peppermint mocha."

"I have no idea what a peppermint mocha even looks like."

"I do, and this is not it." He showed me a cup of black coffee. "I think we got each other's orders by mistake."

"So I guess we should exchange our drinks…"

"Not so fast. Not without some negotiations first."

"Negotiations?"

"I'm an attorney. I negotiate everything."

"Look, what do I have to do to get my black coffee?"

"Drink it with me." He smiled.

That's how it started. Everything moved very quickly after that. And—a few weeks ago—he popped the question over a candlelit dinner at Bourbon Steak, one of Washington D.C.'s most prestigious restaurants. He proposed, I said yes, he gave me a ring and our wedding is planned for a few months from now in the fall.

So that's me right now. A rising star in the FBI. A media celebrity. Engaged to a successful, charming, loving man.

I guess I should be happy. And I am happy. But sometimes —crazy as it sounds—I wish I could be… well, happier.

I still have the feeling that's there's something missing from my life.

Something I wish I could fix.

Even though I've never been able to.

But life can hit you with unexpected twists—shocking changes that turn your whole world upside down in a few seconds.

And that's what happened to me that day in the FBI offices in Washington as I basked in the glory of my newfound fame.

Suddenly, and without warning, everything changed for me.

"Someone called for you while you were taking your victory laps," Alex Del Vecchio said to me. "A lawyer. Said they represented a client in prison who had information about a murder case. Wants to meet with you in prison to discuss it. Wouldn't tell me anymore—said the prisoner insisted only on talking to you."

"Did the lawyer give you the prisoner's name?"

"Yes, his name was David Munroe."

Alex saw the look of shock on my face.

"Do you know him?" she asked.

"David Munroe is the man who murdered my sister."

TWO

My twelve-year-old sister Caitlin was abducted on July 19th, 2008 exactly fifteen years ago this summer. Her body was found days later in a wooded area of the small town of Huntsdale, Ohio where I had grown up. David Munroe was arrested for the murder and had been in prison ever since.

Every year, on the anniversary of Caitlin's disappearance, I had gone to the Ohio prison where he was being held and attempted to talk to him. I wanted to find out why. Why this person did something like that to horribly change my life—and my family—so completely.

But Munroe would never speak to me.

He just sat there silently.

Staring at me—and ignoring my questions—until the hour-long visit was over.

It was almost July 19th again. I'd already planned to fly to Huntsdale on my day off and try once again to confront Munroe in jail. Even though I was pretty convinced at this point that he was never going to reveal anything to me about what really happened to Caitlin that summer day.

Except now. On the fifteenth anniversary of the day he

abducted and murdered my sister he suddenly had indicated he was ready to do just that.

And all the memories came rushing back for me again...

* * *

I had what I thought was a pretty good life back then during that last summer I spent in Huntsdale.

My father Luke Cassidy was the Huntsdale police chief, which meant everyone looked up to him—and to our family too. I was eighteen years old, had just graduated from high school and was getting ready to head for college. The future looked very bright for me, and for my younger sister Caitlin too.

Until the carnival came to town.

The carnival was a highly anticipated annual summer event in the town of Huntsdale where I grew up. Especially for me and the other young people there. The carnival meant riding the Ferris wheel, the Tilt-A-Whirl and other cool stuff; it meant eating great food like chili dogs and cotton candy and winning prizes at the arcades; and—most of all, for me anyway—it meant meeting boys. There were always a lot of boys at the carnival, and I was an eighteen-year-old girl who loved meeting and hanging out with boys. Yes, boys were a very important thing for me back then.

Which is why I was so upset when my mother told me I couldn't go to the carnival on the first day it opened. My mother said she had places to go that day, and she needed me to stay home to be with my twelve-year-old sister Caitlin until she got back home later that evening.

But all my friends were going to the opening of the carnival, and I so desperately wanted to be there with them.

And so, without telling my mother what I was doing, I took my sister to the carnival with me and all my friends.

It was fine at first.

Caitlin seemed to enjoy being there with me and all the older kids.

Except she was afraid of the rides.

We managed to get her to go on the Ferris wheel with us. That seemed safe enough to her, I guess. But when we got to the Tilt-A-Whirl, she was terrified of it. The Tilt-A-Whirl was actually my favorite ride at the carnival. Scary, exciting, but all in a good way. I tried to convince Caitlin it would be fun, but she adamantly refused.

And so, when me and my friends got on the Tilt-A-Whirl, we left Caitlin standing by the ticket counter to watch us.

Even now, all these years later, I still remember what she looked like that day. Wearing tan slacks, a brown-and-white striped top and a Cincinnati Reds baseball cap. Her long blonde hair hanging down her back. Waving at us for luck. She looked a lot like me—well, a younger version of myself when I was 12— and I still thought about that sometimes when I remembered that day at the carnival. It was the last time I would ever see Caitlin alive. When we got off the ride a few minutes later, she was gone.

There was a frantic search for her that went on for days.

Until it finally ended tragically.

Caitlin's body—she had been shot to death—was found by a dog walker in a wooded area called Grant Woods several miles away.

And, in a horrifyingly macabre touch, the killer had placed a wreath of roses on her head in death.

No one ever understood about the wreath of roses.

Since my father was the police chief in Huntsdale at the time, this meant he had to investigate the murder of his own daughter. It was a terrible ordeal for him. I remember that so well. But he did his job as professionally as he could. That was my father: he was always the consummate professional police chief.

The search for the person who did it focused at first on the people working at the carnival. Many of them were temporary workers and drifters and some had criminal records. So it seemed likely one of them killed my sister. But, despite intense interrogation of anyone and everyone associated with the carnival, none of them were ever linked to her death or even named as a potential suspect.

Instead, the murderer turned out to be a person from the area. David Munroe. He worked as a postal clerk in a town near to Huntsdale. People there said Munroe was known as a loner, a bit strange, but no one ever suspected he'd be capable of murder.

Until Caitlin's death.

The key to catching Munroe turned out to be a parking ticket. Later, his DNA and fingerprints were also found at the crime scene. Even more damning evidence came when strands of Caitlin's hair and pieces of her clothing were found inside Munroe's home, which he'd apparently kept as a sick "souvenir" of her murder.

Munroe was quickly convicted and is now serving a life sentence at a high-security prison called Dagmore outside of Columbus, about seventy-five miles away from Huntsdale. He later admitted to Caitlin's murder in a deal with the prosecution to avoid a death sentence. But despite that admission, Munroe had never talked about why he had killed her or divulged any more details about the murder.

For me, my entire world collapsed the very day Caitlin went missing.

And it was a nightmare that has haunted me ever since.

Especially after my father suddenly died that summer, too. It was just a few weeks after my sister Caitlin's murder that my father suffered a fatal heart attack. Many people—including me, I guess—believed the heart attack came because of the stress of losing a daughter in such a horrifying way.

My mother—without a husband and having lost a daughter —didn't turn to me, her only surviving family member, for support.

Instead, she blamed me for everything, saying it was all because I had taken Caitlin with me to the carnival that day.

She constantly laid the guilt over Caitlin's murder—and my father's subsequent death—on me.

What made it even worse was that I was already struggling to deal with my own guilt over what I did. I so badly wanted my mother's love and emotional support to get me through those terrible times. But instead she just made everything worse for me—and still does even after all this time.

My relationship with my mother had always been a bit complicated. I loved my father, and he loved me back unconditionally. On the other hand, my mother and me... well, we had some problems. Especially as I got older and began going through all the teenage trauma that a girl goes through. My mother wasn't much help to me there. So our relationship was never great, even before Caitlin died.

But after Caitlin was gone and my mother was forced to deal with that reality, well, that's when things truly fell apart between us.

We haven't talked in a long time.

I knew back then that I had to get away as quickly as possible. In a small town like Huntsdale, everyone knew everyone else's business. Everyone knew me as the girl who took her sister to the carnival where she got abducted and killed. I desperately wanted to go someplace where people didn't look at me like that and judge me.

Which is what I did. Going away to college first, then joining the FBI in Washington and eventually specializing with the bureau in rescuing missing children.

I couldn't save my own sister.

It was too late for that.

But I could save other children like her from the same fate.

Even now, after all this time, I hardly ever go back. Whenever I do, I feel trapped and uncomfortable and out of place. I never stay for very long. I always rush back to Washington as quickly as I can to escape the nightmares from my past that still haunt me back when I'm in my hometown.

Except I still could never put the memories of my sister behind me. That's why every year, on the anniversary of her abduction from the carnival, I've returned to Ohio and attempted to talk to David Munroe in the prison there. Looking for some answers from this man. Looking for some kind of closure for Caitlin.

But that has never happened.

Every year that I went there to visit him, Munroe just sat there silently and refused to reveal anything.

Until now.

Now Munroe suddenly wanted to talk to me about Caitlin's murder.

And I had to find out why.

THREE

"I want to go to Ohio," I said to Les Polk, the head of the Crimes Against Children Squad and my boss at the FBI.

"What's in Ohio?"

I told him about my sister and David Munroe and the call I'd received from Munroe's lawyer.

Polk didn't look happy about my request. I didn't expect him to be happy.

"It's not appropriate for me to assign you to a case that you have such a personal involvement in, Nikki," Polk said, shaking his head after he heard all this from me. "It's not ethical. It could be a conflict of interest for a law enforcement officer to do something like this."

"If you won't let me do it, I'll take vacation time—I have a lot of it, you know—and do it on my own. But I'd rather do this officially. As an agent for the FBI. That could help me open up a lot of doors with local law enforcement when I get there."

"I don't know—"

"Look, you owe me for all the positive publicity I just got for the FBI with the Mattheu case arrest."

"That arrest could have gone either way," he said, referring to the viral video. "You could have been the next example of police brutality instead of a hero. You got lucky with all the media adoration that followed. You know that as well as I do."

"But it worked out great for us."

"C'mon, Nikki, you're a hell of an agent, but you're also a loose cannon out there sometimes. Especially on a case like this where you have so much personal emotion involved in it. I just worry about you getting out of control again on something like this. Like you have in the past. And that can cause me a lot of problems."

"When have I gone out of control?"

"Uh, Norm Byers."

"Oh. Yeah, that."

"You kicked a U.S congressman in the balls, Nikki."

"Well, he tried to rape me."

"He said he tried to kiss you. He admits he had too much drink, but he said it never went any further than the kiss."

"I was there."

"Still..."

"Okay, maybe kicking Congressman Byers in the balls was a bit of an overreaction on my part."

"And then there was the time you ignored orders and charged a hostage situation on your own—"

"Listen, I promise not to charge any hostage situations on my own in Ohio, and I won't kick anyone there in the balls. Now can I go to Huntsdale?"

I knew this was going to be a tricky decision for Polk. I waited to hear what he said.

"How long would you have to be there?" Polk asked.

"Just time enough to check in with the local authorities, then go to the jail and meet Munroe."

"So we're talking about a day or so, right?"

"I guess."

"Okay, I'll make a deal with you. You go there for a day. You visit this jail in Ohio and talk to the guy, find out what he wants now after all this time. Then you come back and do the job you're supposed to be doing. One day, that's all, okay? In and out. That's all."

"In and out," I agreed.

Greg Ellroy, my fiancé, wasn't happy with me going there either.

"Why do you have to do this?" he said as we were lying in bed at his Washington, D.C. apartment and I'd told him about my upcoming trip to Ohio. "We've got that big party coming up at my senior partner's house. I really want you to be there. And we still have so much to talk about for our marriage plans and everything else that's going to happen for us in the next few months."

"It's my job," I told him.

"Not really. This isn't your job. From what you tell me, it's a personal thing."

I'd told him about my sister Caitlin and the man in jail for murdering her that I was going to see after I got back to Greg's place. And how I had been going back to try talk with him on every anniversary of Caitlin's disappearance. I hadn't really told him much about my sister or her murder before that. I hadn't talked about it much with anyone. The memories were too powerful.

I felt bad about burdening Greg with all this now though. He was never wild about me being an FBI agent in the first place. "Chasing murderers and kidnappers and child molesters and all sorts of disgusting people all over the country. Is this really what you want to do with your whole life, Nikki?" he said, when we were working on our wedding plans.

Greg belonged to a prestigious D.C. law firm that did mostly corporate work for rich and power people in the Capitol.

I think he was sometimes embarrassed by what I did for a living. Probably got a lot of kidding and disapproval and questions from the people at the law firm when they saw me splashed all over the news handcuffing and arresting a suspect.

Now I was focused on this new David Munroe business.

And going back to my hometown in Ohio—where Caitlin's murder happened—to confront him about it.

After all my repeated trips in the past, that had never yielded any answers for me from David Munroe.

"Why?" he asked. "Why would you keep going back like that over and over to this man all these years, even though he never spoke to you during that entire time?"

It was a reasonable question. I'm not sure how the whole thing started. All I know is that as the first anniversary of Cailin's death approached, I became more and more consumed by the need to get some sort of closure about her. To find answers about what happened to her, and why. The only person who could give me those answers was David Munroe.

"He confessed to killing my sister," I told Greg now. "But he never revealed any details about why he did it or how or anything else. He was never called to testify by the public defender assigned to represent him. He just sat there staring stonily as he listened to the prosecutor's case against him, until the jury came back with the guilty verdict. And that's the exact same thing Munroe did when I went to meet him in prison afterward. Just sat there and stared at me. Never said a word during the entire time I was there, no matter how many times I asked him the questions I desperately wanted answers for."

"But you kept going back? Visiting a man who refused to speak with you at all? That's the part I don't understand, Nikki."

"It became a sort of game. I would show up every year, sit there watching him as he stared back at me while saying nothing at all. At first, I kept asking him questions that got no answers. But at some point I stopped even doing that. And the two of us just sat in silence for the duration of the prison visit.

"For some strange reason, it always reminded me of the early scene between Matt Damon as Will and the psychiatrist played by Robin Williams in the movie *Good Will Hunting*. They simply sit there for an hour session, staring at each other without speaking. It was a test of wills to see who would crack and speak first.

"Munroe didn't have to meet with me all those previous times, of course. He could have simply refused my requests to see him there. I was never sure why he didn't do this. And honestly, Greg, I was never really sure why I did what I did: making the trek to see him in prison every year on the anniversary of my sister's death.

"But I didn't know what else to do. So I kept making these bizarre visits in the hopes that one day this monster would finally talk to me. Now his lawyer says he finally wants to do that. And he'll only talk to me. I have to go. I have to find out what secrets he's been holding onto about Caitlin's death for all this time. Don't you understand that?"

"I'm trying. I'm really trying."

Greg massaged his fingers across the back of my neck as we lay in bed together.

"Feel good?"

"Uh-huh."

"Want me to keep going?"

"Sounds like a plan."

"Are you getting as turned on as I am?"

"Absolutely."

"Let me see if I can make you forget about David Munroe for a little while," he said, his fingers exploring my body as he talked.

I moaned softly.

"I believe I can do it," he said.

"I'll betcha you can, too," I murmured.

And, when the lovemaking started, it really did feel good.

As good as it had ever been for me and Greg.

So good that I almost did forget about David Munroe and all the questions I was going to ask him.

Almost.

When it was over, Greg leaned over and kissed me.

"I love you, Nikki," he said.

That's the bottom line about Greg and me and our relationship: he *does* love me. And I love him. Which is why we're going to get married. At least I think I love him. I know I like him. I like him a lot. But do I really love him? Of course, I do. What am I talking about? Just the usual pre-wedding jitters everyone gets, I'm sure.

"Right back at you, big guy," I said.

Later, after Greg had fallen asleep, I lay there awake for a long time. Finally, I got out of bed and went into the living room. I turned on the TV, making sure I kept the sound low enough so it wouldn't wake up Greg in the bedroom. I watched awhile, but my mind wasn't on what I saw on the screen.

I stood up, walked over to the window in Greg's apartment and looked out at the lights and buildings and historic spots of Washington D.C. out there.

"What exactly do you want out of life, Nikki?" Greg had asked me not long ago during a discussion about our future together.

Sitting there alone during the early hours of the morning, looking out the window of Greg's apartment at all the streets and the buildings and the immenseness of the Capitol, I realized I had no answer for that question yet

And now I was going back to Ohio.

Back to my hometown of Huntsdale and all the memories I had back there.

I'd run a long way and for a long time since then to get away from those memories.

But not far enough to escape them.

FOUR

The Huntsdale police station didn't look like I remembered it when I was growing up there and my father was the chief.

It looked smaller.

And less impressive.

Which was logical, I guess. I mean I was just a little kid running around the place where my father worked, and it all seemed so enormous and exciting and significant in my world then.

Like those reruns of the *Andy Griffith Show* that still run on cable all the time. About Andy Taylor, the sheriff of tiny Mayberry, North Carolina. Andy's son Opie was always hanging out at the station and learning about life from his dad. Well, that was me as a little girl. I was a female Opie Taylor to my father Police Chief Luke Cassidy.

Now I was a successful FBI agent who worked out of the bureau's main headquarters in Washington, D.C. Still, walking into the Huntsdale police station again after all this time away was a strange and uncomfortable experience for me.

It was a few minutes after nine a.m. when I pushed open the door of the station house and went inside. I started to show my FBI credentials to an officer sitting at a desk there. But it turned out I didn't have to.

"It's Nikki Cassidy!" he said.

I looked down at the sign on his desk, which said Officer William Weller.

"You know me?"

"Everyone here knows you." He smiled. "You've been all over TV. Local woman becomes FBI hero. You're the most exciting thing that we've had happen in Huntsdale for a long time. Of course, not too much excitement ever happens in Huntsdale."

He smiled again. It was an infectious kind of smile. Very friendly. He wasn't exactly a handsome guy. But he wasn't bad looking either. Reddish curly hair, about my age, nothing really particularly distinctive about him. Nothing at all memorable, except the fact that he had a helluva nice smile.

"Officer Weller, I—"

"Billy."

"What?"

"Call me Billy. Everyone does."

"Okay, Billy. I have an appointment to meet with Police Chief Frank Earnshaw."

"Right. Chief Earnshaw's right in there," he said, pointing toward an office in the back of the station. "Good luck with him."

"What do you mean?"

"You'll see."

"Thanks."

There's a game you have to play when you're an FBI agent working with local police officers. A dance of sorts, that's what I always think of it as. The dance, the game, was to establish your authority to investigate a case while at the same time deferring—and honoring—the authority of the local authorities.

I'd played the game, I'd done this dance with a lot of police officials during my time at the FBI. I was very good at it. But I found out very quickly that the current Huntsdale Police Chief Frank Earnshaw wasn't interested in being my dance partner on this.

He was a big man, well over six feet and two-hundred pounds, I figured, with close-cropped, short grey hair and a meticulously pressed uniform. He stood up ramrod straight to greet me with a perfunctory handshake, then sat down stiffly again. No, Chief Frank Earnshaw didn't seem friendly, like Billy Weller did outside. He seemed... officious. I had a bad feeling about this guy. I've met a lot of local police officials like Frank Earnshaw.

I told him about my upcoming visit to the prison to see David Munroe. I explained my own background to the murder of Caitlin Cassidy, how she had been my sister and my father was the police chief here who investigated the case—just on the off chance he didn't know. And I said I wanted to examine the Huntsdale Police Department's records of the case before I met with Munroe. I said that I wanted to make sure that I was completely prepared for the jailhouse confrontation.

"I didn't know your father, Luke Cassidy," Earnshaw said. "Your sister's murder and all that was before my time here. But I'm in charge now. I'm the police chief, not your father. And I can't let anyone like you just go looking through our official police records, Cassidy."

"I'm not *anyone*—I'm with the FBI."

"Does the FBI have any jurisdiction here?"

"Jurisdiction? What do you mean?"

"Jurisdiction—the authority to investigate a criminal case without the approval of local authorities."

"I know what jurisdiction means," I snapped.

"Do you have any?"

"Not officially."

"Well, you'll need something official."

"Chief Earnshaw, I was hoping we could work together on this in a more cooperative manner."

"We can. But you've got to go through official channels. You can't just walk in here, flash that badge and look through our files."

"Okay then, how do I do this officially?"

"You need to talk to the District Attorney. The D.A.'s office was the one who prosecuted the case against Munroe. Go to them for what you want."

"Who's the District Attorney?"

"Tommy Thompson.'

That surprised me. Tommy Thompson was the same District Attorney back when my sister died and Munroe was arrested.

"Thompson's still in that office, huh?"

"That's right. Done twenty years as D.A. already. Probably will do another twenty before he's finished. No one ever really challenges him or runs against him. Tommy Thompson is a very popular guy in this town."

"I understand, Chief. But I don't really have time to go through whatever it takes to get official approval from the D.A. to examine the police report. I'm only here for a day to talk with Munroe at Dagmore Prison. Couldn't you just let me take a look at what you have here in your files right now?"

"You'll have to deal with Thompson for permission on this, not me," Earnshaw said.

I sighed and stood up.

"Thanks for all your cooperation, Chief Earnshaw," I told him sarcastically before I left.

But I guess he didn't pick up on the sarcasm.

People like Frank Earnshaw rarely did.

"No problem," he said to me. "That's what I'm here for."

On my way out, I passed by Weller's desk again.

"How'd it go with Chief Earnshaw?" he asked.

"Not well."

"I warned you."

He smiled again. That pissed me off at first. I wanted to be mad at Weller. Just like I was mad at Frank Earnshaw for the way he had treated me. I wanted to be mad at everyone who worked for the damn Huntsdale Police Department. But it was tough to be mad at a guy with a friendly smile like that.

"You don't remember me, do you?" he asked now.

"We've met each other before?"

"I went to high school with you."

He did look kind of familiar. But I couldn't place him.

"Sorry. It's been a long time since high school."

"Oh, I understand. No reason you'd remember me. I wasn't one of the cool people in high school like you were. You never would have hung out with someone like me, Nikki Cassidy."

I didn't know exactly how to respond to that, so I started to leave.

"Hey, do you want to catch up over lunch or dinner or something, Nikki? I can re-introduce myself to you since you don't remember the geeky guy I was in high school. But don't worry, I'm cooler than that now."

He smiled again.

"I'm sorry," I said. "I can't."

"Okay. I thought maybe you deserved a little friendly Huntsdale hospitality after your encounter with Chief Earnshaw."

"The thing is I'm not going to be here very long. Just a day or so. And I have to go to Columbus to interview David Munroe. Maybe we can do it some other time—'

"Sure, the next time you have to come to Huntsdale working on some big FBI case here, right?"

Another smile from Weller.

He wrote his phone number down on a piece of paper and handed it to me. I gave him my cell number too. Even though I didn't expect to ever see or talk with him again.

"I've gotta go," I said to Billy Weller. "Thanks for everything."

FIVE

David Munroe's lawyer—the one I'd talked to on the phone—
was a woman named Doreen Trask.

She was waiting for me in the visitors' area when I entered
the prison. Doreen Trask didn't look much like a lawyer. She
looked more like a crazy bag lady you'd expect to see on the
street. A middle-aged woman with dingy blonde hair, a bit
chunky and dressed in baggy jeans and a T-shirt.

Her greeting to me was a quick one, very perfunctory.
Barely a handshake. I wondered if she was going to make some
request or even demands before she allowed me to talk to him.
But instead she simply kept walking with me to the area where
David Munroe would be brought to meet me.

"I've been here before to see him, you know," I said, mostly
to make some sort of conversation. "He's never talked to me
before."

"He'll talk to you now."

"Will I get an entire hour?"

"It won't take that long. That's what he told me. But he said
whatever he had to say to you now would be well worth your
time. That he can give you the answers—or at least some of the

answers—that you've been looking for."

I nodded. We kept walking. This wasn't exactly what I expected.

"How long have you been with Munroe?" I asked.

"I've been representing him as an attorney for the past few months. But I've been with David for longer than that."

"You knew him before you became his lawyer?"

"Yes."

"You were a friend?"

"I'm his wife," she said.

"His wife," I repeated.

David Munroe had never been married at the time of his trial and conviction.

"We got married while he was in prison. Well, not officially married. But we act together as man and wife. David loves me. And I love him. I'm pregnant with his baby."

I looked down at the loose-fitting top she was wearing. I realized now it hid the baby she was carrying in her stomach. David Munroe's baby.

"They allow conjugal visits with the inmates?"

"Not really."

"Then how...?"

"There's an advantage to being his attorney." She smiled. "It allows us to have some private time together. To talk about legal stuff, but also to do other things. That's how we consummated our marriage."

Damn.

David Munroe sure was full of surprises.

So what surprise did he have in store for me?

David Munroe didn't look the way I remembered him from the last time I was here a year ago. Or the times before that. He'd lost weight, his face was gaunt and the prison uniform hung loosely from his body. I wondered if he was sick. Some sort of bad terminal illness. That would be nice, on one hand. But it also meant I'd have to get his secrets from him quickly before he died.

He walked into the room where we were meeting and sat down in a chair at a table across from me. There was a prison guard accompanying him, but I told the guard to wait outside and close the door.

I wanted this to just be about David Munroe and me.

The guard was concerned if Munroe might try something alone with me in the room. I had checked my gun at the prison entrance before I came in, according to regulations. But I wasn't worried about Munroe hurting me in any way. That wasn't why he'd asked me to come here. For some reason, he'd decided to talk with me at last.

"Thank you for coming to see me," Munroe said now.

"I've come to see you before, and you never thanked me. You wouldn't even speak to me."

"Okay, then thank you for coming to see me this time."

I didn't want to waste any more time on preliminaries. I took out a picture of my sister Caitlin and placed it down on the table between us. It had been taken at her twelfth birthday party a few weeks before her abduction and death. She was smiling at the camera, dressed in a party dress and eating a big piece of chocolate birthday cake.

"She was twelve years old," I said to Munroe, trying my best to somehow keep my emotions under control, despite the fact that I was finally talking to the man responsible for murdering my sister. "She had her whole life in front of her. And you took that way from her. You took that away from all of us. Why? That's what I have to know. Why did you do something like this? And why to her?"

Munroe looked down at the picture of my sister. He didn't react at first. Just stared at it.

"Well? Tell me about what happened to my sister."

He looked back at me now.

"You never should have left your sister alone at the carnival while you went on that ride with your friends."

I sat there stunned. The prison guard had been worried beforehand that David Munroe might do something to hurt me physically. But if Munroe had hit me, he couldn't have hurt me more than he just did with those words. The same words I'd said to myself over and over again so many times over the years.

I wondered if he was trying to bait me, to get me upset and rattled and angry for some reason. Maybe that's the only reason he asked to see me on this anniversary of Caitlin's death. To play these kind of mind games with me.

But, just as soon as he said it, he shook his head and smiled at me. A crazy smile. So crazy that it was almost worse than his original comment.

"Nah, she would have died anyway, Cassidy. She was the target. The target all the way. If it didn't happen at the carnival, it would have happened later. So you shouldn't keep feeling guilty about that. She was going to die sooner or later, no matter what you did or didn't do."

"But why did you pick her to kill?"

"Like I said, she was the target."

"What does that mean?"

"You'll need to find that out on your own, Cassidy."

Dammit! This meeting was the closest I had ever come to thinking I might get some answers from him about Caitlin. Instead, it was just getting me more frustrated. But I knew— from interviewing other prisoners who had committed heinous crimes—that it was important for me to not lose my cool and stay professional, even with someone as evil as David Munroe.

"Why did you ask to meet with me like this today? After all this time. Your lawyer said you had something you wanted to tell me."

"I do."

"Okay, tell me then."

"I have cancer. Stage four cancer of the colon. It's untreatable. So I don't have a long time to live. Maybe three months, the doctors say. Six months at the most."

I didn't say anything.

"The appropriate response is something like 'I'm sorry to hear that.'"

"Not for you it isn't."

"I'm dying, Agent Cassidy."

"I only hope it's an excruciatingly painful death."

"No quality of mercy at all from you here?"

"You killed my sister. You didn't feel sorry for her. Karma is a bitch. Now it's your turn. And, when you're dead, I'll celebrate. For myself and for my dead sister too. But I still want to hear from you what happened—and why? Why did you kill an innocent twelve-year-old girl, Munroe? Why did you kill my sister? Why did you abduct her from that carnival? Why did you leave a wreath of roses on her? Why—"

"I'm trying to put things in order before I leave this planet. I made a lot of mistakes when I was young. I did some bad stuff, I know that now. I wasn't willing to confront that about myself for a long time. So I never talked with you all those other times. But I knew one day I would need to deal with everything I've done in my life and try to make some of it right again.

"That's why I'm with Doreen. She loves me, Cassidy. Crazy, huh? And now she's carrying our child. A part of me will live on after I'm gone. Hopefully that child will be a better person than me. And maybe my child can bring some good into the world to balance out all the evil things I did. That's why I'm talking to you here today about this."

Munroe looked down again at the picture of Caitlin in front of us. The little twelve-year-old girl at the birthday party with so much to live for. The little girl who would die for no discernible reason a few weeks later.

"I didn't kill your sister," Munroe said softly.

"What?"

"That's what I need to tell you. I didn't kill your sister. I wanted you to know that."

"What sort of game are you trying to pull, Munroe? You were convicted for her murder. You gave up all rights for an appeal. Of course, you killed her. And you just told me how she was your goddamned target all the time."

"I was there that day. I was tracking her. I was there when she was abducted. But I didn't kill her. There are more people involved than just me. Find them, and you'll get all the answers about your sister."

"More people involved? Who? Where do I go looking for these people?"

"Nowhere." Munroe laughed. "They're... nowhere."

"What does that mean?"

"That's all I've got to say for now. Maybe later."

Munroe stood up and started to leave. He knocked on the door and called for the guard.

"Wait a minute," I said. "I have more questions for you. A lot more questions."

He was on his way out the door now, headed back to his cell.

"If you really didn't kill my sister, tell me who did!" I shouted at him.

Munroe turned around and looked at me.

"Maybe you should have asked your father that question back then."

"My father? What does my father have to do with this?"

"He could tell you a lot about your sister's death. Ask him."

"My father is dead."

"Well, then I guess you can't ask him."

David Munroe laughed again now.

A scary, crazy laugh.

And then he was gone.

SIX

My mother was living in a different house now in a place a few towns away from Huntsdale. She'd moved there a number of years ago after my father died, and she sold the house in Huntsdale where I had grown up a lifetime ago. I guess with Caitlin dead and then my father gone too, there were just too many sad memories in that house for her to keep living there alone.

I had not been to see my mother at her new home very often.

And the last time I was there I'd walked out in anger and bitterness.

But I needed to go back now to ask her questions after my interview with David Munroe.

Especially about his bizarre reference to my father.

I wondered how she would react to seeing me again. I hadn't called ahead. I decided to just show up unannounced. I figured that would be the most painless way. But it still turned out to be very awkward when I got there.

"What are you doing here?" she said when she saw me.

"Hello, Mom. Good to see you too."

"It's been such a long time. And now you just show up on my doorstep?"

That was it. No "how proud I am of you, Nikki." No praise for me saving a girl's life. No congratulations on my success as an FBI agent.

"I guess you're too busy to have any time for your mother."

"There's a lot going on in my job."

"You could still call me."

She was right about that. I could have called her after my big arrest or a lot of other times too. But I hardly ever did. Because I didn't really know what to say to her. And I also knew that, despite her complaint about not calling her, she didn't really want to talk to me, either. I'd found that out the last time I was here.

It was a year ago. The last time I'd come back here to Ohio to try to talk to David Munroe in jail. Before I had left to go back to Washington, I had tried to confront my mother about the emotional gulf that had existed between us ever since my Caitlin died and the loss afterward of my father.

But that effort had ended badly.

Extremely badly.

She broke down in tears and anger when I started talking about that long ago day at the carnival, trying unsuccessfully to convince her to confront the reality of it after all these years, and she finally told me to leave.

You would think that after losing both her other daughter and her husband, my mother would want to cling to me—her daughter—as the one part of her family that she still had left in her life.

But instead, it appeared to be the opposite.

I wasn't comfort or solace for her. No, I was only a constant reminder of everything else she had lost. All the nightmare memories from the past. And so she wanted to get away from the memories I brought back to her, just like she wanted to get away from the memories of the family house she sold, so she could somehow move on with her life. Yes, I was just like that house. My mother wanted to forget about me too.

Unlike my mother, my father had never blamed me for what happened to Caitlin. He was extra protective and extra loving to me throughout that time. He told me I should never feel guilty about Caitlin, that I couldn't have prevented her death. He said he had lost one daughter, and he sure didn't want to lose another. I remember on that last time I saw him how he hugged me and told me how the three of us—him, my mother and him—would be all right. We'd survive this.

And then later that day he suffered a fatal heart attack.

"Why are you here now?" my mother asked me.

"I'm working on a case."

"What case?"

"Caitlin's murder."

She glared at me. I suppose I should have felt more sorry about bringing this kind of pain to her all over again but I didn't. I wanted to find out some answers—about the things David Munroe had shocked me with about my father and my sister— and my mother was the only person I knew to ask.

I told her what Munroe had said at the end about my father.

"He made it sound like Dad knew some kind of secret about Caitlin's murder. Do you have any idea what he's talking about?" I asked her.

"Of course not."

"Then why did he say it?"

"He's a horrible person. He's making up lies."

"Why would he lie about this? About Dad? Is there something about my father—about his investigation of Caitlin's murder—that I should know about?"

"Your father was devastated by what happened to Caitlin, but he did his job. He caught the man who did it. Those are the facts about what happened. I don't care what this child killer says now."

"Munroe also said that Caitlin had been targeted as a victim before the carnival that day. That he followed her there. Is there anything like that you remember hearing?"

"Stop it! Just stop it, Nikki!"

I thought my mother might start crying again. I was prepared for that. But instead she stared at me with a stony look on her face, like I was some stranger probing into her life with these questions, not her own daughter.

"Why are you doing this?" she asked me. "Why are you opening this up all over again? Caitlin is dead. Your father is dead. Let them rest in peace. Haven't you done enough already? Haven't you caused enough damage?"

I didn't say anything. There wasn't much I could say. Not after fifteen years of her still blaming me for Caitlin's death. And my father's death too. Nothing for me to say that would change the relationship between her and me at this point. No, we weren't going to have any fuzzy mother-daughter moments between us.

"Why are you doing this?" she said again. "Asking questions about Caitlin and digging up the past? For God's sake, leave it alone. None of this will ever bring Caitlin back to life again. You can't do that, Nikki. You can't undo what you did. You can't undo what happened in the past."

"No, I can't," I said.

"Then drop this whole thing."

"I can't do that either."

After I left my mother's place, I drove to the cemetery where my father and my sister were both buried.

Maybe I didn't spend too much time talking to my mother.

But I still talked to my father.

And to Caitlin.

They were buried side by side at a cemetery on the outskirts of Huntsdale. I'm not one of those people who believe my loved ones are still there somewhere listening to me at the gravesite, or anywhere else I talk to them. But it still makes me feel better to do it. I'm not really talking to them anyway. I'm talking to myself. It helps sometimes. Especially after a traumatic experience like I'd just endured with my mother.

It was a beautiful spot where they were buried. Next to a pond, surrounded by trees and grass, ducks swimming in the water. But then I guess a lot of cemeteries are in scenic locations like this. Not for the dead, for the living like me who come to pay their respects to the people we loved.

I parked my rental car and started walking to their graves.

I was still thinking about the scene with my mother and didn't pay too much attention to my surroundings until I was almost at the gravesite.

That's when I noticed it.

There was something on both graves.

When I got there, I could see what it was: flowers.

Two wreaths of roses.

One wreath of roses was on my father's grave.

The other wreath of roses on Caitlin's.

Just like the wreath of roses that had been left on Caitlin's body when it was found fifteen years ago.

SEVEN

I called Greg in Washington to tell him I wouldn't be coming back there that night, as I planned. I said I wanted to do some more work on the case—then I'd fly back tomorrow morning.

"I thought you were only going to be away for one day," he said.

"Some things have come up. More questions."

I told him about David Munroe now claiming he didn't kill my sister. About the strange reference he'd made about my father knowing some kind of secrets at the end of our conversation. And about the wreaths of roses I'd found on the graves of Caitlin and my father at the Huntsdale Cemetery afterward.

"Why did he target my sister? Why did he bury her with that wreath of roses on her head? Why does he say now he didn't kill her? If he didn't kill her, why hasn't he told anyone that story before now? Is this just some kind of sick game he's playing before he dies? Or is he telling the truth now?"

"I don't know."

"And, if he is telling the truth about not being the one who killed her, then who did? That means the real killer—or killers— is still out there. Who are they? Where are they? What did he mean when he said the place I had to go looking for them was 'nowhere?' And, if there were other people involved, have they killed anyone else like they murdered my sister fifteen years ago?"

"C'mon, Nikki, let's just—"

"And what about the stuff with my father? Telling me I should ask my father why Caitlin had been targeted for murder. How would my father know anything about that?"

"Well, you said your father was the police chief."

"Yes, he was. Which meant he had to investigate his own daughter's murder. And that's what probably killed him with a heart attack. But why would he have kept anything he found out a secret, like this guy Munroe suggested to me? He's gotta be wrong about that. It makes no sense whatsoever."

"He's a crazy bastard, Nikki. You know that. Hell, maybe the cancer has affected his brain, made him delusional. That's why he told you all this stuff."

"And what about those wreaths of roses I found on my sister and father's graves? What's that all about?"

"Didn't you tell me that the business about the roses found with your sister's body back at the time of the murder all came out during the investigation and the trial?"

"Yes, it did."

"So anyone could have put them there. They heard you were in town, and they figured you would likely visit the graves. Maybe it was some sort of sick joke. Or else, someone just left them there for some other reason. You don't know it's connected with your sister's death in any way. It could just be a coincidence."

"There has to be a better reason than that for all of this stuff happening here now," I told him.

"Look, I understand this is very difficult for you to deal with," Greg said. "It's opened up all sorts of bad memories and feelings of guilt about losing your sister all over again. I get that,

Nikki. But you've been away, off in Ohio, and I've missed you. I miss being with my girlfriend. Can't we just change the subject and talk about other things?"

Change the subject? How could I change the subject with all this happening around me? I knew that Greg didn't like talking about the details of my job, and I knew that my job made him uncomfortable. But this job of mine at the FBI solving big crimes was my life. My passion. And now I felt like I was close —or at least as close as I'd ever been—to finally getting some kind of closure on the biggest crime of my life.

I wondered if Greg was going to put more pressure on me to find another kind of job. I hoped not. Was this the way it was going to be once we were married? I knew what he wanted in a wife, and it was a more traditional wife like a lot of his law partners had in their marriages. Not some gun-slinging FBI chick. But I didn't want to have that conversation with him now.

"Okay, let's change the subject," I said.

"Good."

"What do you want to talk about?"

"Our wedding. We've got a lot of wedding plans to talk about, Nikki."

"Yes, we do."

"Or we could just elope. Go to City Hall as soon as you get back to Washington, get a blood test and be married right away."

"And miss out on all those wedding gifts from the rich lawyers in your firm?"

He laughed.

"Have you thought anymore," he asked me now, "about my idea that you move out of your apartment and live here with me full-time right now—even before we get married?"

"I've pondered it from time to time."

"How about moving up our marriage date? Or at least setting a definite one?"

"Also under consideration."

"Can't we talk about all this, Nikki?"

"Later."

"Later when?"

"Later, when I get back from Ohio. We'll talk about it all then, Greg."

I needed to go back to Doreen Trask right now and see if she had any more details about what David Munroe had told me. Maybe try talking to Munroe in prison again, although that seemed unlikely given the abrupt way he'd walked out of our meeting. Maybe check with people at the cemetery too and see if anyone there knew anything about the roses I'd found on my sister and father's graves.

"So when is that? When do you think I'll see you?" Greg asked.

"Like I said, I'm booked now on a flight tomorrow morning."

"You promise you'll be on it?"

"I promise. Believe me, I want to get out of Huntsdale and back to Washington again as much as you want me to, Greg."

EIGHT

I meant it too. I wanted to get out of Huntsdale as soon as I could. Coming back here—even briefly—was traumatic for me. And this was the most time I'd spent here in a very long time.

It was a hot July day outside after I hung up with Greg, just like it had been a hot July day the afternoon at the carnival when Caitlin first disappeared.

People talk about the summer heat in big cities like Washington, but somehow it always seemed worse to me in the small town of Huntsdale. There was no ocean, no big lake, no river near Huntsdale, and the stifling heat at this time of year seemed impossible to escape. I remembered feeling that way in the summertime when I was growing up here, and the heat felt even worse now. It made me feel even more claustrophobic about being trapped back in this place where I had so many bad memories.

But, like a bad horror movie that you can't stop watching, I found myself replaying many of those memories all over again.

I drove past my old high school—Huntsdale High. It looked the same, even though a new wing had been added to the structure. So did the football field where I'd once been a cheerleader.

I had some good moments in high school, I guess. But also a lot of bad ones. Many of those involved dealing with my mother as I went through all the angst and drama that a teenage girl experiences.

By the time I graduated high school, I was pretty—but during my early teenage years I sometimes felt gawky and insecure about my appearance. I thought my blonde hair was stringy, my complexion bad, my breasts too small, and other parts of my rapidly changing body left me feeling very uncomfortable too. I remember once when a boy at school told me my ears were too big for my head, and laughingly called me "Dumbo." I ran home crying to my mother. She told me to stop bothering her with such nonsense.

Looking back on it now, I realize I was confused and uncertain and angry back then as a young girl, even before Caitlin's abduction and her murder.

Lots of buildings and businesses in the town were changed too or completely gone. But the Burger King was still there. It had been my favorite hangout in high school, and me and my friends spent a lot of time there. That was the first place I ever kissed a boy. Damned if I could remember his name though. I wondered if he was still in town. My good memories of this town were few and far between. I wondered how I'd ever survived Huntsdale to become the woman I was today.

The house where I'd grown up here in Huntsdale—living there with my sister and mother and father until I was eighteen —looked basically the same as I remembered it.

It was within walking distance of town, and also close to the Huntsdale police station where my father worked. I used to walk into town all the time to spend time with my father at the station, and watch him work there. Me and my dad spent a lot of quality time together. Those were the happiest moments for me.

Later, after I went away to college, I hardly ever went back to this house. All it did was remind me how both of them were gone now. And then, of course, my mother blamed me for it all going so terribly wrong for our family.

I stood there looking at the house for a while. It was a white two-story home with a big porch in the front, which I did remember fondly from when I was young. Sitting outside with my father on that porch and listening as he told me his stories about cases at the police station. None of them were really that interesting, I realise now that I'm grown up and handling major crime cases.

But they seemed fascinating to me back then as a little girl, and I loved those one-on-one moments with my father on the porch talking about police stuff.

That's probably why I decided to go into law enforcement myself.

Finally, I swung the car left down a place called Canyon Road and went back to the one place I always visited whenever I did come back. Just like my father and my sister's graves. I always went back to the scene of the crime. The spot where it had all started fifteen years ago. The site of the carnival where I had seen my sister for the last time on that long-ago summer day.

It looked totally different now.

Back then it had been an open area where the carnival people could set everything up. The rest of the time it was just an open lot of land. But the property had become more valuable since then. It was now paved over into a parking lot with a strip mall made up of stores. A mobile phone store; a hairdressing salon; a CVS; and even a Starbucks.

As best I could remember, the Tilt-A-Whirl we rode had been somewhere close to where the phone store was now, and the place where I had last seen Caitlin alive was in the middle of the CVS. Not that it really mattered. But I walked around the area just for the hell of it, hoping that might spark some long-forgotten memory of that day for me.

Didn't help.

But it was jarring still for me to be back here again where my sister disappeared.

I could almost see her again there now.

Standing there in her tan slacks, a brown-and-white striped top and a Cincinnati Reds baseball cap. Her beautiful and innocent face. Her long blonde hair. Waving at us as we got on the carnival ride without her.

Now you see her. Now you don't...

That old refrain runs through my head every time I think about Caitlin.

Even after all these years, it still seems unfathomable to me that my little sister could be gone in an instant like that.

I went back to the motel where I was staying. I wanted to get the hell out of this town as soon as I could. It was just too hard for me to be here again—too many memories I didn't want to remember anymore.

Then I figured I'd be able to do whatever follow-up work I needed to do on Trask, Munroe, the cemetery etc. once I got back to Washington—at least for the time being until I found out more.

That was my plan anyway.

Except it didn't work out that way.

I was just heading out the door of my room the next morning when my cell phone buzzed. At first, I assumed it was either Greg or someone in the FBI office calling me from Washington. But, when I looked down at the number on the screen, it was from a 740 area code. That was the area code for right here in Huntsdale. I answered it.

"This is Billy Weller," the voice on the other end said.

"Officer Billy Weller. I met you at the Huntsdale police station—"

"I remember you, Billy."

"I thought you would want to know that we just found out a young girl here is missing. A thirteen-year-old girl. Almost the same age as your sister was. And... well, she was last seen on July nineteenth."

The same date my sister went missing.

NINE

The missing girl's name was Natalie Jarvis.

She was thirteen years old and a seventh grader at Huntsdale Middle School. Her father was an insurance salesman, and her mother a nurse at a nearby hospital. There was nothing to indicate they were anything but a normal American family. Except for the fact that their thirteen-year-old daughter was now missing.

Natalie Jarvis had gone to the movies on the afternoon of July 19th, with a group of girlfriends her age. The movie was a matinee performance of a Captain Marvel film. At some point during the movie, Natalie said she wanted more popcorn and left the group to go to the refreshment stand. She never came back.

At first, the other girls assumed she had simply changed her mind about watching the movie and gone home. But, when one of them talked to Natalie's parents afterward, she was not there. No one had seen her since she left her seat at the movie theater to go to the refreshment stand.

Unlike with my sister Caitlin's disappearance, there was no immediate panic. Everyone figured she'd show up at home later, that she'd just stopped off somewhere. But, by the next morning there was still no sign of Natalie, and her parents had called the police. As the hours went by, fears grew for her safety. Soon a massive search was underway.

I found this all out from Billy Weller when I showed up at the Huntsdale police station after his phone call. I'd thought about it all as I hurriedly drove over there. No matter how many different ways I approached it though, I still couldn't get past the significance of another young girl from Huntsdale like my sister suddenly going missing on the anniversary of Caitlin's disappearance.

I called Alex Del Vecchio in Washington and informed her about what I was doing.

And why.

"Have you told Polk you're still in Ohio yet?" she asked.

"No, I didn't even tell him I'd cancelled my flight back last night."

"So he couldn't tell you not to do it, right?"

"Something like that."

"And now?"

"I'm going to call him as soon as I hang up with you."

"Well, that ought to be a fun call."

I ended the call and turned to Billy Weller.

"Don't expect too warm a welcome here," Weller said to me.

"What do you mean?"

"Chief Earnshaw."

"He's not going to be happy to see me, huh?"

"No."

"Not exactly a surprise. He wasn't very happy to see me here last time either. I'm used to that kind of reception. Local police frequently get their feathers ruffled when the FBI shows up. It's part of the job. I can deal with Earnshaw, don't worry about that. This is my career."

"Do me one favor, Agent Cassidy."

"You can call me Nikki."

"Okay then, Nikki. Don't tell him that I was the one who called to alert you about this."

"You're afraid Earnshaw won't like that?"

"Absolutely. Hey, this is my career."

He smiled when he said it. It sure was a nice smile. He wasn't the most handsome guy in the world. Not as good-looking as Greg Ellroy, that's for sure. Greg dressed really well, he was in great physical shape, he had terrific hair, he was tall and impressive. He looked like he came out of a fashion magazine.

Weller was a lot more... well, ordinary. He was medium height, kind of gangly, and his uniform was kind of wrinkled, almost looking like he could have slept in it. Nothing special about Billy Weller when it came to outward appearance. But that infectious smile and personality made up for a lot.

It made him interesting to me.

It made me wonder why I hadn't paid more attention to Billy Weller in high school. Not that it really mattered now, of course.

I just needed to focus on finding Natalie and then I could go back to Greg and to Washington and to my life there.

"I don't understand why you're here about this," Chief Earnshaw said, when I went into his office with Weller to meet with him.

"You didn't understand why I was here last time we talked either."

"Well, that was about your sister from a long time ago. This is a local girl who disappeared right now. What is the FBI's interest?"

"Because she disappeared on the exact same date as my sister."

"That was fifteen years ago. This girl, Natalie Jarvis, wasn't even alive then. There's no real indication that there's any kind of connection between the two cases."

"Well, it is all very peculiar. I get a message from the guy in jail for killing my sister. He says he didn't do it, that the real killer is still out there. And now a girl nearly the same age as my sister goes missing on the exact same date my sister disappeared fifteen years ago. I see a pattern there. You must too, Chief Earnshaw."

"But Natalie Jarvis isn't dead, as far as we know. She's only missing. Until we know any more—"

"How many missing girls have you had in Huntsdale since you've been here, Chief?"

"Well, not many, but—"

"And you are searching for Natalie Jarvis right now?"

"Yes, we are."

"Then let me help you."

I was playing a tricky game here with Earnshaw. The FBI's jurisdiction in cases like this depends on a lot of factors—things like evidence of transport of a victim over state lines, or links to other similar cases around the nation. I might be able to get official FBI clearance to join the investigation, depending on what happened next in this case. But I didn't have it now.

I was hoping to be able to convince Earnshaw, though, to voluntarily let me into the investigation. I had a feeling he hadn't handled any potential major crimes like this in Huntsdale since he'd become chief. And, if Natalie Jarvis was indeed dead, he'd want—and he'd need—my help. So I tried to play "good cop" with him as best I could.

"Look, Chief, I've had a lot of experience with finding missing persons. Especially missing young girls like Natalie Jarvis. I'm assigned to the Crimes Against Children Squad at the FBI. I'm sure you could use that kind of experience. It will be your investigation, I'm just here to observe and assist in any way that I can. I'll do everything I can to help you find Natalie

Jarvis. And then, if it turns out to have no connection with the disappearance of my sister, I'll go back to Washington."

I didn't say that I was going to stay around Huntsdale for this whether he wanted me to or not.

But maybe he already knew that.

And he also knew he could use my help at the moment.

"Okay," Earnshaw said finally. "You can go with Officer Weller right now. He's headed out to interview the parents again and some of the girls the Jarvis girl was with at the movies. But remember, this investigation is about Natalie Jarvis. Not your sister."

TEN

Natalie's parents, Michael and Anne Jarvis, were waiting for us when we got there. Sitting together in the living room and looking at Weller and me expectantly when we came inside. I guess they were hoping we had some answers—good answers. But we didn't have any kind of answers. All we had was questions.

"When is the last time you saw Natalie?" Weller asked them.

I decided to let him take the lead in the questioning because he was local. They likely knew him and might feel more comfortable talking with him than they would with an FBI agent from Washington.

"That afternoon," the mother said. "Right before she left for the movie theater. We had lunch here. It was around noon, I guess. I remember Natalie saying she had to be at the theater before two because that was when the picture started."

"I drove her," her husband said. "I dropped her off at the theater where her friends were waiting for her out front. She got out of the car, waved goodbye to me, and that was the last time I saw her..." He hesitated, suddenly realizing the significance of saying "the last time I saw her..." Then he quickly added: "I mean the last time I saw her on that afternoon."

Michael Jarvis looked what I expected an insurance agent to look like. Wearing a bland jacket and tie, short cut hair and he talked in a business-like manner as if he was trying to sell a policy right now. Anne Jarvis, on the other hand, didn't look much like a nurse. But then I'm not really sure what a nurse is supposed to look like these days. She had a big head of blonde hair, was wearing some kind of a workout suit and had a trim body that looked like she used it for exercise a lot.

"Did you know all the other girls?" Weller asked.

"Of course," Mrs. Jarvis said. "They were her friends. We knew them all. That's why we weren't worried at first. We figured she was just with them."

"What happened after you dropped her off at the theater?" Weller asked her father.

"I came home, did some work around the yard. Then a few hours later—between four and five, I guess—I drove back to the theater to pick up Natalie."

"You drove back there?" I asked now.

That surprised me.

"Yes. Of course."

"You didn't usually let her come home from something like that by herself?"

"Natalie's at that 'in-between' age," her mother said. "Where she wants to do things on her own, but we want to make sure she's under parental supervision as much as possible. So we worked out this compromise. She could do things like this with her friends. But one of us would take her—and then pick her up afterward. She wasn't happy with it, but that was the deal that we had with Natalie."

"Then what happened when you got to the theater?" I asked Michael Jarvis.

"I waited for her in the car. But she didn't show up like she was supposed to. Finally, I went into the theater and talked to the manager or someone there who said he remembered the group of girls. But he said they had all left. I was angry at Natalie for doing that, but I came home and waited for her here to ask what happened. Why she left with her friends and didn't wait for me like we had agreed on. But instead, we got the call from her friends asking if we had any idea where she was."

At some point, Anne Jarvis turned to Billy Weller and me with an anxious look on her face.

"Do you think she's still alive?" she asked.

"Of course, we're very hopeful," Weller said. "We're doing everything we can to make sure she comes home safely and—"

"No, don't give me that prepared speech," she said, cutting him off in mid-sentence.

Then she said to me: "You know more about this than anyone. Can you get my daughter back to me again?"

Mrs. Jarvis was clearly talking only to me now. Not to Weller at all. I assumed she had seen me on TV news rescuing the Mattheu girl, and she hoped I could somehow do the same with her daughter Natalie. That I could work another miracle and bring her daughter back home safe like I did Julie Mattheu.

"I know my Natalie," she said. "Natalie's a responsible girl, even at thirteen. She didn't run away. She didn't do something stupid. If she was in an accident, we'd have heard about it by now. Someone did something to her. Someone took her. I know this, and you know it too. You're the only one who can understand how I feel."

"You mean because of my experience in bringing Julie Mattheu home. Well, all I can say is—"

"No, it's not just that. You know what I'm feeling because of what you went through with your sister all those years ago. I remember that. I remember feeling so sorry for you. And now... now I'm feeling sorry for myself. I know it was too late to save your sister Caitlin. But I'm hoping it's not too late for you to save Natalie for me."

Of course, she knew me from Caitlin. Huntsdale was a small town. If she lived here then, she'd remember my sister's disappearance at the carnival and everything that happened afterward. She looked to be about the same age as me, probably early thirties. But then why didn't I know her? From high school or somewhere around town?

"I didn't live in Huntsdale then," she explained, when I asked her if we'd known each other. "I lived in Orangeburg."

Orangeburg was a few towns away.

"But I knew your sister," she said.

"How did you know Caitlin?"

"From summer camp. She was attending a camp that summer where I was a counselor and swimming instructor. I spent a lot of time with her there. She was a really good swimmer, and I was working with her to swim competitively when she got to high school. So it was a terrible shock to me too when... well, when it happened to her."

Summer camp. I remembered now how Caitlin had been going to a day camp that summer. She was still living at home, but my mother or father would take her there in the morning, then pick her up at night. I'd done it a few times too. I'd just gotten my driver's license, and I liked being able to use the family car whenever I could.

"Caitlin was a lovely girl," Anne Jarvis said. "Just like Natalie."

I asked them if I could see Natalie's room. She offered to show it to me, but I said I'd find it myself. I preferred to look at Natalie's stuff without her or her husband looking over me. I said Billy would stay in the living room and ask them more things that might be beneficial in the search for their daughter.

Natalie Jarvis' room was on the second floor of the house, and it looked like what a typical thirteen-year-old girl's room

would. At least as far as I knew and could remember from my
own past.

One thing I saw right away was that Natalie liked music.
There was a big retro-style record player in a prominent spot—
along with a stack of old-fashioned vinyl records from popular
performers like Taylor Swift, Miley Cyrus, Selena Gomez and
Dua Lipa. I'd read somewhere that old-style record players and
records were a trend of young people who wanted more than
Spotify or downloading music from streaming sources. What's
old is new again, I guess.

There were stuffed animals all around the room. On
shelves, windowsills and even on the bed. Giraffes, dinosaurs
and more. A movie poster on the wall next to the bed for *Black
Widow* with Scarlett Johansson. In another part of the room
were combs, brushes, hair braids and even some basic makeup,
which Natalie must have just been beginning to use. Everything was neat, including the clothes in her closet, even though
there was such a large number of things in the room.

I went through it all, not knowing exactly what I was
looking for.

And then, even when I found something, I wasn't sure what
it meant.

It was a card. A simple greeting card, the kind you can buy
in any store.

But, for whatever reason, Natalie Jarvis had displayed it
prominently on a shelf next to her bed. The card was unsigned.
It said simply:

> *Roses are red,*
> *Violets are blue.*
> *Want to know a secret?*
> *This is just for you.*

ELEVEN

"I guess you've had to do a lot of that, huh?" Billy Weller said to me after we'd left the Jarvis house and were back in the car.

"Talking with families of missing kids?"

"Yeah, or families of any crime victims."

"I've done my share. How about you?"

"Not really. One or two times for the notification of a traffic accident. Or some kid who got hurt on the playground or at school. Maybe even a drug overdose. But this was a lot different."

"It shook you up to see the Jarvis family like that. I understand."

He shook his head sadly.

"It's not easy when you haven't done that kind of thing very much."

"It's not easy even when you have," I said.

Weller and I drove in silence for a while. Him still behind the wheel, me in the passenger seat. I hadn't said anything to Weller about the card I found in Natalie's room because I didn't know if it meant anything or not. And I still wasn't a hundred percent sure I could trust him, even though he seemed to be on my side. I'd privately asked Mrs. Jarvis if she knew where the card came from when I went back downstairs, but she didn't know anything about it. Still, it was a weird coincidence—a card making references to roses—after the new roses I'd found on my father and sister's graves.

"Where to next?" Weller asked me.

"The movie theater where she disappeared."

"What about talking to the girls that were there?"

"Let's go back to the theater before we do that."

"Why? There's nothing still there at the theater."

"It's the crime scene. I always like to go back to the crime scene."

"Whatever you say, you're the hotshot FBI investigator. I'm just a small-town cop who gives out parking tickets."

He didn't say it in a smart ass or sarcastic way though, like Chief Frank Earnshaw might have done.

Billy Weller smiled when he said it.

That damn smile again.

The movie theater was still an old-fashioned theater. It had never been transformed into one of those multiplex places like you see everywhere these days.

It looked pretty much the way I remembered it from when I was a teenager living in Huntsdale and went to matinees there with my girlfriends or on a Saturday night date.

The theater manager was different though. He was a young kid named Nick Eaton. He said he'd been in the job for six months. He seemed impressed—and probably intimidated—by a police officer like Weller there to question him. Even more impressed and intimidated when I showed him my FBI credentials. Eaton was eager to cooperate. The problem was he didn't have much he could tell us.

"We didn't really know anything about this until later," he

explained. "I mean the other girls with Natalie went home before they became concerned and started calls to her parents and then the authorities got involved. We had no idea here that anything was wrong."

"Did you notice anything suspicious at all that afternoon?"

"No."

"Anyone acting strangely out in the lobby or anywhere else in the theater?"

"Not at all."

"You're sure?"

"As far as we knew, it was an ordinary afternoon audience."

I asked to see the section where Natalie and the other girls had sat. They were in the center section of the theater, about ten rows back from the screen. I examined the seats themselves, the floor underneath them and the area around. There was nothing there.

Hey, you never know.

I thought about Natalie Jarvis sitting in this seat in front of me, and then suddenly disappearing from the theater. I tried to get some feeling of what she might have been thinking or doing in those minutes before she left her friends to go to the refreshment stand and never came back.

I used to do the same thing at the spot where the summer carnival had once been. I'd stand there at the exact place—even though the carnival was long gone by then—and try to imagine what Caitlin was feeling and doing. I never found out with Caitlin, and it didn't work for me with Natalie Jarvis now either.

"Do you have security video from that afternoon?" Weller asked.

"Not for the seats, but out in the lobby."

"What about the refreshment stand?" I asked.

"That would be on the video too."

We went into Nick Eaton's office to watch the security

video. It showed Natalie and her friends entering the theater shortly before two p.m. Then they bought some things at the refreshment stand. After that, I asked Eaton to fast-forward until the time she left her friends inside and went back to the refreshment stand.

Sure enough, at 3:02 on the video time stamp running across the bottom of the screen, Natalie appeared. First, she went into a bathroom. Then she reemerged and you could see her standing in line at the refreshment stand. There didn't seem to be anything unusual going on. She didn't look upset or scared or anything like that. She simply waited in line, got a box of popcorn and something to drink and then moved away from the refreshment stand.

"Nothing there," Weller said.

"Keep the video running," I told Eaton.

I wanted to see if it would show whatever happened next. That was the crucial part. We watched as she walked away from the refreshment stand, presumably headed back to her seat. But then suddenly she stopped. It wasn't clear why. It was as if she had seen something off screen. Something that got her interested enough to head in that direction. Then she made a left turn, away from the theater seats, and disappeared for good.

I went back out in the lobby from the manager's office and retraced her steps from the refreshment stand. I made a left at the same spot it appeared she had turned away. That's when I saw it. A big set of double doors ahead of me. I pushed the door open and found myself in an alley behind the theater.

"Was this door open that afternoon?" I asked Eaton.

"Not from the outside."

"But from the inside?"

"Yes, you could use this as an exit. We have to do that. In case of a fire or other emergency."

"That's where she went," Weller said. "Out this door. But

why not use the front door? Maybe she didn't want anyone to see her. Or—"

"Or maybe she didn't have a choice," I said.

"I'm sorry I don't remember you from high school," I said to Weller, once we were back in the car and driving away from the theater.

"Hey, I wasn't that memorable. I had bad skin, bad hair and I was pretty scrawny. I also had a terrible case of inferiority complex. I could barely get up the courage to talk to anyone, much less a girl like you, back then. Even thought I had... well, I had a big crush on you."

I gave him a surprised look.

"But you never did anything about it."

"You were too popular."

I wasn't sure exactly what to say.

"Well, that was a long time ago."

"Yeah, a long time. We're both a lot different though. Although it is funny how we both wound up in law enforcement."

"How did you decide to join the Huntsdale force?"

"It just happened. I enlisted in the army and wound up being an MP. When I got out, there was an opening on the Huntsdale police force. I took the job. I figured it would be good until I decided what I wanted to do with my life. That was three years ago. I'm still here though."

"Nothing wrong with that."

"I'm taking some criminal justice college courses in the evening. Hopefully, that can help me get a better job in law enforcement someday. Bigger city. Bigger department. Hell, maybe I can even get in the FBI like you."

I smiled.

"Do you have a family?" I asked.

"Nope."

"Not married?"

He hesitated for a second before answering, then gave me a big smile. That same smile again. I sure liked Billy Weller's smile.

"Well, I was married. Once. Not now."

"What happened?"

"Oh, my wife wanted something more in a husband than a small-town cop, I guess. How about you?"

"How about me what?"

"Are you married?"

"I'm engaged. Getting married later this year."

"That makes sense."

"Why?"

"A woman like you has to be either married or engaged."

I tried to think of a way to switch the conversation back to the Natalie Jarvis case, but I didn't have to. Weller did that for me.

"Do you think she's dead?" he asked.

"I don't know."

"Best guess."

"I don't guess, Billy. I investigate."

"So let's go investigate," Weller said.

TWELVE

There were three young girls who had gone to the movie theater that day with Natalie Jarvis. Their names were Hanna Weiss, Emma Cunningham and Barbara Howard. All of them were understandably traumatized over what had happened, and it wasn't easy to get information out of them.

And—in one case—that was true of the parents too.

"We don't want to talk about any of this with anyone, and we don't want Emma to either—even with the police or the FBI," James Cunningham said emphatically when we went to the Cunningham house to question their daughter Emma. "That could be Emma who is missing or, most likely, now dead. Whoever did this thing might be crazy and sick enough to come after her next."

"We don't want our daughter linked to this case in any way," the mother Dorothy Cunningham said. "We don't want her to get involved."

She wasn't as belligerent about it as her husband, but she seemed just as insistent.

"We will make sure that no harm comes to your daughter," Weller said to them both now.

"You couldn't stop what happened to Natalie Jarvis," the father said sarcastically.

"We didn't know someone like this was out there then, Mr. Cunningham," he said. "Now we do."

"We'll make sure your daughter Emma is protected," I told him.

"How can we be sure of that?"

"You have my word on it."

"Hell, Cassidy, you couldn't even protect your own sister."

I hadn't expected that. But I guess I should have. Just like with Anne Jarvis earlier. People in Huntsdale remembered me and my sister and my father too for what happened here fifteen years ago. I needed to suck it up and ignore Cunningham's comments and do my job.

We finally convinced the Cunninghams to at least let us talk to their daughter Emma, but she was so upset—and, I suppose, scared too—that we didn't get very much from her that was useful. It was just an afternoon movie outing with Natalie and her other friends, she said. Nothing more than that. Until Natalie disappeared.

The second girl we talked to, Barbara Howard, was more forthcoming and willing to cooperate, but didn't tell us anything of significance that helped us figure out what might have happened to Natalie.

She talked a lot about the movie and why they all were so excited to see it.

"It was the new *Captain Marvel* movie with a female hero," she said. "We'd seen the first one, and we were eager for this one. I mean it was Captain Marvel! This woman was out there really kicking ass to save the planet! It was great stuff. You know all about Captain Marvel, right?"

I didn't know much about Captain Marvel. But then I

wasn't a thirteen-year-old girl. I tried to get her to focus less on the movie and more on what actually happened when Natalie and the girls went to the theater.

"I don't remember anything unusual," Barbara Howard told us. "I'm sorry. I've tried to go back and think hard about everything from there. But I don't know anything that might help you on Natalie. I mean we waited for her outside the theater, we bought tickets and went inside, we watched the movie. Not really anything else for me to say."

"Tell me about when Natalie left her seat," I said.

"Uh, she simply got up and left. I didn't think much of it at the time."

"Did she say anything?"

"I'm not sure. Maybe something about going to the restroom, I guess."

"She didn't tell you about going to the refreshment stand for more popcorn and something to drink?"

"Uh, maybe. Not sure. But I was watching the movie, so I didn't pay a lot of attention. I figured she'd go the restroom or the refreshment stand or whatever, and then come back when she was done."

"Were you worried at all when she didn't come back to her seat?" Weller asked.

"Not really worried. Surprised, I guess, when we didn't see her. We went looking for her after the movie in the bathroom and around the refreshment stand and outside. But she was nowhere around. We figured that she must have left for some reason and would let us know soon. We texted and tried to call her phone. But there was no response from her. That's when we started to become concerned. Natalie always texted back quickly to everyone. So we called her house and talked to her parents. Later, well... that's when you people got involved. And that's really all that I can tell you."

"How long was it from the time she left her seat until you went looking for her in the theater after the movie ended?"

"Forty-five minutes. Maybe an hour."

"And no one thought about going to look for her before that?"

"No, I guess we didn't."

"Why?"

"We didn't want to leave the *Captain Marvel* movie. I mean it was really good!"

Right.

It wasn't until we interviewed the last young girl—Hannah Weiss—that we found out something that might really be significant.

"I think Natalie might have had a boyfriend," Hannah said to us.

"She told you that?"

"Not in so many words. But she was excited about something. Or someone. She didn't talk about it with me that day at the theater. We didn't have much time to talk, we just got our tickets and went inside. But she'd told me bits and pieces in the previous days that made me think someone was interested in her."

"One of the boys in your class at school?"

"I don't believe so."

"Why not?"

"I assumed... I assumed it was someone older."

"What made you think that?"

"Well, a few of the things she'd said. They didn't sound like the things any boy we knew at our school would do. It seemed to me like it must have been someone older than us."

"How old?"

She shrugged.

"All I know is that from the things she told me she seemed to have some sort of secret admirer. Someone who she thought was very romantic. Because she told me someone was giving her gifts."

"What kind of gifts?"

"The only one I know for sure is the flower. I was there when she found that."

"A flower?"

"Yes, she said someone sent her a card and there was a flower with it."

I thought about the card I'd found in Natalie's bedroom.

"What kind of flower?" I said to Hannah Weiss.

"It was a rose."

"A rose," I repeated.

"Yes, a single red rose."

THIRTEEN

"There's a lot of things bothering me about the disappearance of Natalie Jarvis," I said to Alex Del Vecchio on the phone.

"Like what?"

"Mainly that there are more and more similarities to my sister's case fifteen years ago."

I was back at the hotel after leaving Natalie's friend who told me about the rose. I was trying to sort through everything I'd found out over the past few days in Huntsdale. It was easier to do that with Alex. So I called her at home back in Washington.

"The killer placed a wreath of roses on my sister's body fifteen years ago," I said. "Then someone placed the same kind of roses on my sister and my father's graves after I'd visited David Munroe in jail. And now I find out that someone sent a single red rose to Natalie Jarvis before she went missing. There's gotta be a connection."

"The most logical explanation is that whoever killed your sister is back after fifteen years. He left the roses on your father and sister's graves as some kind of a sick calling card to you. And he sent the single rose—which seems to have some unknown significance to him—to the Jarvis girl before he abducted her. Except that theory doesn't work, does it? Because the man who murdered your sister has been in prison for fifteen years and couldn't have done any of this other stuff now."

"Thanks for the recap, Alex. I already know all that—"

"Hey, I'm sitting here three hundred miles away. You're at the crime scene. If you can't figure it out from there, how do you expect me to do it here?"

"Which is one of the reasons I called you. I could really use you up here with me. I need someone I can trust on my side. What if you asked Polk to assign you to this case, too?"

"I'm way ahead of you."

"Huh?"

"I put in a request to Polk to be assigned to the Natalie Jarvis case with you. I said you needed a partner up there. And what better partner do you have than me, right? Anyway, I hope to get an answer from him tomorrow."

I exhaled a sigh of relief. "That's great, Alex."

I heard a commotion on the phone from her end.

"Sorry. That's my kid. Jonathan is very well behaved unless he is hungry. And right now he's hungry. Come to think of it my husband is the same way. Bob's the greatest guy in the world when I feed him. But if I don't... well, let's just say I better get back to making everyone's dinner."

She was married to a senior foreign policy analyst with the State Department, and they had a young son who had just turned four years old. It was a lot for her to juggle, but her mother helped raise the boy when they were busy with their careers. As a result, Alex was usually able to deal with balancing her personal and professional life pretty well.

"How do you do it, Alex?"

"Cook dinner?"

"No, I mean how do you manage to be an FBI agent and a wife and a mother all at the same time—and do it all so well?"

She laughed. "I have my good days, and my bad days."

"I worry about that. About after Greg and I are married. He wants a wife, I think. He wants a more traditional wife than I am. I'm not sure I can balance my professional and my personal lives as well as you do."

"You'll be fine, Nikki. You'll figure it out, just like I did. One of the keys to me doing what I do is that I make sure to always stay in constant communication with Bob when I'm on assignment or out of town on a job. That's very important. Are you doing that with Greg?"

"Of course."

"When's the last time you talked to him?"

"He's my next call after I hang up with you."

Greg wanted to talk to me about a lot of things. About wedding invitations. About a church where he thought it would be perfect for us to be married. About a big new case that he was working on for his law firm. About a new series he'd started watching on Netflix. About a pizza place he'd heard raves about and had ordered his dinner from that night.

"Dinner for one, I might point out," he said.

"I'm sorry."

"When are you coming back?"

"As soon as this case is over."

"How long will that take?"

"I'm not exactly sure yet."

"You have to be back here next weekend for that party at my senior partner's house. It's very important. I need you to be there for me, Nikki."

"I'll be there."

"Are you sure?"

"I promise. I'll be back in time for the party."

I wasn't certain I could keep that promise, but I didn't want

to argue about it with him now. I didn't have the time or energy
to explain my job to him one more time. Going to a party at the
house of his law firm's senior partner was not exactly a priority
for me right now. What was going on here in Huntsdale was my
priority.

"I still don't understand... you were originally going to be up
there for only a day."

"It's getting complicated."

I ran through it with him, like I had done with Alex.

"A lot of facts that don't add up to me. The fact that Natalie
Jarvis was almost the same age as when my sister Caitlin disappeared—and was eventually murdered. The fact that Natalie
disappeared on the exact day of the fifteenth anniversary of my
sister's death. The fact that David Munroe—after years of
silence—summoned me for the meeting at the prison just before
Natalie went missing. And now—on top of all that—I find out
about the possible connection with the roses.

"If that's all coincidence, it's a hell of a series of coinci-
dences. Something is going on here. Something more than just
the search for a missing girl. Yes, I want to find Natalie Jarvis
and save her. That has to be my primary mission back here in
Huntsdale. But, more than ever now, I believe that finding out
the answers to what happened to Natalie Jarvis might help me
answer some of the questions that have haunted me about
Caitlin too over all these years."

We talked a bit more until his doorbell rang and he said he
had to go get his pizza that was being delivered.

"I miss you, babe," he said.

"Miss you too."

I think he wanted to keep talking after he got the pizza, but
I got off the phone then as quickly as I could. I didn't want to
waste any more time. I had to get back to work here.

FOURTEEN

I needed a place to start on trying to find a link between Natalie Jarvis and my sister's murder.

And the best place was to go back and pick up my own father's investigation on Caitlin from fifteen years ago.

Which meant I needed to read my father's police report.

Chief Earnshaw had said he wouldn't let me see it without getting approval first from the District Attorney.

So I drove over to the D.A.'s office.

I was surprised when I first found out from Earnshaw that Tommy Thompson was still the prosecutor here. Thompson had been the District Attorney in Huntsdale for a long time. More than twenty years. Which meant he would have known—and worked with—my father when he was the police chief. I'd never paid much attention to Thompson back then. It wasn't until he prosecuted the case against David Munroe for murdering my sister that I became aware of him.

But then being a D.A. in Huntsdale wasn't like being a D.A. in Washington, D.C. or New York or some other big city. My sister's murder was probably one of the few big crime cases he ever became involved with. Someone like Tommy Thompson could just keep getting re-elected every four years or so, handling a lot of small-town, mundane things, without anyone trying very seriously to replace him.

Maybe my father was like that too. He'd been police chief for years. Probably would have kept on in that job for a long time too, just like Thompson.

Tommy Thompson knew all about me and what I'd been doing since I left Huntsdale after my sister's death. And, unlike Chief Earnshaw, he seemed happy to see me back in town.

"Well, well, Huntsdale's famous crime fighter comes home. This is an honor, Nikki."

"I always thought my father was Huntsdale's most famous crime fighter." I smiled.

"Your father never got a million hits on a viral video during an arrest."

"You saw that?"

"Who didn't? That was a helluva video. A helluva arrest for you. A helluva thing you did to save that young girl. Huntsdale is proud of you. Your father would have been very proud of you too."

"Thank you," I said. "That means a lot."

Thompson looked like he hadn't aged too much over the years. His hair was gray, and he'd probably put on a few too many pounds around the middle. But he still looked like he could be the Huntsdale District Attorney for another twenty years or so.

There was a picture on his desk of his family. I remembered my father had a picture like that on his desk too. Me, my mother and Caitlin. For the rest of Huntsdale, for people like Tommy Thompson and his family, life had gone on as normal for the past fifteen years. But my family's life—the life as we knew it—had been gone for a long time.

"I'm helping the local police on the Natalie Jarvis case," I said. "But the real reason I came back to Huntsdale—"

"You interviewed David Munroe."

"Who told you?"

"Chief Earnshaw."

"He didn't seem happy about me doing it. About going back on my sister's case again. Are you?"

He shrugged. "Hell, you've been coming every year on the anniversary of your sister's death to try to do that. So now he decides he wants to talk to you? Why wouldn't you follow up on an offer like that?"

"You're very well-informed," I said.

"I wouldn't last long in this job without being connected to a lot of people in law enforcement. So what did David Munroe tell you?"

"He said he didn't do it."

"You know what they say, right?" Thompson laughed. "There are no guilty men in jail. If you don't believe that, just ask them. Every one of them will tell you how they're really innocent. That they were framed. That someone else really did the crime they're serving time for. Is that basically what Munroe told you?"

I nodded.

I told him then about the rose someone had sent to Natalie Jarvis before she disappeared. And about the roses I found on my father and sister's graves. I said it made me wonder if there could be some connection between the disappearance of Natalie Jarvis and what happened to my sister all those years ago.

"If Munroe really was telling the truth about someone besides him killing Caitlin, maybe that person—or persons—is responsible for Natalie's disappearance now too," I said to Thompson. "And Natalie Jarvis went missing on the same date, July nineteenth, that my sister did at the carnival."

But Thompson quickly dismissed the idea.

"It most likely is a copycat at work here. Someone who

knew about the roses with your sister. And knew about the anniversary date too. It was a high-profile murder, one of the few we've ever had around here that got so much attention. But that's all it could be now, a copycat. One thing I am certain of is that David Munroe—and no one else—killed Caitlin. So whatever is happening with Natalie Jarvis, it has nothing to do with Munroe. Or with your sister's murder. All these years he's never said one word in his defense or claimed that he wasn't the one who killed her. Why now? Why suddenly out of the blue come up with a story about being framed for the killing? He's just playing games with you, Nikki. What other reason could there be?"

"He's sick."

"Yes, I know about that too. Happy to hear about it. Hope he suffers a lot from the friggin' cancer."

"Maybe he's trying to make things right because of that."

"It is right. We got it right when we arrested him—it was your father who did that—and put him in jail for life. End of story."

"So you're certain that he murdered my sister. You never had any doubts at all about David Munroe's guilt?" I asked Thompson.

"None whatsoever. It was a slam-dunk conviction. Hell, he even confessed."

I said I still wanted to go back and try to talk to Munroe in prison again. To get more information from him about his claim that he wasn't the one who killed my sister. Before I did that, I said, I wanted to go through the official police report on the case that my father wrote up at the time. I explained how Earnshaw wouldn't give me access to it without approval from the D.A.'s office.

"No problem," Thompson said.

"You'll tell Earnshaw to show me the report?"

"I will. Even though you're not going to find out anything

significant, I'm afraid, beyond what all of us—including your father—were able to learn back then at the time. I know it's always been difficult for you and your family to accept, Nikki. That there was no reason for your sister to die the way she did, that it was just one sick son of a bitch who caused all this agony. You want more answers. And I wish I could give you those answers to make you feel better somehow. To make some sense out of it all. But David Munroe did it, he was arrested and convicted of murder, and he'll never kill anyone again."

"The D.A. is certain he got the right guy, huh?" Alex Del Vecchio said when I called her at the FBI office in Washington and told her about my conversation with District Attorney Tommy Thompson. "But you're not, huh?"

"Think about it, Alex. This is the only major crime case this guy Thompson has ever prosecuted in his entire career. He's been living off the fame from this for years, getting elected over and over again because people remember him from this high-profile case. That's really the only thing he's ever accomplished. Everything else in his career has been small time. What if it turned out he got it wrong? Or at least didn't get it all right, and other people were involved? His entire reputation would be destroyed. Even if there were just questions being raised about Munroe being the sole killer, it would look bad for him. He's going to make sure he does everything he can to make sure everyone believes he got it right."

"Well, I do have some good news from this end."

"I could use some good news."

"I just heard back from Polk. He okayed the assignment."

"So...?"

"I'll be in Huntsdale with you in the morning, Nikki."

FIFTEEN

The Huntsdale police file on my sister's case was separated into two parts.

First, there was the initial investigation into the disappearance and massive police search for her after she vanished.

Then came the discovery of her body; the murder investigation; the search for a suspect; and the arrest of David Munroe.

The key to catching Munroe turned out to be a parking ticket. Huntsdale cops had been out in force for the carnival, ticketing any cars that parked illegally at the scene. They wound up giving out a lot of tickets before Caitlin's abduction. All were from people in town or people who had an obvious reason for being there except for one, my father discovered. That one was issued to David Munroe, whose car was registered in a town some thirty miles away in southeastern Ohio. This was enough to question Munroe about his reason for being there—and soon led to his confession.

It should have given my father some kind of satisfaction, I suppose, to have caught the man who killed Caitlin. But instead I think it left him with an empty feeling. When he was investigating the case he had a purpose. Now he was just left with the tragic loss of his daughter.

Not long afterward, they found him slumped over the wheel of his police car in the station parking lot. His morning coffee and glazed donut were still on the seat next to him. He'd suffered a massive coronary.

The entire file he'd compiled on Caitlin's case was large, just what you'd expect in a town where most of the other crimes consisted of traffic violations, domestic disputes and high school kids who partied too loudly on the weekend.

But it was also very clear, concise and to the point. I could almost hear my father's voice in the words I was reading, and I knew he had written most of it. I thought again about how horribly difficult and traumatic it must have been for my father to keep doing his job in such a professional manner even though the victim was his own daughter.

There were autopsy documents, evidence lists, forensic analysis, photos of the crime scene, both from the carnival and later from the woods where Caitlin's body was found; written statements and summaries from my father as well as other officers who had worked on the case.

I started from the beginning, with the report of the first officer to arrive at the scene of the carnival, soon after Caitlin went missing:

At 1530 hours, the department responded to a report of a missing girl at 221 Canyon Road, which turned out to be the site of a carnival in Huntsdale that week.

Officer Gary Lawton spoke there to Nikki Cassidy, 18, who said she couldn't locate her 12-year-old sister, Caitlin Cassidy. Caitlin Cassidy was last seen by Nikki and her two friends—identified as Carol Ladzinski and Katie Gompers— standing next to the Tilt-A-Whirl while the girls were riding it.

A search, first inside the immediate area, then the entire carnival, turned up no sign of the missing girl.

There were interviews after that with potential witnesses. With me. With Carol Ladzinski and Katie Gompers, the two girlfriends with me that day. With the guy who operated the Tilt-A-Whirl. With the ticket taker at the park. And with anyone who attended the carnival that day who might have seen my sister—either before or after she disappeared.

State troopers were called in for the search; volunteers from the town knocked on doors and talked to anyone who might have seen her; and various theories were put forward about what might have happened. She was dead, she was kidnapped, she had an accident, she ran away, etc. etc.

You could almost feel the desperation of my father and the rest of the Huntsdale force as the days went by without any trace of Caitlin.

The more time that passed, the likelihood grew that Caitlin was dead. I'd worked cases like this in my career, and I knew how the forty-eight-hour rule worked. The key to finding a missing child was in those first forty-eight hours after the victim went missing. Everything after that decreased the odds that the case could be solved and he or she would be brought home safely.

Reading through all of this now, it brought back memories of me living through all this back then—sitting at home waiting for word of my sister as my father went out to look for her each day and my mother yelled at me and did everything possible to make me feel guilty for allowing this to happen.

I thought my life couldn't get any worse during those first hours and days after Caitlin went missing.

But I was wrong.

It got worse very soon.

Much worse.

When they found Caitlin's body.

The second part of the file dealt with that and the subsequent arrest of David Munroe for her murder.

The writing was still official sounding and non-emotional, like this was just any other case. But I could only imagine the pain and anguish it caused my father to write and to read this report. It was the biggest case of his career, but it involved the death of his own daughter. I suppose he might have had a heart attack at any point during all this. But he somehow made it another few weeks—until Munroe was in jail—before he died.

I read a portion of the account about finding Caitlin's body:

Six days after she disappeared, a dog walker discovered the body of Caitlin Cassidy in Grant Woods, located a few miles away from the carnival site. She was lying on her back, her arms crossed in front of her and someone had placed a wreath of roses on top of her head.

Michael Franze, the medical examiner, conducted an autopsy and said she had been shot in the head by a single .45 caliber bullet, which killed her instantly. There was no sign of physical or sexual abuse. Although there were marks on both her wrists and her ankles to indicate she had been restrained for an extensive period before her death.

The time of death was estimated to have been fairly recent, apparently several days after she was abducted from the carnival.

There were photos and diagrams of the crime scene. An X marked the location of Caitlin's body. Another X showed exactly where the roses had been found. The photos were tough to look at, especially the ones of Caitlin's body being removed. I'd been to a lot of crime scenes, but never seen one so personal for me. So it must have been almost unbearable for my father to have been there and later to have to look at these pictures.

The last section of the report dealt with the arrest of Munroe for Caitlin's murder several days later.

> *Officer Rudy Delgado of the Huntsdale Police Department discovered that a parking ticket had been placed on the windshield of a car near the carnival site that belonged to David Munroe of Cloverfield, Ohio, about thirty miles from Huntsdale, at approximately the same time period when Caitlin Cassidy went missing.*
>
> *Delgado visited Munroe, who—when questioned by the officer—appeared nervous and defensive. After further questioning, Munroe simply told Delgado: "You got me. I'm the one you're looking for."*
>
> *Officer Delgado and other officers then obtained a search warrant for the Munroe residence. They found jewelry that had belonged to Caitlin Cassidy; a piece of her clothing; and strands of female hair that were later determined to be hers.*
>
> *Munroe was arrested and formally charged with the murder of Caitlin Cassidy.*

The police summary at the end of the file was concise and almost matter-of-fact in its confidence that the case had been solved.

> *Based on all the available evidence, the inescapable conclusion is that David Munroe abducted, then later shot and killed Caitlin Cassidy.*
>
> *The accused confessed—but offered no explanation for carrying out the crime.*
>
> *It has been determined by the Huntsdale Police Department that Munroe carried out the abduction and murder of Caitlin Cassidy on his own. There is no evidence to warrant any further police investigation of this case, and it has been handed over to the District Attorney's Office for prosecution.*

I'd been taking notes the entire time I'd been reading through the file. I'd skipped through a lot of pages very quickly —the ones covering routine police procedures. But I still had plenty of stuff I'd written down.

There was a lot of information in the report, all right.

But not enough.

I wrote down the names of people that I wanted to go back and talk to again now:

Gary Lawton, the first police officer on the scene at the carnival that day.

Rudy Delgado, the officer who arrested Munroe.

Carol Ladzinski and Katie Gompers, the two friends who had accompanied me and Caitlin to the carnival on that long ago summer day.

Michael Franze, the medical examiner who did the autopsy on Caitlin's remains.

And—most of all—David Munroe. Again.

I needed to go back to the prison to find out what secrets Munroe was still holding on to after all this time—and if he and my sister's murder fifteen years ago really had anything to do with Natalie Jarvis now.

I needed to go back and restart the investigation my father did fifteen years ago before he died.

I needed to start at the beginning and follow the trail of evidence all over again.

Wherever that might take me...

SIXTEEN

Alex Del Vecchio was in Huntsdale with me now too. As soon as she arrived, I explained to her how my top priority was to try to talk to David Munroe again. In order to do that, I had to make another request for a visit to him in prison. That meant dealing with his lawyer, Doreen Trask. So, I reached out to Trask and asked if Alex and I could stop by her office.

As it turned out, Doreen Trask didn't have an office. Well, not a real office anyway. She said she pretty much worked out of her home and her car.

"Her legal practice must not be exactly a booming success," Alex said.

"You think?"

Alex and I got the car office. She pulled up to meet us in front of the Huntsdale police station in a battered old Honda Civic filled with files, paperwork and what looked like a lot of clothes as well. Maybe she lived out of the car too.

I'd tried to prepare Alex for how strange this female attorney of Munroe's really was, but she still seemed a bit surprised by her arrival and her appearance when she parked the car and got out to meet us.

"Not too many successful lawyers work out of their car instead of an office," Alex said.

"Matthew McConaughey did in *The Lincoln Lawyer*," I pointed out.

"That ain't no Lincoln," she said, looking at the battered Honda.

"Well, let's go talk to her."

"Do you think there's room for us inside that car with all the junk piled around?"

Fortunately, instead of getting in the car, we all sat together in a park in the center of Huntsdale. Doreen Trask looked pretty much the same way she had that first day I'd seen her at the prison. Baggy jeans, a sweatshirt, stringy and unkempt hair. She clearly wasn't a woman who spent a lot of time on fashion or making herself look good. I wondered what Munroe saw in Doreen to want to "marry" her. But then Munroe was in jail for the rest of his life, so he didn't have much of a choice when it came to female companionship.

I asked her how she and David Munroe had first met. Had he turned to her for legal advice?

"No, I was the one who found him," she said. "I read about him and the case, and I was intrigued. So I wrote him a letter in prison. I thought he might be a good fit for me romantically. He wrote me back. Then I asked to come see him as a visitor. And, after that, well... things just clicked between David and me. He was just what I was looking for in a romance."

"You wrote a letter to a prisoner convicted of murder because you thought he might be a good fit for romance with you?" Alex asked incredulously.

Thank you, Alex, I thought to myself—I had the same question.

"That's what I do," Doreen Trask said.

"Excuse me?" Alex asked.

Again, my question.

It's good to have a partner who thinks like you.

And right now we both thought this woman was pretty weird.

"I'm what they call a 'jailbird dater.'" She laughed. "I've been doing this for a long time. I've had relationships with a lot of men in prison before. None of them were as serious though as my relationship with David. David and I are soulmates. That's why I married him. And it's why I'm having his baby."

She talked about her fascination with dating prison inmates. Others at first, then finally David Munroe. It was a bizarre story, and I wasn't sure if it had anything to do with Munroe's new comments about my sister's murder. But I wanted to hear everything, so I talked to Doreen Trask about being a "jailbird dater."

"I'd read about women who did that sort of thing—sometimes even with inmates on Death Row—and I wanted to do it myself. There's something wild and daring and kinkily crazy about it—it just gives me a thrill I could never get out of dating normal men on the outside of prison walls.

"Is it dangerous? No, it's probably the safest dating you can do. I mean they're in prison. They're under control twenty-four-seven. So don't you see? Meeting up with a prison inmate like that is not as dangerous as picking up some strange guy in a singles bar or on Tinder or any other dating spot or app.

"As for sex, it's not easy—but it can be done. As David's lawyer, I'm able to meet with him one-on-one for conferences. It's not technically a conjugal visit, but we're able to manage being alone for long enough to get the deed done! Hey, that's how I'm pregnant right now with David's baby."

She explained how she managed to get a law degree—albeit from a less than well-known or prominent law school—and used it to become David Munroe's official attorney as well as his lover.

"David's not a bad person," she said. "He just made some bad decisions. He got involved with the wrong people. He regrets that now. But he says he's innocent of your sister's murder—and I believe him."

"He admits he was there when my sister died?" I said.

"Yes. But he says he couldn't do anything to stop it."

"He's never told this story before."

"He was afraid to."

"Afraid of what?"

"Powerful people."

"What powerful people?"

"That's all I know."

I looked over at Alex and shook my head. I wasn't sure where this was going. I could tell she had the same feeling.

"Then why is he talking about it now?" I asked.

"He's sick. He's convinced he doesn't have much longer to live. He wants to make amends. He wants to right the wrongs. But he's still afraid. He won't even tell me the specifics of what really happened with your sister. But he says he never meant to hurt you—or your little sister. And he thinks you have a right to know more about what happened to her—and why. That's why he met with you."

"We have to talk to him again," I said.

"Why?"

"Because there's a lot of things he still has to tell us if he wants us to believe his story about not being my sister's murderer. Like who the real killer is if it wasn't him. He claims there were other people involved. But when I asked him where I could go looking for them, he said: 'Nowhere... they're nowhere.' What the hell does that mean? He also said something strange about my father knowing more about all this before he died. It's not enough. I need more from David Munroe."

"David said he told you all he can. That you'll have to find out the rest by yourself."

"Why doesn't he just tell me it all himself? Or tell you so

that you can pass that information on to me. Why all these games?"

"He says there are people who would kill him if they knew he was going to give up information about them. He says he wanted you to figure it out. That you should be able to do it."

"I need more information from him, Doreen. Can you set up another meeting with him at the prison?"

She nodded.

"Okay, I'll do my best to try to get you in to see him again," she said.

"With Alex too. She's my partner. I want her to hear his story as well."

"Let me see what I can do," she said.

As we walked back to her car, I asked about her baby.

"It's going to be a boy," she said.

A son.

David Munroe—the man I've been convinced for fifteen years murdered my sister Caitlin—was now going to have a son roaming the world too.

I wasn't sure how I felt about that.

I wasn't sure I believed anything that he—or this crazy Doreen Trask woman—had told me.

I wasn't sure about anything.

SEVENTEEN

The search for Natalie Jarvis continued relentlessly each day. Between Alex and me and the local police, we must have knocked on every door in Huntsdale. Talked to residents. Searched what seemed like every inch of the town and surrounding area. But no one knew anything about what happened to Natalie Jarvis.

"It's like the ground opened up, and she fell through it," Alex said in frustration to me. "Or a flying saucer dropped down from outer space and took her away to another planet. She's just... gone."

Of course, she could be dead. We were obviously keenly aware of that possibility. But, at least for now, we were operating on the theory that Natalie Jarvis had been abducted and was still alive somewhere. My father had operated on the same premise fifteen years ago when Caitlin disappeared. Until he found her body. Hopefully, this would turn out to have a better ending. Meanwhile, at the moment, all we could do was keep looking for Natalie.

It wasn't like we didn't have a lot of leads in searching for her. We had plenty of leads. Except every lead, every tip we received and followed up on turned out to be a dead end.

Someone called into the hotline we'd set up for information about Natalie and said they'd seen her at a mall in a nearby town buying clothes at Gap. Which made sense, the caller suggested. She'd need a change of clothes if she was running away from home, and where better to get some new duds than at Gap. A clerk at Gap told us a girl resembling Natalie's description had been in the store, and she tried to shoplift several articles of clothing. She was caught by a security guard before she could leave the mall and taken into custody. She was not Natalie Jarvis.

Another potential lead came when an Instagram photo was emailed to us at the station that showed Natalie on the back of a motorcycle with a biker gang. She was wearing black jeans, boots and a leather jacket with chains hanging from it. It sure looked like Natalie in the photo and—since there were a lot of biker gangs in the southern Ohio area—it seemed at first like she had joined up, or else been kidnapped, by one of them. And it was Natalie in the picture, but only her face. It was quickly determined that someone had photoshopped the picture on another woman's body from the gang. No idea why, some sort of sick prank, I suspect.

There was even a psychic in the mix. A man who claimed he was clairvoyant and said he had been experiencing strong visions of Natalie Jarvis' location. He said she was still in the Huntsdale area, but that he sensed she was in a body of water. She might be dead, or she might still be alive—he wasn't sure about that. But he said if we found the body of water in Huntsdale, we'd find Natalie. He also asked us if we could help him get on the *Dr. Phil* show or Fox News or CNN with his story. The problem was there was no real lake or river in Huntsdale, which is pretty much a landlocked area. The psychic probably should have checked his geography before coming to see us.

Meanwhile, the real search for Natalie went on.

I went back to the Jarvis family home every day. Sometimes by myself, and then later with Alex.

Partly to assure them we were doing everything we could to find their daughter. But also to try to pick up any kind of information about Natalie that might help us. I learned that Natalie loved cats—they had two Siamese named Ollie and Otto; Captain Marvel movies, which is why she went to the theater that day; chocolate fudge sundaes; playing soccer on the middle school team where she attended—she was the goalie; and was already talking about wanting to be a teacher when she grew up because she loved school so much.

Hundreds of fliers and pictures of Natalie were distributed around town. At supermarkets, at bus stops, at the schools— even though there were only a handful of students and teachers there for the summer session—and even to people simply walking down the street in Huntsdale.

We must have walked that route from Natalie's house to the theater and back dozens of times. Looking over and over for some clue we might have missed about what changed for this thirteen-year-old girl on that seemingly normal afternoon trip to the movies.

We went back to the movie theater too.

I sat in the seat Natalie sat in that day. Then I made my way up to the lobby. Then to the ladies' room, where she apparently went first. And then to the refreshment counter where she bought a big bag of buttered popcorn. After that... poof! She was gone.

I'm not sure what exactly I was hoping to find at the theater. A hidden note from Natalie telling me what happened? A secret code or map scratched on the ladies' room wall or back of a theater seat? A trail of popcorn kernels she left behind as a trail so that we could follow and find her?

But there was nothing.

The same way there had been nothing with my sister Caitlin's disappearance either, until they found her body.

God, I didn't want that to happen again with Natalie Jarvis.

And what about boys? Was there someone romantic in the picture? She did get that single rose, according to one of her friends. And there was that card about roses I found in her room. That all bore a shocking similarity to the roses that had been placed on top of my sister's head when it was discovered. But lots of people give other people roses. It could have been something innocent.

Does a thirteen-year-old girl even have a boyfriend at that age? Her parents didn't know about anyone. But then a thirteen-year-old girl might not tell her parents something like that. Especially if her romantic interest was someone older. I tried to remember if I had any boyfriends when I was thirteen. I didn't think so. I mean I had crushes on a couple of boys back then, but I never went out with anybody on a date or anything until I was older, in my teens.

But the rose still bothered me.

Someone had sent her a rose.

Who?

A secret admirer?

Or maybe the person that abducted her.

And maybe it was somehow linked to the roses found with my sister's body.

I looked at a picture of Natalie Jarvis. She was thirteen years old. She loved cats, she loved Captain Marvel, she loved chocolate fudge sundaes, she loved playing soccer and she wanted to be a teacher one day because she loved school so much.

And then one summer afternoon she went to a movie and never came back.

Just like Caitlin.

I stared at the picture of Natalie Jarvis for a long time.

Tried to imagine where she might possibly be right now.

But I came up totally blank.

Where are you, Natalie Jarvis?

EIGHTEEN

"Tell me what it was like for you," Billy Weller said.

"What do you mean?"

"Being here in Huntsdale. After your sister died."

"It was terrible. The funeral. My father's death. All of it was just terrible..."

"No. I mean what was it really like for you? How did you cope with it? How did you survive that time and somehow become the woman that you are today?"

I hadn't really talked about that with anyone. Not really talked about my feelings and what I went through back then. Not even with the grief counselor I met with a few times that summer before I went away to college. I just kept all those emotions and trauma and guilt bottled up inside me.

Weller and I were having lunch at a diner in downtown Huntsdale. I was eating a triple-decker tuna fish sandwich with sliced hard-boiled egg and lots of mayonnaise. He had a big cheeseburger and fries. Everything tasted great. I'd forgotten how good the food can be at a small-town diner like this. Oh, they had diners and coffee shops in Washington and other big cities where I've been. This diner though was a place I used to come to a lot when I was growing up in Huntsdale, and it held some great memories for me.

But that was all B.C., of course.

Before Caitlin died.

This was the first time I'd been back in fifteen years.

Alex was in her hotel room on a Zoom call with her family in Washington. So it was just me and Billy having lunch together.

"It was the summer after I graduated high school," I said slowly to Billy Weller now. "I was headed to college. This was my last summer in Huntsdale before I left for school. I had... well, I had a lot of fun for those first few weeks before the carnival. I was really enjoying myself, looking forward to going to college and getting ready for the rest of my life.

"After my sister died, my own life was never the same. Those immediate days afterward were terrible, of course: the funeral, the arrest of David Munroe and all of the rest of it that was going on. But the most difficult part for me came when it was all over. And I was left with just the memories, the sadness and the guilt over my own part in what happened to Caitlin.

"My mother hardly ever spoke to me. She could barely look at me. When she did say something, it was to make clear that she blamed me for Caitlin's death. That was a lot for me to deal with as an eighteen-year-old girl.

"For a long time, she kept Caitlin's bedroom the way it had been that last night she slept there. She never even changed a calendar Caitlin had in the room: it remained at July nineteenth, the day of the carnival. She wouldn't throw away any of Caitlin's clothes or things, she cleaned the room regularly and changed the sheets as if Caitlin was still there.

"Like she was waiting for Caitlin to come back. Maybe I was too. Sometimes, when no one else was around, I used to sit on Caitlin's bed and try to talk to her. I'd tell her how much I missed her, how I hoped she was okay wherever she was, how sorry I was for not helping save her somehow that last day.

"I suppose I hoped her spirit might still be floating around somewhere in that bedroom, and I could get my message through to her. That she would hear me wherever she was. That she would respond with some kind of a sign. But there was never anything. Caitlin was gone. At some point, I accepted that reality."

"What about your father?" Weller asked. "Did he blame you for her death? Did he make you feel guilty?"

I shook my head.

"My father helped me. I don't know how I could have gotten through it without him. He said we all make decisions in our lives that have repercussions we didn't expect, and that I had simply done what any teenage girl might have done when I disobeyed my mother about staying home with Caitlin and instead took her to the carnival with me. I loved my father. He was the best man I ever knew."

"But then your father died, right? When was that?"

"Later that same summer. Only a few weeks after my sister. He had the heart attack, he was gone and then things got even worse. I felt guilty about that too, figuring the heart attack might never have happened if he wasn't dealing with all the trauma of Caitlin's death and the trauma and stress of directing the police investigation into her murder."

"And your mother?"

"My father's death really pushed her over the edge. She continually lashed out at me now, blamed me for him and Caitlin and everything. You would think losing my father and sister might have wound up pushing us closer together as the only people remaining from our family. But it was the exact opposite. It was like she couldn't stand to look at me anymore. I reminded her of everything she had lost—her husband and her daughter. That was the worst time of all for me. So, yes, those days before I left Huntsdale for college were a nightmare. I don't remember all of it, a lot is a blur. All I knew was I had to get out of Huntsdale. So that fall I left and pretty much never came back. I went to college at Georgetown in Washington. I took criminal justice courses there. Thought about being a lawyer, but then decided on a career in law enforcement. Worked for a local police department in Virginia for a while, then joined the FBI."

I finished off the last of my tuna fish sandwich. I suddenly realized that I was eating the same thing—the same sandwich— the last time I was at this diner that long ago summer. The diner looked exactly the same. Even the menu was basically unchanged too. The only thing that had changed since the last time I had been here was me. So much has changed for me since then.

"I remember thinking about you that summer," Weller said now. "Worrying about how you were doing. Obviously, everyone in town knew about what happened and I hoped you were all right. I thought about reaching out to you to offer condolences, but I never did. I guess... I guess I was afraid you might..."

"Not remember you?" I smiled.

"Yes, not remember me. Who's this Billy Weller guy? So I did nothing. I regret that now."

"Like I said, I'm sorry I didn't remember you when we met. And thanks."

Neither of us said anything for a while. We just finished our meals.

"Look," Weller said finally, "I hope I wasn't out of line in bringing all this from the past up again. I didn't want to stir up any old memories that you would prefer not to deal with again."

"I'm fine, Billy," I said.

Alex walked into the diner now. She gave me a surprised

look when she saw me having lunch with Billy. Then she sat down in the booth with us.

"What are you two doing?" she asked.

"Just finishing up lunch, that's all. Did you eat?"

"Yeah, I grabbed a salad before my Zoom call home. I'm getting back to work now. I have a lead on a few other girls that might have known Natalie Jarvis pretty well. So I'll try to interview them, see if they know anything more about her that might help us. How about you?"

"I'm going to spend some more time digging into my sister's case."

"Doing what?"

"I'm going to look for Carol Ladzinski and Katie Gompers."

"Who are they?"

"The two girls—my high school friends—that I went to the carnival with on the day my sister disappeared."

NINETEEN

I hadn't talked or been in contact with either Carol Ladzinski or Katie Gompers since we graduated.

But I was able to get enough information from Huntsdale High School alumni records and other stuff online to track the trail of both since our days together back then when we were teenagers.

Carol Ladzinski had never left the area after high school. Gotten married and started a family right here in Huntsdale. That was the good news I found out. But the bad news turned out to be that she had died a few years ago. From breast cancer not long after her thirtieth birthday. That was the problem working on a cold case as old as this one. People died or disappeared or forget things over the years. It's always difficult doing an investigation so long after the crime.

I got the information about Carol's death when I called the most recent number I'd found for her. I said I was an old friend who'd gone to high school with her and expressed my condolences, even though I didn't really know Carol Ladzinski anymore. I mean, we'd been friends in high school, she was with me that day at the carnival and after that we hardly ever spoke anymore.

I felt bad about Carol, felt bad for her husband and family. But I didn't really have any overwhelming grief about her death. Mostly it was frustration over the fact that this was another dead end in my investigation.

Katie Gompers wasn't as easy to track down, but at least she was still alive. Not living in Huntsdale though. I found out from her parents that she worked now as a fashion designer for a department store in Pittsburgh. They gave me a number to contact her. She said that it was only an hour's drive from Pittsburgh to Huntsdale and she'd meet up with me here later that night at a place called the Hickory Bar. Which we both found pretty funny. The Hickory Bar had been around when we both lived here as teenagers and it had a reputation as a really swinging, fun place. Katie and I always wanted to go there, but we were too young. Now we were finally going to get to see the inside of the Hickory Bar.

I told Alex what I was doing, and I asked her to keep trying with Doreen Trask to set up a new interview with David Munroe.

I also told Alex to try to find the two police officers from back at the time of Caitlin's murder—Delgado and Lawton—who had been specifically mentioned in the police report by my father.

Then I called Les Polk at the FBI offices in Washington to fill him in on the status of what was going on in Huntsdale.

I told him about the search teams out looking for Natalie Jarvis, about my conversations with her family and friends and about the way she simply suddenly disappeared off the security video at the movie theater.

And also about the links I kept finding between her disappearance and my own sister's abduction and murder.

"How are you getting along with the local authorities on this?" Polk asked me when I was finished.

"I'm coping."

"What about the police chief? You said he didn't like you very much."

"Hard to believe, huh?"

"Just remember you represent the FBI."

"Don't worry. I'll behave myself. Besides, I've got the local District Attorney on my side, along with one of the cops on the Huntsdale force. So I'm doing okay despite any opposition from Police Chief Frank Earnshaw."

"One more thing, Nikki: you're there to investigate the disappearance of this Natalie Jarvis girl, not to reopen the case of your own sister, whatever suspicions you might have."

"Funny, that's the same thing Chief Earnshaw told me."

Not long after I hung up with Polk, I got another phone call. This time from Greg in Washington. I wasn't expecting him to call then. And I sure wasn't expecting what he told me.

"I'm flying up there tomorrow to see you, Nikki."

"What? Why?"

"Because I miss you. And, if you won't come back to Washington to see me, I'll come there to see you."

"What about your job at the law firm?"

"I'll just take the day off. Fly up to Huntsdale tomorrow afternoon, spend the night with you—and then fly back to Washington the next morning. Maybe I can even convince you to come back with me."

Later that evening, I headed to the Hickory Bar to talk with Katie Gompers.

I had no idea what to expect from a woman I hadn't seen or

talked to since we were in high school here a long time ago. I wondered if she felt the same way about meeting me.

Katie Gompers turned out to have aged pretty well. I recognized her as soon as I walked into the bar.

"You look great!" I said, after we'd hugged and sat down at the bar.

"You too."

We ordered some drinks and began to talk more comfortably after we each had a few sips of the alcohol. Surprisingly comfortably for two people who hadn't seen each other since we were kids growing up. It made me remember how much I liked Katie back then, and I guess why were such good friends in high school.

"I wasn't sure what to expect of you," I told her. "You could have put on fifty pounds or whatever. But then I guess you weren't sure what to expect when you saw me either, huh?"

"Oh, I knew exactly what you would look like. I saw you on TV."

Of course.

"And online too."

The viral video.

"You're famous, Nikki."

"Only for a little while." I smiled.

We reminisced a bit about our days together in high school. She didn't know about Carol and seemed shook up when I told her how Carol had died. "That's tragic," she said. "I'm really sorry to hear that."

She seemed to mean it too. Which made me feel a little guilty I didn't react more personally to the news when I found out about the death from Carol's husband. But then I wasn't looking up these women from my past just to reconnect, I was focused on doing my job.

She asked me questions about my work at the FBI—"It

sounds so exciting!"—and she told me about her career as a fashion designer.

"Tell me everything you remember about that day we were at the carnival and Caitlin disappeared," I finally said to her.

"Okay. But why? Why now? I didn't really understand that on the phone when you told me how you needed to talk with me again about it."

"There's been a similar case in Huntsdale," I said.

I told her about Natalie Jarvis.

"My God! Who would have ever imagined something happening like that in quiet little Huntsdale? But what does this have to do with your sister?"

"I'm exploring the possibility that both incidents could be connected."

"Fifteen years apart?"

"Yes, I believe that there is some kind of a link between my sister's death and the disappearance of Natalie Jarvis."

Katie sighed, picked up her drink and took a big swig. Then she shook her head.

"I still don't understand. They guy who killed your sister is in prison. David Munroe. How could he have had anything to do with this new missing girl?"

"Munroe says now he didn't do it."

"What?"

"He told me he didn't kill my sister. He said that someone else did it, but he won't tell me who. If he's telling the truth, then the real killer is still out there."

"Jeez, you mean...?"

"Yes, that means the police got the wrong man for Caitlin's murder."

I asked her to take me again through everything she remembered about that day at the carnival. I said I wanted every detail, no matter how small, that she remembered. I was hoping that something she said might point me in a different direction in the investigation after we talked.

Most of it though was just a repetition of everything I already knew.

Our excitement about going to the carnival because we wanted to meet some boys we knew were going to be there. My frustration after my mother told me I couldn't go and had to stay home with my sister. My decision to take Caitlin along so I could be there with Katie and Carol after all. The rides at the carnival we rode with Caitlin at first, like the Ferris wheel and go-carts; the booths we played games at; the refreshments like cotton candy and popcorn and lemonade we ate and drank.

And finally, how Caitlin was afraid to get on the Tilt-A-Whirl with us, and I went with Carol and Katie, leaving Caitlin behind.

"I still remember the moment we got off the ride, and you couldn't find her," Katie said to me now. "You were frantic. We told you to calm down, that she'd probably just wandered off. But, of course, well... I'm so sorry. I still can't believe what happened. I'll never forget it. And my heart goes out to you for what you had to live through. It all seems so wrong. Like we should be able to go back and somehow reverse time and make sure it never really did happen. But we can't do that. And poor Caitlin is dead."

"Just to be certain, you never saw Caitlin at all—you never saw her where she was supposed to be waiting for us—when we got off the ride?"

"No. She was gone."

"And you didn't notice anything strange at all?"

"Not after the ride."

"What do you mean?"

"Well, I happened to look back on Caitlin waiting at the gate when we got onto the Tilt-A-Whirl. And I saw her talking to a man."

"Who?"

"I didn't know him."

"What did he look like?"

"Older. Not a kid."

That didn't sound like David Munroe.

"I didn't think much about it at the time. I figured maybe he was just someone asking her a question or something about the carnival. But, once she disappeared, I realized it could be important. So I told the police who questioned me about it. But it turned out it wasn't anything significant, after all. The man wasn't David Munroe and once Munroe was arrested for the murder, the police told me it didn't really relate to the case."

The police.

She told the police about a man talking to my sister just before she went missing.

But that was never included anywhere in the Huntsdale police report on the case that I'd read.

Why?

"Who was the police officer you told this to?" I asked Katie Gompers.

Was it Delgado?

Lawton?

Or someone else on the Huntsdale force that could be covering up a secret about my sister's abduction and murder?

"I told it to the chief of police," Katie Gompers said. "I told it to your father, Nikki."

TWENTY

I was still thinking about what Katie said—about how she'd told my father about some man talking to Caitlin right before she disappeared, but he'd seemingly never followed up on the lead —when I picked up Greg at the airport the next day and drove him back to Huntsdale.

Greg was excited to see me. I was excited to see him, of course. Just not as excited as him. I wasn't thrilled that he decided on his own to come up here on the spur of the moment like this. I knew that meant I would have to stop working to spend time with him tonight, when what I really wanted to do was keep looking for answers about Natalie Jarvis and about my sister.

We went out to eat at a restaurant near my hotel, and I guess I pretty much talked non-stop during the meal about everything going on in Huntsdale. He'd spent most of the time in the car trying to convince me to get on the flight back to Washington with him the next morning. I told him I couldn't do that.

"This is my job," I said, the same as I'd explained it to him so many times before.

Which wasn't actually true. I mean Les Polk had only let me come here to interview Munroe as a favor to me. And, as Huntsdale Police Chief Frank Earnshaw had pointed out to me, I had no jurisdiction in the Natalie Jarvis case. But the "this is my job" reason I gave Greg was still my story for being here, and I damn sure was going to stick with it.

"So you're not concerned that this guy Munroe—the one who you've always been certain murdered your sister—calls you out of the blue to suddenly claim he didn't do it?" he asked. "And then another girl goes missing? And there are all these links between this missing girl and your sister's death? Plus, the wreaths of roses—just like the one found with your sister's body —that mysteriously appear on her grave and your father's grave right after you talk to Munroe? David Munroe is somehow, for some sick reason, drawing you into it all. This case is personal for you, Nikki. Too personal. But it seems like its personal for someone else too. That's what I'm worried about. I'm worried you could be the next target. Doesn't that worry you at all?"

"No, I'm not worried," I said, even though I knew that wasn't exactly true.

"Well, I am. Come home to Washington with me when I go back tomorrow. Then we can talk about your job with the FBI or maybe some other career choices or whatever once you're back home safely with me. What do you say?"

"Look," I told him, "the bottom line here is I'm no longer certain David Munroe was the one who killed my sister. Or at least I'm not sure he did it alone. Whatever really happened to Caitlin, I think, yes, Munroe is playing some sort of game with me now. But there has to be someone else out there.

"That person could have abducted Natalie Jarvis—and made it seem similar in all the ways it is to Caitlin's disappearance and murder. We found out about Natalie Jarvis on the anniversary of Caitlin being gone; same pattern of a mysterious abduction; the connection with the roses on Caitlin's body and the rose someone sent Natalie before she was taken; and then the roses on my father and sister's graves.

"I think it all has something to do with Munroe. I'm not sure how. But I need to find out. Not just because of Natalie Jarvis now, but to look for any more clues connecting this to Caitlin. I have to be sure about Caitlin. I just can't live with that kind of uncertainly. Can't you understand that, Greg?"

He shook his head in frustration.

He knew he wasn't going to get me to change my mind about giving up on this.

He probably knew that right from the beginning, but he tried one more time.

"Are you sure you won't come back to Washington with me?" he asked.

"I can't, Greg."

"Last chance."

"I'll be home very soon."

"Promise me that."

"I promise."

"And take care of yourself. Promise me that too."

He leaned over and kissed me.

"I hope that kiss will be enough to keep you thinking about me while you're still in this goddamned place."

"I will think about it constantly," I said.

Once we got to the hotel later, it didn't take long for us to jump into bed together.

It started out as a normal sex thing between me and Greg. Good and fun, but nothing spectacular. Just the kind of sex that goes on between two people who have done this a number of times together and know all the erotic moves and all the erotic buttons that the other person is going to push.

But then, at some point in our lovemaking it all changed.

Greg wasn't there anymore, at least in my mind.

The face I was now seeing—the face of the man I was making love with—was someone else.

Someone with curly red hair, a friendly grin and... well, yeah, this face belonged to Billy Weller. I clawed at Greg's back wildly, our bodies moved in perfect rhythm and—at the end—I let out loud moans of passion and yelled, "I love you! I love you!" over and over again until we both collapsed onto the sheets.

"Wow!" Greg said. "That was really something."

"It sure was."

I could tell that he was especially happy at the way I'd told him how much I'd loved him during the lovemaking.

But who exactly was it that I was saying, "I love you!" to?

"You better get some sleep," I said afterward. "You've got that early flight back to Washington in the morning."

"How long do you think you'll have to stay here in this town?"

"As long as it takes."

He sighed loudly.

"Don't let me make you choose between me and this case, Nikki."

"What does that mean?"

"I don't know... I'm just frustrated about having to leave you up here."

"This case will be over eventually."

"But then there will be another big case you're chasing."

"Let's talk about this some other time."

TWENTY-ONE

Gary Lawton was the first police officer on the scene at the carnival that summer day when Caitlin disappeared.

I remembered him from that and also from the Huntsdale station when I would visit my father there. Even fifteen years ago, he was no kid. Balding, overweight, a cop who'd already been in the Huntsdale Police Department for a long time. Which was never that difficult or challenging a job in the quiet peaceful little town of Huntsdale. Until my sister was abducted and killed.

Lawton had retired a while back and moved out of the area, Alex had found out from people at the station. She tracked him down to Florida. He had retired to some place not far outside Sarasota down there.

Alex and I weren't going to go all the way to Florida to talk with him, even though I always preferred interviewing someone face to face. Alex came up with the answer though. FaceTime. Lawton was on Facebook, and he agreed to link up and Face-Time us there. He said one of his grandkids had showed him how to do it.

And so there Alex and I were in the Huntsdale police station, drinking coffee Billy had brought for us—and talking to Gary Lawton.

Lawton hadn't changed that much from what he used to be when he was on the force—he'd lost a bit more hair, and he'd put on some more pounds—but he was still the same affable, likable guy I remembered from when I was a kid.

He talked a bit about his retirement in Florida, his house down there, his kids and grandchildren—and how much he loved being retired. Alex and I listened politely. He asked me about my life too, told a few stories about my father, said my father would have been proud of me as an FBI agent and brought up the viral video of me that he said he'd seen.

"But you didn't look me up after all these years to talk about old times, did you, Nikki?" Lawton said finally. "What's going on that you're so interested in? And why are you back in the Huntsdale police station."

"David Munroe."

"The guy who killed your sister."

"I went to see him in prison."

"Why?"

"I've gone to see him every year on the anniversary of what happened to Caitlin. Looking for some kind of answers about her. He never talked to me before. Not until this time. He says he didn't do it, Gary."

Lawton snorted disgustedly.

"And you believed him? C'mon, Nikki, you've been around law enforcement all your life. First, with your father. Now you're a big star as an FBI agent. You should know better than anyone that every prisoner says they're innocent."

He was right.

Tommy Thompson had said the same thing when I told him about Munroe's sudden reversal about being innocent.

"David Munroe admitted he killed Caitlin before," I pointed out to Lawton.

"Exactly. So why believe he's innocent now?"

"I didn't say he was innocent."

"Then why are you doing all this? What in the hell are you investigating?"

"There's been another missing girl case in Huntsdale. A young girl about the same age as Caitlin. I think it somehow could all be connected, Caitlin's murder and the missing girl now. Maybe there was somebody besides Munroe who killed Caitlin. That's what I'm investigating."

I could see the look of shock on Lawton's face on the screen. Here he was living a peaceful life of retirement, and I suddenly showed up from the past and brought up these questions about the one big case he'd ever been involved with as a police officer.

"My partner, Alex, and I are trying to go back on everything that happened with Caitlin—the entire investigation my father and you and the rest of the Huntsdale police force did back then—in the hope that we might come across some new clue or piece of evidence to help explain what's going on in Huntsdale now."

Lawton nodded.

"What can I do to help?" he asked.

"Tell us everything you recall about the day you showed up at the carnival after Caitlin disappeared."

Which is what he did then...

"I didn't think much about it being a big deal at first," he recalled. "I mean kids go missing all the time at carnivals. And this was a twelve-year-old girl. I figured she'd probably met a boy, another friend, or just went home or something on her own.

"But when I got there and found out it was your sister, I began to be more concerned. I knew you pretty well from your father, and, even as a teenager, you were a responsible kid and not someone who would panic without good reason.

"Yes, I was the first one there. But I soon called for some backup—and of course your father arrived. He was more upset than I'd ever seen him. Which made sense, of course, since this involved his own daughter. I still was hoping she'd show up, and this would all be over. But... well, it turned out to be worse than any of us could ever imagine."

He continued to describe the details of the search for Caitlin that summer afternoon.

"Did you talk to a lot of people at the carnival?" Alex asked.

"Sure. As many as I could. I talked to you, Nikki, too. You didn't know anything except for the fact that she was there when you got on the ride, but then gone by the time you got off."

"Did you talk to Katie Gompers?" I asked him.

'Who?"

"One of the girls who went on the ride with me."

"Not sure."

"She said she told my father about seeing Caitlin talking to some strange man right before the ride started. Did she tell you that too?"

"No. First time I heard that."

"But you were there and—"

"Yes, I was there. But your father took complete control of everything as soon as he arrived. Handled all the questioning, the interviews with everyone at the carnival scene himself. He never told me anything about someone seeing a man talking to your sister. I mean we would have been all over that if we knew. Do you think this Gompers girl is telling the truth to you?"

"She'd have no reason to lie after all these years."

"Then why didn't your father tell anyone else about it?"

Why didn't he?

Why was the mystery man at the carnival not in my father's police report either?

Why did my father seemingly ignore such an important piece of information that might have led to finding out what happened to my sister?

But, most disturbing of all, why were these questions about my father and his actions at the time coming out now everywhere I looked?

TWENTY-TWO

Rudy Delgado, the police officer who arrested Munroe, was not happy to see me. It turned out he didn't have a lot of warm memories about Huntsdale. Or the Huntsdale Police Department. Or my family either, for that matter.

Delgado had left the force at some point after Caitlin's murder and the Munroe arrest. We found him working for a security firm in southern Ohio. Providing protection for businesses and stores and the like.

He quickly made it clear to me that he missed being a police officer, but that it wasn't his choice to leave the force.

"Your father really messed me up," he said to me. "Okay, I had some issues, I had some problems. I understand that. There were a couple of drinking incidents on duty that got me suspended a few times. And then one time I used a bit too much force, well, quite a bit of force, on a suspect and we got sued for police brutality.

"But my David Munroe arrest, that was a big deal. That should have turned it around for me. The biggest thing that ever happened to me in my career. A once-in-a-lifetime dream bust. It should have been my ticket to undo all that bad stuff on my record in the Huntsdale files. Maybe gotten me a bigger job on a bigger police force somewhere.

"I went to your father and asked for his help. I said I wanted to get my record cleaned up. Could he go through my personnel file, take out some of the bad reports and reprimands he had put in there for me, and give me a commendation and praise for the Munroe arrest? I mean I was the one who did that. Tracked down Munroe because of the parking ticket and arrested him. That was me."

"What happened then?" I asked.

"Your father said he would think about it."

"But he never changed your personnel file?"

"No, he died before he could get around to doing that. Can you believe that bad luck?"

"Yeah, awfully inconsiderate of him to do that," I said.

"Sure was."

I guess Delgado had no idea how his words sounded to the daughter of Luke Cassidy, or maybe he simply didn't care.

"I applied for the post of chief after that. I figured I had as good credentials as anyone to replace your father. But they hired another guy. He and I didn't get along, he knew all about my background from the records too and he wound up firing me. They've had a few police chiefs in Huntsdale since then. I've tried them all to get reinstated, but they always turn me down because of the reprimands and suspensions still in my record. Same thing with any other town where I've applied to be on the police force. They check my record in Huntsdale and then, well, that's why I'm working with security guards and night watchmen now."

None of this seemed to have anything to do with my sister's murder, so Alex and I tried to steer Delgado back into talking about the arrest of David Munroe.

"So it was your idea to check the parking ticket records to

see if anything unusual happened there around the time of Caitlin's disappearance?" Alex asked.

"Well, to be honest, it wasn't really my idea. Nikki's father suggested it. This was after Caitlin's body was found in the woods. We'd run into a wall on any other leads we were chasing. This was one of just a lot of other things we tried—it was pretty desperate. But we got lucky on this one.

"I found out that David Munroe had gotten a parking ticket on a street near the carnival site just before Nikki's sister went missing. We had a bunch of cops out ticketing cars there to control the crowds and traffic jams we expected from the carnival. There was more than one parking ticket, not just Munroe's.

"I checked through all of them. Everyone else who'd got ticketed seemed to have a reason to be there. Except Munroe. He didn't have any connection with the carnival or anyone there, at least that we could see. And he lived several towns away. So I drove to his address to find out what he was doing in Huntsdale that day. It was still a long shot at that point.

"But as soon as he opened the door, I knew. I knew he was the guy. I was a pretty good police officer back then in Huntsdale, no matter what your father thought of me. And I just had this cop instinct about it. Munroe tried to act casual at first, but I could tell he was nervous and twitchy as he answered my questions. Finally, I simply came out and said to him, 'Did you murder Caitlin Cassidy?' He should have refused to talk to me anymore or demanded a lawyer at that point. But he didn't. Instead, he just caved and gave it all up. 'You got me,' he said. 'I'm the one you're looking for.' After that, we got a search warrant and found stuff from Caitlin in his house."

"Munroe said, 'I'm the one' not 'we?'" I asked.

"Sure. Why wouldn't he?"

"Just wanted to make sure he didn't say anything about working with anyone."

I told him about the missing Jarvis girl and how I was trying to figure out if there was any connection with Munroe after all this time.

"Was there anything unusual you remember from the arrest? Anything that didn't really make sense to you at the time?"

Delgado thought about that for a minute.

"He seemed to be okay in the beginning. Like he even expected us to show up and arrest him at some point. And he confessed on the spot. But then, once we got a search warrant and found the items he'd taken from your sister's body—the strands of hair, the pieces of clothing, the jewelry—well, that seemed to upset him. He kept denying he'd taken them or put them there."

"Why? He already admitted to doing the killing?"

"That's just it. He didn't deny the killing. But he did deny putting her stuff in his house. It didn't make any sense."

No, it didn't make sense.

Not if David Munroe was the lone killer like everyone had thought all this time.

I remembered the words that he had said to me when I went to see him in the prison: "I was there that day. I was tracking her. I was there when she was abducted. But I didn't kill her. There are more people involved than just me. Find them, and you'll get all the answers about your sister."

More people?

But who?

Well, maybe the same person who put Caitlin's stuff in David Munroe's home.

The same person who could have planted this evidence to make everyone think Munroe was the only person responsible for my sister's abduction and murder.

So that the real killer was free to kill again...

TWENTY-THREE

"What's going on with you and this Weller guy?" Alex asked
me on the drive back to Huntsdale after our meeting with
Delgado.

"Huh?"

"Because you and he sure have a good opportunity to do
whatever you want, now that Greg has gone back to
Washington."

"What are you trying to say, Alex?"

"I'm picking up on definite sexual tension between the two
of you. There's some kind of connection with you and Weller.
I'm very good at sensing sexual tension in people. It's a specialty
of mine."

"I like him as a friend, that's all."

"Did you have some kind of a relationship with him when
you were growing up here?"

"No. Not at all."

"You did tell me you went to high school together. He's got
quite a crush on you, no question about it. Anyone can see that.
The question is, how do you feel about him?"

I sighed. "There's nothing going on between Billy Weller

and me. Weller seems like a nice guy, and he seems like a good cop. That's all there is to my relationship with him. Once this is all over here, I'll go back to Washington and marry Greg and we'll live happily ever after. Satisfied, Alex?"

We drove in silence for a few minutes.

"Then everything's fine between you and Greg?"

"Absolutely."

"So why did he fly up here to Huntsdale yesterday? To check on you?"

"He misses me."

"Do you miss him?"

"Of course, I do."

I hoped Alex was finished with this conversation about me and Greg, but she wasn't.

"How's the sex?" she asked now.

"Excuse me?"

"The sex with Greg. Is it good?"

"What kind of a question is that?"

"Sex is a very important part of a relationship."

"Jeez..."

"It makes up for a lot of other shortcomings in a person you're with."

"I know how important sex is, Alex."

"So how is the sex with you and Greg?"

"The sex is good. Very good."

The first time I had sex was in the back seat of a car when I was still in high school.

We'd gone to a movie together, picked up a six pack of beer afterward, driven around for a while drinking the beer in the car until we wound up in a lovers' lane and then... well, one thing led to another until I was no longer a virgin.

The boy—Mark Andrews—had been as inexperienced as I was in sex, and it turned out to be a less than magical moment. He fumbled around a long time before we could consummate the act, it was over very quickly after it began and he managed to rip the new blouse I'd bought myself for our date that night.

On top of that, neither one of us had come prepared with any kind of protection. I spent the next several weeks worrying about whether or not I might have gotten pregnant. Finally, in the worst moment of all, we got pulled over by a policeman who found the beer cans in our car.

The cop wound up taking me to the Huntsdale police station to meet with my father—where I had to explain it all, including the ripped blouse, to him.

I told myself back then, when I was still the young Nikki Cassidy, that sex had to be more fun—sex had to be better—than it was that first time for me.

And it was.

Yes, sex with Greg was good.

Just like I'd told Alex that it was.

Hell, it was more than just good. It was great. Greg was good-looking, smart, personable, affectionate—the guy was everything a woman could look for in a man. I had slept with other men since that first high school encounter, of course, some of whom were not so perfect. But Greg was different. Greg was special. And he and I shared something together that was really special and good and wonderful.

Except...

Well, except if it was so special and so good and so perfect, why was I fantasizing about Billy Weller the last time Greg and I had sex together?

"Where to now?" Alex asked.

"I want to go back to the place where my sister's body was found days after she disappeared at the carnival."

"In the woods?"

"Yes."

"Why?"

"Everybody's out looking for Natalie Jarvis. Knocking on

doors, looking in homes and buildings, trying to find some place where whoever abducted Natalie might be holding her. But no one's found anything yet. That could mean—much as we don't want to acknowledge it—that she's already dead. And if she's dead, the killer would have to get rid of her body somewhere. So if I'm right that the same person is somehow responsible for Natalie as well as my sister's death, then..."

"He might have buried Natalie's body near where your sister's body was found fifteen years ago," Alex said.

"It's a possibility."

"What is this place?"

"It's called Grant Woods."

TWENTY-FOUR

Grant Woods was a place I knew about growing up in Huntsdale long before they found Caitlin's body there.

It was an area of trails and trees and creeks and even a lake. When I was young, me and my friends used to go hiking there or swimming in the lake. Later, after I got to high school, Grant Woods was a "make out" place for us. Boys would take their girlfriends in cars there, park in one of the remote areas and kiss and neck and... well, do whatever teenagers did back then.

But that all changed for me after Caitlin's body was found in Grant Woods. It was days after she disappeared at the carnival. Until then, every one of us had this hope, prayers for a miracle, that Caitlin would turn up alive somewhere. That hope, those prayers were ended forever—just like Caitlin's too-short life ended—when her body was discovered in Grant Woods.

I used to come back to these woods every year when I returned to Ohio to try to interview David Munroe. The last time was a year ago. My routine was always the same—first I'd go to the prison where Munroe would simply stare silently at me for an hour, then I'd visit Caitlin's grave, sometimes go to the old carnival site, and finally come back to the place where her body was found with the roses in Grant Woods.

Now I was back here again.

Back looking for another girl who might have died here—someone else besides Caitlin.

I knew the exact spot where Caitlin's body had been found, of course. So I led Alex through the woods from where we parked the car for about a half-mile until we got there. The spot was underneath a big elm tree and surrounded by grass and other foliage.

It was a place I would never forget. I sometimes thought about Caitlin's body lying out here. And that wreath of roses on top of her head. That was a horrific image I would carry around with me for my entire life.

"Do you really think we might find something out here?" Alex asked as we trudged through the woods.

"It's a long shot."

"The longest of long shots."

"We're probably just wasting our time," I agreed.

Except it turned out we weren't.

I knew something was different as soon as we got to the spot where Caitlin's body had been all those years ago. There was no grass or other foliage like I remembered there. It was gone, and the ground around the area looked like it had been dug up since the last time that I was there.

Someone else had been here and done this.

I grabbed a stick from a tree that was strong enough to move some dirt and began digging. Digging in the same spot where my sister had lain dead. It was a bizarre feeling. But I had to see if there was something—or someone else—here now.

Sure enough, a short time later, I found something hard in the ground.

At first, I thought it was a rock.

But then I realized it was a bone.

It was just a small piece of bone, but I knew now that there had to be more down there under this ground.

"We've got to get Earnshaw and a lot of people with excavation equipment out here," I yelled to Alex.

But she was already on the phone to Billy Weller at the Huntsdale station.

Very quickly after that, the area was overrun with people as a large number of Huntsdale police officers and emergency personnel showed up. The medical examiner was there too to deal with whatever they found under the ground. And, of course, Chief Frank Earnshaw was running the show.

If Earnshaw was grateful to me and Alex for finding this, he sure didn't show it.

"This is a local case, not federal," he said to us. "So stand back from all the official activity."

"We found it—we found whatever it is you're digging up there!" I pointed out.

"Yes, we just want to help out in any way we can," Alex said.

"You have no jurisdiction with this. You're just observers."

"We're not here to argue with you about jurisdiction, Chief..." Alex started to say.

"Good, because if you do, I'll have my officers throw you out of this crime scene."

Then we heard a noise. It was a van driving up from one of the area's local TV stations. They'd obviously found out that an official digging operation was underway here looking for a body —presumably the body of poor Natalie Jarvis. More media coverage would no doubt be following them and arriving here very soon to cover the story.

"Do you want to be on camera having a confrontation with FBI agents at the crime scene like this?" I asked Earnshaw.

"Video like that will go viral very quickly. Believe me, I know what I'm talking about when it comes to viral video. So let's not cause a public scene here about jurisdiction or anything else. You do your job, and we'll do our job. Who knows, we might even be able to help each other."

Earnshaw agreed to let us stay, but kept us—along with the media and other onlookers who had shown up—away from the workers digging up whatever was buried there.

It didn't take them long to find something.

It was a body.

The body of a young girl.

Buried at the exact same spot my sister's body had been left by her killer.

A short time later, I heard the sound of another vehicle arriving.

Then I saw Anne Jarvis emerging from a car, crying hysterically and running toward the body.

Her husband followed behind her.

Along with a group of Huntsdale police officers, trying in vain to restrain her and calm her down.

Not a surprise to see a family member falling apart in emotional distress like that. Hell, that's what happened to my family too with Caitlin. Earnshaw, Weller and the other officers did their best to try to calm down the distraught mother.

But what happened next was a surprise.

We heard a scream from the mother—and then she collapsed at the site.

"It's not her!" Weller said as he ran back toward me and Alex a short time later.

"What do you mean?"

"This body is not Natalie Jarvis. The ME says—based on the condition of the body—it's been there for weeks, maybe months. Not just a few days like Natalie has been gone. That's why she screamed and collapsed."

I thought about all the emotions that must have been running through the Jarvis woman. First, she believes her daughter is dead. Then she discovers that the body buried here is not her daughter after all. Except she still doesn't know where her daughter Natalie is, or if she's still alive or not.

Which, of course, left one very big question.

"If the girl in this grave isn't Natalie Jarvis, who is she?" I asked Weller.

"We have no idea," he said.

TWENTY-FIVE

The medical examiner for the town of Huntsdale was a man named Michael (Big Mickey) Franze.

Like District Attorney Tommy Thompson, he'd been in the office for a long time. All the way back to when I was growing up when my father was the police chief. They called him Big Mickey because he was a huge man, probably at least six foot five and weighing in at somewhere over three hundred pounds.

But he was a big man in Huntsdale too besides just his stature, or that he had held the ME's job for so long. Franze was a familiar face all the time around town—showing up at council meetings and hearings; at a local coffee shop every morning; at sporting events and concerts and parades. Wherever you went in Huntsdale, you could see Big Mickey.

For a guy who dealt in death for his job, he sure brought a lot of life to the town.

I went to his office later to find out more details on the dead girl they'd found in Grant Woods. I'd tried to ask him about it at the scene, but Earnshaw whisked him away before I could do that. I was pretty sure Earnshaw wouldn't be too happy about the medical examiner's office sharing key information with me about the case, and I was right.

"Chief Earnshaw told me that any information I find out about the body we just found is totally confidential," he said now as we sat in his office. "He said I should tell no one anything about the medical findings besides him. Especially— and I have to tell you that he particularly emphasized this part— 'that damn FBI woman.'"

"I really need to find out what happened to her," I said.

"I get that."

"So could you maybe just bend the rules from Earnshaw a bit and..."

"Of course, I can."

I stared at him.

"I don't work for Chief Earnshaw. I don't even like Chief Earnshaw very much. He's sure not the man your father was as police chief. I run this office the way I see best. I've done that for a long time, and I'll keep on acting that way for as long as I'm here. I'm happy to share what I know with the FBI. Hell, it will be a lot more productive I'm sure than sharing it with that jerk Earnshaw.

"Besides," he said, smiling at me as he did so, "I owe it to you, Nikki Cassidy, because of your father."

I remembered how close he and my father were back then. Not just as friends, but as combined forces against whatever enemies they perceived were working against the best interests of the town of Huntsdale. I was happy—and I suppose proud too—that Big Mickey Franze put me on the same level of respect that he did my father.

"I still miss your father," he said. "In a lot of ways."

"Me too."

"He went far too soon."

"I still blame myself for that. If I had watched out for my sister better that day at the carnival. Even more so, if I hadn't even taken her there that day. Well, then Caitlin would still be alive. And maybe my father would be alive too. A lot of people think the stress of losing Caitlin and having to investigate his own daughter's murder, well... maybe that was the cause of the heart attack that later killed him."

Franze shook his head no when I said that.

"That's not true, Nikki. I know there is a popular perception that people die of a 'broken heart' after a tragedy like that. But it doesn't happen that way. People die for actual medical reasons. In your father's case, he had a weak heart. He'd been diagnosed with heart damage earlier. He would have died very soon anyway, no matter what happened or didn't happen to Caitlin. He didn't tell many people about his condition. Maybe he didn't even tell your mother so you wouldn't have known that. But his time was up. That's simply the sad truth. It had nothing to do with you or anyone else. I'm telling you this not only as a friend of your father's so that you don't feel guilty about his death for the rest of your life, but also as a medical expert."

"Thank you," I said, fighting back tears I felt forming in my eyes.

"I knew Luke Cassidy better than anyone," he told me. "And I want you to know he'd be proud if he could see you right now, Nikki."

I lost the battle with the tears at that point.

"So let's talk about Jane Doe," Franze said afterward, reaching down for a folder on his desk and opening it up to take out a sheaf of papers.

Jane Doe.

The name that law enforcement—and other official offices—use for a crime victim that remains unidentified.

Jane Doe always sounded so cold and unfeeling whenever I heard it.

Like this person, even in death, wasn't even given the dignity of a real name or identity.

"Let's start with the cause of death," Franze said, reading from the documents in front of him. "At first, we thought she might have been beaten to death. The body was in pretty bad condition. But then we discovered a gunshot wound. A single shot to the head that must have killed her instantly. We found the bullet too. It was still inside her. So cause of death was officially death by gunshot."

The same as my sister Caitlin.

"The bullet was damaged, but we were able to ascertain the gun it came from. The wound in her was from a .45 caliber pistol."

Same as the .45 caliber wound in Caitlin.

"As for the victim's age, we were quickly able to estimate that from the condition of the body as being a young Caucasian girl between twelve and thirteen years old."

Basically, the same age as Caitlin, too.

"The body itself was in a condition that indicated she had died some months ago. Probably about a year."

"Were there fingerprints still on what was left of the body—something that you could use to try to figure out her identity?"

"There were fingerprints, and we have them here in this file now. But that didn't help us very much. You need something or someone to compare fingerprints with to confirm an identity. And, as you might expect, not too many twelve- or thirteen-year-old girls have their fingerprints on file with law enforcement or anywhere else. Now dental records though, that's an entirely different story. You can compare them with anyone's dental files, which is what we did. Except you need to know which dental records to compare her with. So we did a check of missing girls in Ohio or surrounding states. We found one who seemed to fit the age and timetable of disappearance. So we asked for those dental records. And guess what?"

"Are you telling me you now know who she was?"

"We just found out. Erica Kent is our Jane Doe. She's from Louisville, Kentucky. That's a few hundred miles from here. She was abducted there, and we believe transported for some reason to Huntsdale—and very possibly was actually murdered at the spot in Grant Woods where we found the body. So at least she has a name now. She won't go through eternity as Jane Doe."

"When did Erica Kent disappear from Louisville?"

"Exactly a year ago. On her way to school one morning. She simply vanished from the school bus, and no one has ever known what happened to her or been able to find her since then. Until she turned up dead here in Grant Woods."

"Did anyone find a rose—or roses—anywhere near the grave?"

"No. But, like I said, the body had been there probably for almost a year. Anything like that would have been washed away by rain and wind and whatever else after that much time out there in the woods."

I had one big question left to ask.

"What date last year did Erica Kent disappear?"

"July nineteenth."

The anniversary of Caitlin's disappearance.

And the same date that Natalie Jarvis vanished at the movie theater too.

That meant three girls dead or missing—potentially by the same person.

Someone who was still out there playing a deadly game.

That was a scary thought.

But even more scary was not knowing what might happen next...

TWENTY-SIX

The identification of the Jane Doe murder victim as Erica Kent, a twelve-year-old who had been missing from Louisville, Kentucky for a year, accomplished another positive thing besides making her more than just a girl without a name.

The victim had gone missing in Kentucky, then her body was found here in Ohio after she was murdered. That meant she had at some point been transported across state lines to Huntsdale. Which made it now a federal kidnapping/murder case. This development gave the FBI and other federal agencies the jurisdiction to investigate the case along with local law enforcement authorities.

I was on the phone to FBI headquarters in Washington with my boss Les Polk as soon as I left the ME's office.

"Yes, it definitely seems like the inter-state aspect gives us the authority to step in on this," Polk said. "But I still don't understand what's going on here. I mean you went there to interview the man who murdered your sister fifteen years ago. Now all of this has suddenly exploded why you're there. How can any of the rest of this be connected with a murder that was closed fifteen years ago?"

"That is the question, isn't it? I have no idea what's going on here. But I want to find out. Look, I need to get official authority —ability to obtain warrants, examine evidence, question witnesses and potential suspects—as soon as you can. It's really important that I get all that officially."

"Okay, you got it. But isn't that really all a formality? I know you've had trouble dealing with the local authorities there. But once they find out about the multi-state aspect of this—that the dead girl was transported there from Kentucky—they should welcome our help. The police chief can't handle something like this on his own."

"You haven't met the police chief here," I said.

"He's really that uncooperative?"

"I'd take 'uncooperative' at this point. He's also defensive and surly and a general pain in the ass. But then I understand he has trouble getting along with a lot of other people in this town in his role as the police chief of Huntsdale. Chief Frank Earnshaw is not exactly what you'd call a people person."

"Didn't your father used to be in that job of police chief?"

"That's right."

"I would have figured that might help you in dealing with this guy."

"I think it hurts me more than it helps. Makes him more defensive about his job when I'm around. He knows how everyone used to love my father when he was in that job. Maybe I'm a reminder to him of that. Anyway, he took an instant dislike to me. Oh, well, I was probably getting too big a head from all the attention of the Mattheu case and that viral video. I'm sure not a big star to Chief Frank Earnshaw."

We talked a bit more about the case—or, to be more specific, all of the cases.

Especially the search for Natalie Jarvis.

"Do you figure she's dead?" Polk asked.

"I keep waiting to hear the news that her body has been found."

"So that's a yes?"

"It makes sense."

"What about this body you did find? Any idea how long between her disappearance and when she was murdered?"

"The ME's office can only make a general estimate from the condition of her body that she's been dead a long time. So presumably she was killed sometime shortly after being abducted or whatever on the way to school in Louisville—even though the body wasn't discovered here in Ohio until now. But the medical examiner's office speculates from the evidence they have that she was likely murdered here—not back in Kentucky. So we're probably talking several days between the abduction and the murder."

"And how long was it between the time your sister disappeared at the carnival and her body was found in those same woods?"

"Six days."

"How long has it been since the Jarvis girl went missing?"

"Five days."

"So the clock is ticking rapidly."

"Yep, I had that same thought."

Before hanging up, Polk said he had one more thing to tell me.

"I'm sending you some more help. A third agent to work on all of this there with you, Nikki."

"Alex and I are fine for the time being."

"You can always use someone else."

"Is this because we're both women? You think two women together can't handle things without a male agent?"

"You're getting another agent," Polk said. "End of story."

"Who?" I asked.

"Phil Girard."

"Oh, c'mon..."

"Girard is a good agent."

"Correction. He used to be a good agent. The guy's just mailing it in, counting the days until his retirement."

"He has an extensive amount of experience in handling cases like this. More experience than you or Alex. If you think about it, you'll realize that this is a good thing for you. But, whether you agree or not, Girard is going to board a plane later today and join with the two of you in Huntsdale. That's it."

"You're killing me here, boss."

"You want the official documents giving you federal jurisdiction to investigate all that's going on there in Huntsdale, right?"

"Of course, I do."

"Well, you're getting Phil Girard along with the documents. In fact, he'll bring them to you just to make sure you don't forget to pick him up at the airport or something. It's a package deal. The authorization to investigate the Jarvis case and the Kent case and even to go back on the one in the past with your sister. Along with Girard to work with you. Got that?"

"Got it," I said.

TWENTY-SEVEN

People in the FBI office in Washington have told me that Phil Girard used to be a pretty good agent once.

But that was a long time ago.

During the time I'd been with the FBI there, Girard had been mostly a burnout case—someone who had stayed in the job too long and lost his edge and his energy and his commitment to the job.

He'd been with the bureau since the eighties and now the guy was clearly only putting in time to get the maximum amount of retirement pay in another year or so.

He talked a lot about how great retirement was going to be for him—telling us about his retirement home in Florida, the boat he was planning to buy, all the fishing he was going to do, and a lot of other stuff I didn't have much interest in hearing.

In the office these days, he spent most of his time reading travel brochures, or books on fishing, or playing all sorts of puzzles and word games. Girard was very big on crossword puzzles for a long time. He used to do the *New York Times* and *Washington Post* crossword puzzles regularly. Probably still did.

But now he'd added many of the newer, online word games that you can find on your computer or iPhone or iPad.

His favorite was a game called Wordle that a lot of people seemed to be playing at the moment. You get a word a day, or something like that, that you have to guess or figure out by trying different letters. Girard seemed obsessed by it.

Alex and I picked him up at the airport, drove him to the hotel where we were staying to check in, and then we all went down to the hotel bar where we briefed him on everything going on with our investigation.

"Are there any good restaurants in this town?" he asked, when I had finished going through it all.

"What?"

"Gotta be a good steak place, right? I mean I don't expect there's a lot of Chinese or top-quality sushi places in a small town in southern Ohio like this. But maybe there's some decent Italian, huh?"

"You want us to give you a Michelin restaurant guide to Huntsdale?" Alex asked him.

"It would be helpful."

"Dammit, we're here to work on a big investigation, Phil," I said.

"Look, I know you two have a lot of stuff going on here that you need to be working on. And that's fine, you should. Especially Nikki. I realize you have a personal connection to all this going on here. But me, I've been through this kind of thing too many times in my career to get all excited about solving some murders or missing girls here in Huntsdale, Ohio. Polk sent me to cover his ass. To make sure you two don't do anything stupid. I'm not planning to do your job."

"Polk told me he was hoping your experience could help advise us and maybe point us in the right direction on things," I said.

"Let me tell you something, ladies. The best experience

advice I can give you is how to pad your expense on an out-of-town assignment like this. That's FBI Crime Fighter Rule Number One that I learned from all my years on this damn job. Eat and drink well, and make sure you don't pay for any of it out of your own pocket."

He picked up a menu on the bar.

"What about a good wine list? Not much here on this. Do they have any places where we can get a really nice bottle of wine?"

"Glad to see you have your priorities in order, Phil," I said.

"Nikki Cassidy, how are you?" somebody said behind me.

I turned around. It was Tommy Thompson, the longtime District Attorney. He was with a woman. A middle-aged black woman.

We made introductions all around.

"This is Stacy Harris," Thompson said of the woman with him. "Or I should say she's Mayor Stacy Harris. She was elected last year. Nikki, of course, is one of our most famous Huntsdale people who've gone on to fame and acclaim as a crime fighter for the FBI in Washington."

"Well, I've certainly heard a lot about you," she said, shaking my hand. "Good to meet you and glad to have you back in Huntsdale. Even if it is only temporary and certainly not under the best of circumstances. A missing girl and a dead body in just the past few days. We're not used to that kind of crime in Huntsdale, as I'm sure you're aware."

"Glad to meet you, Mayor Harris. But I am a bit surprised."

"Why?"

"Well, when I was growing up in Huntsdale, I'm not sure anyone would have imagined that one day a woman—an African American woman—would be elected to the mayor's job."

"We've made progress since then." She smiled. "Not

enough. But progress. So tell me, Agent Cassidy, have you made any headway on the cases?"

I liked Mayor Stacy Harris. I liked District Attorney Tommy Thompson too. So I told them the truth. About the problems I'd had getting local police cooperation from Chief Frank Earnshaw. But I also talked about how I'd now received official authorization from Washington giving us jurisdiction in the investigations here.

"I just hope that Chief Earnshaw recognizes our jurisdiction here now," I said. "I don't want to have to keep arguing with him about it. I want to work together with your people here in law enforcement to find the Jarvis girl and find out the other answers that we're looking for in our investigation."

"Don't worry about that," she said. "I will speak with Earnshaw and instruct him that he is to cooperate fully with you going forward. I'll do my best to clear out any obstacles you have involving Chief Earnshaw."

"You won't have any more trouble establishing your jurisdiction, believe me," Thompson said. "Mayor Harris will see to that. And I'll help out in any way I can too, Nikki."

After they left, I turned to Alex and Girard with a big smile on my face.

"Damn, that's going to make things a lot easier for us, huh?" I said.

"Absolutely!" Alex agreed.

I looked over at Phil Girard.

"What do you think, Phil?"

He was staring at his phone.

"Hey," Girard said, "I just got my best Wordle score ever!"

I was still complaining to Alex later about the arrival of Girard after he went to his room for the night.

"Hey, don't judge him too quickly," she said. "You might

want to cut the guy a bit of slack before writing him off as useless."

"Girard? Why?"

"Look, I know he comes across as kind of a Neanderthal and he can be a pain in the ass. But I've worked with him on a couple of cases in the past. He's actually really smart and really good underneath all that B.S. he puts out. And he works hard, even though he'll never admit it. Take my word for it—Phil Girard can surprise you sometimes."

"Yeah, well, I'm still waiting for the first surprise from him," I said.

TWENTY-EIGHT

Once we received the official authorization to be involved in the investigation, I set up a "war room" at police headquarters. It's what I have done in previous cases to go over all the details and the evidence. This time I wanted to also coordinate as best I could the local police investigation and a federal probe at the same time. We needed to work together as an entire unit, whether Earnshaw wanted to or not.

The meeting consisted of me, Alex, Phil Girard, Chief Earnshaw, Billy Weller and a few other officers with the Huntsdale Police Department.

There was a bulletin board on the wall, and I used it to post pictures of all three of the investigations that would be covered —Natalie Jarvis, Erica Kent and my sister Caitlin Cassidy. Also pictures of the burial site in the woods; the movie theater where Natalie Jarvis was last seen; and even the site of the long-ago carnival I'd gone to with Caitlin.

We had a chalkboard in the room too, and I used that to list everything we knew about the case, about what we didn't know and ways all of it might be connected.

I stood up and began running the meeting. I wasn't sure

who was technically in charge of it. Girard was senior to me at the FBI. And it was Earnshaw's police station that we were in. But these were my cases—all of them, Natalie, Erica and Caitlin —and I wasn't going to give that up. So I just took the initiative.

I picked up a cup of coffee, stood in front of the bulletin board and ran through a list of everything we knew so far and the forensic evidence, putting together a timeline of all three cases.

I walked over to the bulletin board and pointed to a picture of Erica Kent. She had long auburn hair, big brown eyes and a hauntingly endearing smile in the picture. A girl about to embark on her teenage years and with her whole life seemingly in front of her. But instead she wound up dead in a makeshift grave in Grant Woods. Just like my sister Caitlin had.

"Let's start with Erica Kent," I said. "She's the one we know the least about because the initial case didn't begin in Huntsdale. I asked my partner, Alex Del Vecchio, to coordinate with local authorities in the Louisville area where she disappeared over the details about what happened to Erica. Alex?"

Alex walked over to where the picture of Erica Kent was on the board, pointed to it and then began reading from her notes.

"Erica Anne Kent, twelve years old. Her parents are Robert Kent, a real estate broker, and Margaret Kent, a dietician at a health center in Louisville. Erica was their only child. They lived all their lives in the Louisville area, although not in the city of Louisville itself. They come from Elizabethtown, a smaller town outside metropolitan Louisville. That's approximately two hundred and fifty miles from us here in Huntsdale.

"On July nineteenth a year ago, Erica Kent boarded a bus that was supposed to take her to the summer camp which she attended that month of July. No one is sure exactly what happened. Her mother drove her to the bus and saw her outside waiting for it with a group of other girls. She left her there, assuming she was fine because she was in a group of other teenagers.

"Except Erica Kent never made it to the camp. When the bus arrived, she was not on it. One of the other girls said she thought she saw Erica talking to someone right before the bus arrived to take them. A man. The girl said she thought at first it was Erica's father, but it wasn't. Her father was at work in his real estate office.

"Local police tried to get a description of the man from the girl—and even used a sketch artist to try to draw an image from her recollection. But it wasn't of much help. There was really nothing about the man that was specific or noteworthy that she could remember.

"A massive search of the area was carried out by local police. Then it was expanded to other areas near Louisville—and much of the rest of the state of Kentucky. Flyers were handed out, pictures of Erica Kent posted everywhere, pleas made on TV news for information about the missing girl. But no leads ever turned up. It was like Erica Kent just vanished. One minute she was there, the next minute she was gone. Just like happened with Natalie Jarvis and before that Caitlin Cassidy. No trace whatsoever of Erica until she turned up in the woods here."

There was a lot of discussion after that. Questions. Comments. Theories being floated. I noted that Earnshaw directed his conversation to Phil Girard, not to me or Alex. I figured it was some kind of a male macho thing. He simply felt more comfortable talking with another man instead of us women. Hell, Earnshaw and Girard deserved each other.

I was still determined to run this all on my own terms.

And so I marched over now to the bulletin board and got everyone's attention.

I pointed to the picture of Natalie Jarvis.

"This is obviously our immediate priority. She's been

missing for five days. My sister was missing for six days before she turned up dead. We can't be sure about the timeline on Erica Kent. But, based on the condition of her body, the best estimate is it also was a limited amount of days between her disappearance and her death. So we may not have much time to save Natalie Jarvis. We have to do whatever we can to find her quickly."

"We're already looking for her," Earnshaw said. "We've been looking for her."

"Then we need to look harder."

"Where?"

"Everywhere. This is your town," I said to him. "We need to knock on every door, go into every building, talk to everyone in Huntsdale, because in another day or two—based on the timetable of the two earlier cases—we have to expect Natalie Jarvis will be dead."

I paused, letting the impact of that statement sink in for everyone.

"If she isn't alive, we have a pretty good idea of where her body might be. In Grant Woods like the other two were. So we need to send everyone we can into those woods looking for her remains, if they are there. Let's use firemen, sanitation workers, volunteers from the community—everyone we can round up and use on this. Looking for any signs of a body like we found with Erica Kent and with my sister fifteen years ago." I looked around the room. "Any questions? Comments?"

Billy Weller nodded.

"You left one thing out, Agent Cassidy," he said.

"What's that?"

"Well, you said we should be looking for some kind of remains, assuming the worst, for Natalie Jarvis—just like the bodies found in those woods for both Erica Kent and your sister. Like those are the only two cases we have to worry about."

"What's your question?"

"What about the others?"

"Others?"

"These are only the cases we know about."

I understood what Billy Weller was saying.

And he was right.

Damn, Weller was a smart cop.

"What if there are more dead girls out there that we don't know about yet?" he asked.

TWENTY-NINE

The discovery of Erica Kent's body—on top of the disappearance of Natalie Jarvis—had managed to finally get me official FBI authorization for us to be in Huntsdale to join the police investigation.

That was the good news.

The bad news was that all this also meant that the media was coming to town. Newspapers throughout the area from Ohio, Pennsylvania, West Virginia and Kentucky. Some national outlets like *USA Today*. Local TV stations. Cable news too like Fox and CNN and MSNBC. And, in this era of instant social media news, news websites like TMZ had sent bloggers here to report on every new detail—or rumor—they could find.

There was going to have to be a press conference very quickly. I knew that. My team of Alex and Girard knew that. Billy Weller knew that too, once we explained the situation to him. But Chief Frank Earnshaw was harder to convince. He'd never had to deal with a big crime story like this during his time as chief in Huntsdale, and I could tell he was very uncomfortable about the whole thing.

In the end though, he had no choice. So we set up an area in front of the station to meet with the press. There was a podium with a microphone on it, which Earnshaw stood behind for the big public event. Alex, Girard and me were behind him along with Billy and several other members of the Huntsdale police force.

Earnshaw, somewhat nervously and awkwardly I thought, began running through the main facts of the Natalie Jarvis and Erica Kent cases as we knew them.

The disappearance of Natalie at the movie theater.

The discovery of Erica's body in Grant Woods.

The massive search for clues to the whereabouts of Natalie.

The efforts to find out why Erica's body turned up here—a few hundred miles from where she had been abducted a year earlier—at almost the same time as Natalie vanished.

He did not mention anything about my sister Caitlin. Or that Natalie Jarvis and Erica Kent had gone missing on the same date—July 19th, the same as my sister. Or that Natalie might have been given a rose prior to disappearing, similar to the roses found on my sister's body. Or, even more significantly, that we found Erica Kent's body at the same spot in Grant Woods as Caitlin.

None of these facts were known to the public yet, and I knew Earnshaw wanted to keep them out of the media for as long as he could.

He was still operating on the premise this could be the work of a copycat—or copycats—not the same person who murdered Caitlin.

The questions came fast and furious after he finished giving his prepared account of the situation.

"Do you believe the Jarvis abduction and the Kent death are the work of the same person?"

"Should other young women in this area fear for their safety now too?"

And the biggest question of all: "Do you believe there is any connection between these two cases and the abduction and murder of twelve-year-old Caitlin Cassidy in this town fifteen years ago?"

Earnshaw had an answer for that last question. Not a good answer, but he tried to get by with a stock police response.

"There is no evidence of any connection between the murder of Caitlin Cassidy fifteen years ago and what is happening here today," Earnshaw said. "The man responsible for the Cassidy girl's death, the lone perpetrator of that horrendous crime, has been in prison for the past fifteen years. Therefore, he could not possibly be involved in any way in either the Jarvis or Kent cases."

"Then why is Caitlin Cassidy's sister here for the FBI investigating these two new Huntsdale cases?"

"Agent Cassidy and the other two FBI agents here with me today came to Huntsdale because of the discovery of the body of Erica Kent, who was from Louisville, Kentucky. It is believed she was abducted there and then murdered and buried for some unknown reason in the woods outside Huntsdale where she was recently found. This makes it an interstate murder case, which is why the FBI is assisting in the investigation."

"But we've been told that agent Nikki Cassidy arrived here in Huntsdale before Natalie Jarvis went missing and Erica Kent's body was found. How do you explain that timing, Chief Earnshaw?"

Earnshaw looked over at me, confused and with a look of panic.

"Can Agent Cassidy answer some of these questions for us, if you can't?" the reporter yelled now at Earnshaw.

I nodded and walked over to the podium, where Earnshaw had been standing. I thought at first he might not want me to talk, but he made room for me and stepped aside. I think he was glad to get the media spotlight focused on someone else after all of this.

I knew Earnshaw wanted me to stay on point and follow up on what he had just said about Caitlin and the new cases. Yes, there were similarities. But it could well be the work of a copycat or two copycats. Because the killer of Caitlin Cassidy was already in jail, and he'd been there for fifteen years.

At first, I thought I probably should do that.

Stick to the official line for now.

Don't rock the boat or make more headlines.

But, looking out at the media in front of me, I knew that wouldn't work. They were hungry for sensational news. Like a hungry lion looking for meat to eat. And the only way to deal with a hungry lion so it doesn't eat you alive is to feed it. So I did the same with the media. I fed them what they were looking for.

"Fifteen years ago this month," I said, "my sister Caitlin Cassidy was abducted and murdered right here in Huntsdale. I was recently contacted by the man convicted of that crime, David Munroe, who said he wanted to talk to me. During this conversation, he recanted his confession and said that someone else was responsible for my sister's death.

"My return to Huntsdale was at that time personal, not officially for the FBI. I simply was looking for answers about what happened to my sister fifteen years ago and why. I am still looking for those answers.

"Soon after my visit to Huntsdale, these other cases occurred. First the disappearance of Natalie Jarvis and then the discovery of Erica Kent's body in Grant Woods, where my sister's body was found fifteen years ago.

"There are a number of other circumstances—not all of which we have made public yet, but which have been uncovered in the investigation—that link these two new cases to my sister's case.

"Not the least of which is the fact that the murder of my sister was the only major murder here in Huntsdale history until I came back and started looking into it again. Then

Natalie Jarvis went missing and we discovered Erica Kent's body near where my sister's body was found, too.

"As a trained investigator, it would be foolish and dishonest for me to deny or ignore all these similarities in the three cases."

There was stunned silence for a few seconds, then a reporter yelled out: "Are you saying that you now believe that the person who murdered your sister is responsible for these two new crimes too?"

I looked over at Earnshaw's face. I think he wasn't quite sure what I was going to say next. Then I looked at Alex and Girard. I was pretty sure they did know. Finally, I looked at Billy Weller who was smiling at me. That damn smile. I guess he knew what was coming too.

"Yes," I replied. "I believe that the same person or persons responsible for the murder of my sister Caitlin fifteen years ago is also responsible for the abduction of Natalie Jarvis and abduction and murder of Erica Kent. And I believe that David Munroe is the key to everything, the person who can give us the answers—the real answers this time—to hopefully find Natalie Jarvis in time to save her and to find out how and why Erica Kent died. I'm going back to the prison to interview him again, and I won't stop until I know everything David Munroe has been hiding all these years. I came here looking for the answers about my sister from Munroe, and I won't stop until I solve all three of these cases and find justice for all three victims. Natalie Jarvis, Erica Kent and my sister Caitlin Cassidy. I won't stop until I can do that for them. I give you my word on that!"

A few minutes later, I was trending all over social media again as #NikkiCassidyFBI.

And the video from the press after I made that dramatic vow was being spread and shared all over the internet.

Just like that, I'd gone viral again.

THIRTY

"I'm really, really worried about your safety, Nikki," Greg said.

He had called me as soon as my press conference appearance had exploded on cable news shows and across the internet. I knew he would. After our recent conversations here in Huntsdale, where he kept trying to get me to go back to Washington with him, this was his worst fears coming true. Another murder case in Huntsdale linked to my sister and to me and everything else.

"I'm fine, Greg."

"There's a crazy killer out there."

"I've dealt with crazy killers before."

"Not when it becomes personal for you like this."

"I've told you over and over again, this is my job."

"And I'm going to say this again. You need a new job. A different kind of job. A normal job where I'm not worried about you all the time. I mean you're talking on national TV about tracking down a possible serial killer of women. What if you're the next target? What if someone comes after you with a gun and tries to shoot you?"

"Then I'll shoot them back."

"This isn't a joke, Nikki."

"Sorry, but what do you want me to say?"

"I want you to say you're going to drop all this and come back to Washington. That you're going to get out of that goddamned town. We can talk later about your job and other options you might have so that we can live a normal life together. We can talk too then about maybe even moving up our wedding date so we can get married this summer instead of waiting until fall. We can talk about—"

"We'll talk about everything when I get back to Washington."

"When is that?"

"When this case is over. When I find out for certain who killed my sister. And after I catch the person who killed Erica Kent and abducted Natalie Jarvis."

Les Polk was on the phone to me from Washington too as soon as the press conference was over. My comments were all over CNN, which Polk always had playing on a screen next to his desk. So he had heard everything I said about Munroe and all the rest. He was not happy with me about that.

"Jesus, you really dropped a helluva bomb there, Nikki," he said.

"I know that, Les."

"You essentially—acting as a representative of the FBI—said that we think there's a serial killer in Ohio who murdered your sister fifteen years ago and is now still abducting and murdering young girls out there. The media is going to go wild with this. What the hell, they already have gone wild!"

I knew, like Polk knew, that the bureau never liked this kind of publicity. We were taught to be low key and stay out of the public spotlight as much as we could. I sure hadn't done a very good job of doing that in Huntsdale.

"I needed to shake things up here," I told Polk.

"Well, you certainly did that."

"It's the only way I could think of to rattle some information loose and maybe give us some kinds of leads so we could solve all these crimes suddenly going on here."

"Are you sure that's the only reason you did it?"

"What does that mean?"

"Look, Nikki, you became famous for a while with that viral video of you from the Mattheu case. Now you're going to be famous again because of this performance. I'm just saying—"

"Do you actually believe I did this just to get my picture on TV and all over the internet?"

"No, I don't. But other people might think that about you. Including some of the top people here at the bureau. I'm going to have to answer a lot of questions now thrown at me by these guys."

"I don't want to get you in trouble over this, Les. If there's a problem, I can fight my own battles. It's my fight, not yours."

"This is part of my job. Cleaning up after the messes made by some of my agents."

"I'm sorry about that. But I wanted to do something dramatic to jump-start this whole investigation. If I did nothing, more girls might be abducted and killed. And we might not catch whoever has done all this so far. I thought we needed to do something about it. So I did something. I think it will shake some stuff loose. Trust me on this, Les."

He sighed.

"Okay, I'll deal with all the fallout on this end as best I can."

Chief Earnshaw was upset with me, too.

No big surprise to me there.

"You made me look stupid at that press conference, Cassidy,

saying all that stuff after I told them there was no known connection between these crimes and your sister."

I wanted to tell Earnshaw he didn't need my help to look stupid, but I didn't.

I simply let him rant on at me after the press conference, yelling a lot of unpleasant stuff until he finally went silent.

And then I left.

Yep, no question about it, Chief Earnshaw was mad at me.

My boss Les Polk was mad at me.

And my fiancé was mad at me, too.

I'm very good at making people mad at me sometimes.

But I had accomplished what I wanted. I'd gotten the word out on my conversation with Munroe about my sister, and that I believed it was somehow linked to Natalie Jarvis and Erica Kent. Now I just had to connect the dots in all three cases to track down a dangerous and bloodthirsty and clever killer.

And the person that could do that for me was David Munroe.

I needed go back and get him to talk to me in prison again, like I had vowed at the press conference.

I had to convince him somehow to tell me all his secrets—about Caitlin and about everything else.

THIRTY-ONE

"There's one big question about all this," Alex said. "Why would David Munroe take all the blame for your sister's murder and not tell anyone all this time if someone else was involved?"

"That is a problem," I agreed.

Me, Alex and Girard were back at the Huntsdale station talking about David Munroe—and my plans to go back and interview him again at the prison. Well, Alex and I were talking about it. Girard had been sitting at a table working on a newspaper crossword puzzle since we got there. He seemed completely focused on the puzzle and tuned out of our conversation.

"I mean I know he's sick and all, maybe he wants to meet God with a clean slate on everything he did," Alex said to me now. "But still..."

"Yeah, he's done fifteen years in prison, and he never said a word about anyone else."

"I've never heard of something like that happening in any case."

"It doesn't make any sense," I muttered.

Phil Girard looked up from his puzzle and added something then, which was not what I expected.

"It does make sense to me," he said. "And it has happened before. One guy—a patsy or whatever you want to call him—taking the blame for a heinous crime when other people might have been involved."

"When?" Alex asked.

"The biggest murder mystery in our country's history."

"Which is?" I asked.

"The assassination of President John F. Kennedy."

Girard had read a lot of books about all the conspiracy theories on the JFK assassination. He told us many times in the past about how he was convinced Lee Harvey Oswald was not the lone gunman on November 22, 1963 in Dallas.

"I'm not saying Lee Harvey Oswald was innocent," Girard said to us now. "I don't think he was. He was involved. But so were other people. He knew who they were too, but he never identified them by name during the forty-eight hours or so he was questioned by cops, or even had an exchange with reporters at the Dallas police station. He did say though that he was being set up as a 'patsy.' Maybe David Munroe was a 'patsy' the same way for your sister Caitlin's murder."

Alex shook her head.

"I don't see any real comparison. I mean that's just a political conspiracy theory anyway, Phil. We're talking about a real crime here. A murder. Maybe a series of murders. I don't think I've ever heard of another murder case where something like that happened."

"Son of Sam," Girard said.

"David Berkowitz?" I asked. "The one who killed all those women on the streets of New York City in the seventies?"

"That's right."

"You're saying that Berkowitz took the blame for someone else who really was Son of Sam?"

"Maybe. Have you ever read a book called *The Ultimate Evil*? I have. There was a Netflix documentary recently based on the book, too. It's by an investigative journalist named Maury Terry who says there was a lot of other people involved in the Son of Sam shootings besides David Berkowitz, the one we all know as Son of Sam. That it was a cult of killers. Berkowitz just happened to be the one who got caught.

"Berkowitz said he never told cops about any of the others because he was afraid someone would find a way to kill him in prison. But he found religion and gave interviews in the book saying he wanted to tell the truth now. He was there for all of the killings, he was part of the murder plot, but didn't do all of the shootings himself. He said—and said this for the first time years after his conviction—that there were others besides him who carried out the Son of Sam murders. But he still refused to give any specific names. He said he was too afraid to do that. Sound familiar?"

I thought again about what Munroe had said to me about Caitlin at the prison this last time: He was there when she was abducted and murdered, he said, but he wasn't the one who killed her.

"And you think that might be the reason why David Munroe refuses to give me any more specifics about who killed my sister and who may well be responsible for Natalie Jarvis and Erica Kent too. Because they are still out there?"

Girard shrugged.

"I can only tell you why David Berkowitz said he hadn't talked about other people in the Son of Sam killings. Like I told you, he was afraid they would kill him if he talked, even in prison. And he was guilty too. So he kept quiet for a long time. But then he got seriously into religion, became some kind of an ordained minister through mail order courses in prison, and said he had finally decided to tell the entire truth. Or at least part of the truth. Maybe that's what happened with David Munroe too."

I looked up at the pictures of the three victims we had here on the bulletin board next to us.

Erica Kent. Natalie Jarvis. And, of course, my sister Caitlin.

Caitlin was twelve years old in the picture, and she would never get any older. That was the way she was frozen in time for me forever. I tried to imagine what Caitlin would look like if she were alive today—a woman in her late twenties, beautiful, probably successful in her career.

My sister.

For fifteen years I'd blamed David Munroe for taking her away from me. Taking her away from our family. Maybe even causing my father's death too by putting him through such a horrific ordeal. But now I wasn't so sure. Maybe it wasn't just Munroe. Maybe there were other people involved too. People still out there doing bad things to Natalie Jarvis, Erica Kent and other young girls like Caitlin.

I looked over at Alex.

"What do you think?" I asked.

"Interesting theory," she said.

"Possible, you think?"

She hesitated for a second, then nodded her head.

"Yes, I think it's possible."

"Damn straight it is," said Phil Girard.

Then he picked up the newspaper and went back to working on his crossword puzzle.

"Anyone know a good six-letter word for houseplant?" he asked.

THIRTY-TWO

"Does your husband ever give you a hard time about your job?"
I asked Alex.

We were sitting in a bar around the corner from the station
house having a few beers, trying to unwind after the meeting
we'd just had there and everything happening now that we'd
found Erica Kent's body.

"Like how?"

"Too long hours. Too dangerous. Too strange to have your
wife packing a gun and catching bad guys and all that kind of
stuff."

"Uh, no. I think Bob actually likes the idea. He always
introduces me to new people at parties as "my wife, otherwise
known as the female Eliot Ness." Of course, sometimes we have
to explain to people, especially the young ones, who Eliot Ness
was. He's very supportive of me in this job, whatever it takes."

"Okay, I just wondered."

I took a sip of my beer and didn't say anything else.

But I knew Alex wouldn't let it drop at that.

"Why are you asking something like that?"

"Greg."

"Problem?"

"Maybe."

"Serious problem?"

"I don't know, Alex. Greg just doesn't understand my job. He doesn't want me doing my job with the FBI. He's been giving me a hard time about it. And I'm concerned about being able to live the life I want to live once we're married. Which is doing what I'm doing now. Just like you are."

"Can I give you some advice as a woman who's been married for a while?"

"I would welcome it."

"Talk to him about all this. Don't talk to me or anyone else about your problems. Talk it out with him."

"I've tried to talk to him, but—"

"No, I mean *really* talk. Be completely honest with him about how much his attitude is upsetting you. Open up to him, just like you're doing now with me. Make him understand how important the job is to you. How good it makes you feel doing what you do. How happy you are when you're doing this kind of work, the same way as his work as a lawyer makes him happy. Hopefully, he'll eventually understand. But don't simply get mad at him and brood. That's a recipe for disaster in any marriage. I know that first hand."

"You? I always thought you had the perfect marriage."

"Nobody is perfect. Not me. Not my husband. Not you. And not Greg either."

Alex was right about that.

Okay, a lot of people have told me I found the perfect guy in Greg. I mean he's good-looking; has a fit, attractive body; he dresses well; he's extremely successful in his job as an attorney; he's smart; he's kind. It's almost like someone created the perfect man for me... dropped him down from outer space or something.

Except the guy's not totally perfect.

Even before our fight about my job at the FBI and what I was doing here in Huntsdale I knew that.

Actually, he's not perfect in a lot of ways. Little ways, mostly. Still, they sometimes bothered me when I thought about being with him as man and wife for the rest of my life.

Like he leaves his clothes on the floor when he takes things off, so I have to go behind and pick them up—I'm much neater than him. He eats very slowly, savoring every bite—which can drive me nuts because I tend to wolf down food in a hurry. He tends to go on and on talking about some of his corporate cases, which I don't find nearly as interesting as he does. He sometimes licks his fingers when he turns the pages of a book or magazine or newspaper, which I also find annoying. And he prefers to watch "serious TV" on PBS or one of the news channels, while I'm much more of a guilty-pleasure watcher of shows like *The Real Housewives of Beverly Hills* or *Jersey Shore*.

But the bottom line about Greg is he loves me.

And I love him.

Except...

Well, except, I worried sometimes that Greg loved me more than I loved him.

And I wasn't sure that was a good thing.

Billy Weller came into the bar just as we were getting ready to leave.

"Doreen Trask called the station looking for you," he said to me. "She says she talked to Munroe about seeing you again at the prison. He agreed. She said she'd try to set something up there for you to see him again in the next day or so."

"That's great news, Billy!" I said.

"Yeah, I figured you'd be happy. That's why I came over here to tell you."

"How about another beer to celebrate?" I said to him and Alex.

"Not me," Alex said. "I've got to go call my kid. It's a bedtime ritual. Mom needs to tuck him in, even if it's virtual by phone or Zoom."

"I'll have a beer with you," Billy said.

I ordered two beers for us as Alex was leaving. She gave me a questioning look before she went out the door, but I ignored it. I was just having a beer with the guy, that's all. No big deal.

We wound up having more than one beer. We drank a number of them, Billy and me, and hung out there for quite a while. We talked about Natalie Jarvis and Erica Kent. We talked about my sister. We talked more about our memories from high school in Huntsdale. I even told him details about my estrangement from my mother.

"Maybe you should cut your mother a little slack," he said, when I was finished. "She's your mother. She's all that's left of your family. In a sense, you have to be the adult now in the relationship. Don't blame her for things she does or doesn't do, just be there to support her as best you can. Even if she didn't do that for you. You need to be better than your mother."

"Wow! That's almost kind of profound, Billy."

He smiled broadly.

That damn charming smile of his again.

When we finally left, Billy walked me back to the hotel where I was staying. He stood there at the door with me before I went inside. Him looking at me, and me looking back at him without saying anything.

"Good night, Nikki, I'll see you at the station in the morning," he said.

Then he turned quickly and walked away.

"Tomorrow," I called out after him.

I thought about Billy lying in bed afterward and wondered if it was my imagination or if he had really been contemplating trying to kiss me goodnight.

I thought about something else too.

I'd wanted him to kiss me.

I really did.

Even though I wasn't sure what might have happened after that.

THIRTY-THREE

There was a pounding on my hotel door that woke me up.

I looked over at the clock next to my bed. It said 6:30 a.m. Who in the hell was waking me up at 6:30 in the morning? I grabbed my gun from the nightstand and carried it with me as I got out of bed and made my way to the door. I yelled out before opening it to make sure who was there.

It was Alex.

"Wake up!" she shouted. "Let me in!"

I opened the door and she burst into the room.

"He's dead, Nikki."

"Who's dead?"

"David Munroe."

"What are you talking about?"

"It's on the news right now. David Munroe fell in the prison shower last night, crashed his head against the wall and died of a brain hemorrhage. Preliminary ruling is 'accidental death.'"

"They're calling it an accident?"

She nodded.

"They said he slipped on a piece of soap in the shower," she said.

"So one day after I tell the entire world Munroe has secrets I plan to find out about my sister and Natalie Jarvis and Erica Kent, he just happens coincidentally to slip on a bar of soap in the prison shower and accidentally kill himself?"

"That's the official line from the prison on it at the moment."

A short time later, we were in a car heading to Columbus and Dagmore Prison to see the warden there in order to find out more about the circumstances of David Munroe's sudden death.

I was driving. Alex was in the passenger seat next to me. Girard and Billy Weller were in the back. Weller didn't really belong with us, since this was an FBI visit, but he asked me if he could come along, and I said yes. Professional courtesy and all. At least that's what I told myself. Hey, it was better than admitting to myself that I liked spending as much time as I could with the guy.

"Do you really think someone definitely knocked off David Munroe in prison?" Alex asked me.

"I think it's hard to imagine any other possibility given the timing when he died just as all these new developments were occurring."

"I thought you said he had terminal cancer and looked very sick," Girard said.

"He did. But it wouldn't have killed him this fast. I think someone decided to expedite the process. Much easier for him to slip on a bar of soap and be done with it all quickly. They didn't want him to talk to me anymore."

"They?"

"Could be more than one person."

"A conspiracy?"

"Maybe."

"Wow, I thought you didn't believe in all that conspiracy stuff I was talking about, Cassidy."

"I thought you did, Phil."

"Oh, I do. I think you're probably right on the conspiracy angle with Munroe. But I just wanted to hear you say it."

I knew I bore some of the responsibility for what happened to David Munroe. Once I went public at the press conference with the revelation that Munroe had been talking to me—and I was going to try to get more information out of him—that very likely was the motivation for someone to make sure he wouldn't be alive to tell me anything else.

I didn't feel any real guilt about his death though. Munroe was a horrible person, whether or not he was the one who pulled the trigger on the gun that killed Caitlin. No, my reaction was more disappointment and anger. I'd been hoping Munroe would finally reveal secrets that could help me find the answers I was looking for. But now he was gone, taking those secrets to the grave with him.

And all I could do was find out what happened to him—and why.

"What do we know about the warden we're going to see at Dagmore Prison?" I asked Alex.

"So far, he seems straight. Been there about two years. The newly elected governor appointed him then to replace the previous warden after a big prison corruption scandal was revealed during the campaign. Involved payoffs to guards and prison officials for special favors and for looking the other way, or even aiding and abetting prisoners to carry out illegal acts from behind bars. Since then, things seem to have dramatically improved. The last report from a prison watchdog group gave this place high marks."

"Doesn't mean guards aren't still taking payoffs," Girard grunted. "They might simply be more careful about it. There's still something that really smells wrong about all this. Did you see the report on Munroe's death from the prison? I mean the guard who was supposed to be watching Munroe just happens to not be around when he slips in the shower and kills himself? C'mon."

"There's more than a hundred guards there," Billy Weller said. "I checked before we left. This warden, no matter how good or honest he is, can't know what every guard in his jail is doing every minute."

"No, but he can help us find out more about what really happened to Munroe," I said. "Hopefully, he'll cooperate fully with us. If not, well, there's an advantage to being in the FBI, Billy. We can always get our boss to use some clout from Washington to help us get what we need from him."

"How far away are we from the prison?" Girard asked.

"We should be there in about twenty minutes."

It was a few minutes later when I looked in the rearview mirror and saw a big, black SUV behind us.

That normally wouldn't mean too much.

Except I remembered seeing the black SUV behind us earlier when we left and later on the road.

Was someone following us?

The SUV was moving fast. Very fast. And closing the gap between us until it was pretty much tailgating right behind our car.

"Hey!" I shouted to everyone in the car. "What's this guy behind us doing?"

They all saw the black SUV right on our tail, too. I began to speed up in an attempt to pull away from it. The SUV speeded up too. I had a rented Toyota, and it was no match in power and speed against the SUV. The SUV quickly closed the gap between us even more.

"Jesus!" Girard yelled as everyone realized what was happening.

"Get off on the side of the road," Alex said. "We're all

armed. There's four of us. Once we're stopped, we can handle anything that comes at us."

But I didn't have time to do anything before the SUV driver sped up even more, pulled up alongside of us and then rammed us with the side of the SUV. I tried to hold onto the wheel and control the car. But the Toyota had no chance against the much bigger SUV.

Seconds later, our car spun wildly off the highway.

Everyone was screaming.

And I remember wondering if this was how I was going to die.

THIRTY-FOUR

The Toyota with the four of us in it smashed through a barricade along the highway and down a steep incline into a grassy and wooded area below.

We were lucky though.

The car did not flip over or catch fire.

Instead, we finally hit a group of trees that smashed up the front of the Toyota, but also helped us come to a stop.

I'd been thrown forward toward the steering wheel, but my seat belt protected me from being injured.

"Everyone all right?" I yelled.

"I'm good," Alex said from the passenger seat.

"Me too," Billy said from the back.

"I'm alive," Girard said, "but damn that was close."

We got out of the car, took out our weapons and made our way back up to the highway. The SUV was no longer in sight. Probably assumed he'd accomplished the mission by forcing us off the road and thought that we were dead. And he didn't want to stick around for any witnesses or police to show up.

Amazingly enough, the car was still drivable. I eventually managed to get it back up onto the highway again. Still just regular traffic there, a car or two passing by. But no sign of the SUV or whoever in it who had tried to kill us.

"Anyone have any idea who was driving?" I asked.

"Couldn't see much, just that it seemed to be single person —looked like a white male—inside the vehicle," Alex said.

"Same here," I said. "That's what I thought too. No one happened to get a license plate number, did they?"

"You're kidding, right?" Girard said.

"Yeah, I know. Me too. It all happened so fast."

"So what now?" Billy Weller asked.

"We go try to find this guy in the SUV who tried to kill us, right?" Girard said.

"I'll call the basic description in to Chief Earnshaw back at the station," Billy said. "Earnshaw can reach out to neighboring police districts around here to be on the lookout for a black SUV."

"Good luck with that," Girard grunted. "There's a helluva lot of black SUVs out on the roads these days."

But there was something else I was worried about. A priority concern I had now that I knew we were all safe and sound.

"Think about it," I said. "First, Munroe gets bumped off right after it becomes known that he's been talking to me. Then someone tries to kill all of us working on the case. Someone who was afraid of whatever secrets David Munroe might have told me, or what they feared he was about to tell me. Someone who was willing to go to any lengths to prevent those secrets from coming out. Kill Munroe. Kill a car full of FBI agents and a police officer. And then what after all that? Who else was there that was close enough to Munroe to know his secrets?"

"Doreen Trask," Alex said.

"She could be the next target," Billy agreed.

"We've got to get to her first," I said.

Doreen Trask lived in a town that was a short distance away from where our car crash had happened. It only took a few minutes for us to get on the phone and track down a specific address for her. Then it took another fifteen minutes to drive there. We drove at high speed all the way.

But when we got there it looked like we might be too late.

There was a vehicle sitting out in front of Doreen Trask's house. It was a black SUV. There was even a big dent along the right side on the passenger door, which had obviously been made when the SUV collided with our car.

The front door of Doreen Trask's house was already open.

Billy quickly called in to Huntsdale to get the closest police station to send us backup right away. Billy wanted to wait until they got here—and Girard and Alex too, which was the by-the-book approach. But I wasn't going to wait. If someone else was in that house, then every extra minute or even second could be fatal for Doreen Trask.

"I'm going in," I announced to the three of them, drawing my 9mm Glock out of my holster and heading for the house.

"Okay, then we're all going in," Alex said, pulling out her weapon too.

Billy and Girard nodded too, and we made our way across the lawn and toward the open front door.

That's when we heard gunshots from inside the house.

THIRTY-FIVE

"FBI!" I said in a loud voice when we got to the door. "We are armed, and we are entering this house."

There was no response.

I said it again.

Still nothing.

We went inside, down a short hallway and then into the living room. It was empty. We kept our weapons in front of us as we checked the entire living room out completely to make sure no one was hiding there.

"Clear in this room," Alex finally said.

There was a longer hall leading from the living room to the bedrooms and to a bathroom too.

"FBI!" I said one more time. "If anyone is here and you're armed, give up your weapons now."

No answer.

We began moving toward the bedrooms and the bathroom. I was in front, the others right behind me. I was the first to see it. Blood on the carpeting in the hall ahead of us. Blood splatters. Lots of them.

"Jesus, it looks like we're too late," Billy said.

"She might still be alive," I told everyone.

"Yes, and that asshole who did it might still be here in one of these rooms," Alex said.

"Not exactly what I was expecting when I came to Ohio for what I thought was a nice easy assignment in my last days before retirement," Girard muttered.

We made our way down the hall further, our guns still drawn and pointing ahead of us as we walked.

The bathroom was empty.

So was the first bedroom we checked.

The blood was coming from the second bedroom in the house, and that's where we got a big shock.

There was a body inside the bedroom. Lying on the floor. Covered in blood, the body in front of us was very dead.

"We're too late," Billy blurted out.

"Maybe not," Alex said.

She was right. As we got closer, we could see that the body was not Doreen Trask.

It wasn't a woman at all.

This was a man's body.

But where was Doreen Trask?

We found that out soon enough once we all went into the room, guns still drawn and ready for anything at this point.

There was someone in the room. Sitting on the bed. She was covered in the blood of the dead man on the floor. And she was holding a sharp knife in her hand, which was also covered with blood.

A gun lay on the bed next to her.

"He came here to kill me," she said, staring down at the body and seemingly still in shock from whatever had gone on here before we arrived. "He told me that. He said David was already dead in prison. And that he had just finished killing you people from the FBI on the road. He said I was next. He had the gun in his hand. He was going to shoot me next. All I had to do was die now, and his job was finished—that's what he said when he broke in here."

She looked down at the blood-splattered body of the gunman lying on the bedroom floor in front of us.

"But how...?" I started to ask.

"I guess I surprised him. He wasn't expecting me to put up a fight like I did. But I grabbed the knife and stabbed him before he could shoot me. Then I just kept stabbing him. Over and over. After that, I grabbed the gun he was holding and shot him until it was empty. I wanted to make sure he was dead.

"I had to do that. You understand why, don't you? It wasn't just about saving my life. All I could think about was my baby. My unborn baby inside me. David's baby. I couldn't let him kill David's baby. David's son.

"Now that David is dead, his son is all I have left of him. I wasn't going to let anyone take that away from me. I wasn't going to let anyone harm him. Now David will live on through him once my son David Jr. is born."

Yes, David Munroe was dead.

And his son had somehow survived.

I wasn't exactly sure how I felt about that.

THIRTY-SIX

"I knew David was dead before he broke in and told me," Doreen Trask said. "They notified me from the prison this morning before all this happened here. Since I'm his lawyer, as you know, and his legal representative. Also, because I was listed on his contacts list as next of kin, even though we were never officially married.

"So I'd heard this news just before the man with the gun showed up. I couldn't believe it at first about David. I had talked to him recently, and he was fine. I kept hoping that there had been some mistake. But then this man—the intruder—he laughed to me about David being dead. I was still in shock about David and I guess... I guess I lost it and went berserk."

The body of the gunman was gone now. It had been taken away by the crime team sent to the house a short time ago.

We still didn't know who he was or anything about him. There was no identification found on him, which had probably been intentional on his part. The crime people had taken his fingerprints and hoped to come up with a match on that soon. I mean he seemed like the kind of guy who would have had a criminal record.

The gun he'd brought with him was a Luger, not a .45 like the weapon used on both my sister here fifteen years ago and Erica Kent several months ago. Not that I expected the weapons to be a match. There were too many moving parts to this whole thing now, which meant there had to be more than one person involved. I was pretty sure of that.

There was still blood all over the floor and rug of the bedroom where Doreen Trask had stabbed him to death and shot him. She appeared to be unhurt. All the blood came from the man with the gun she said had wanted to kill her.

Which was a pretty amazing story.

"Tell me exactly what happened," I said to her.

"I was in bed. I was crying and trying to hold myself together after I had gotten the news about David. So that's all I was thinking about. I guess that's why I never heard the guy come in or anything. But I assume he must have broken into the house, right?"

"We found the front door had been broken down. That's how he got in."

"All I know is he suddenly burst into the bedroom and was standing in front of me, pointing the gun. That's when he talked about David being dead, what he'd done to you and how he was going to kill me next. He thought it was funny about David and about you. He said now there would be no one left to tell anyone anything. He was gloating about it. He seemed so happy. I guess that's what set me off. That and the baby inside me. David's baby. I knew I had to protect my baby no matter what else happened.

"He was looking for something though before he killed me. He said he knew David had given me a letter at the prison on one of my visits. If I gave him the letter, he said he'd kill me quickly and painlessly. But if I didn't, he would make me suffer horribly until I told him where it was.

"I glanced over at my handbag on the end table next to the

bed, and said it was in there. I reached for the handbag, and he didn't stop me. But there was no letter in there. Just the knife I keep in there. The knife had been David's idea. He wanted me to always carry it with me in case I ever got attacked. I'd never used it before, but I used it now.

"I was lucky, I guess. He didn't expect me to fight back. He was intent on seeing the letter he thought was in the handbag. He grabbed for me and for the bag himself, and that gave me the chance to take the knife and stab him in the hand holding the gun. The gun dropped to the floor, and he screamed out in pain.

"He let go of me, and that's when I stabbed him again. This time it was in the face, I aimed for his eye, and I think I hit it with the blade of the knife. Now he was screaming even more, and he couldn't see. So I stabbed him again. And again. And again. And then I used his own gun to shoot him over and over. Until I was sure he was dead. And then... well, then you showed up just as it was happening."

My God, I thought to myself. It all sounded crazy. But so crazy that it made me believe her. This woman had summoned up all her courage and her strength and her determination to save her baby and killed the killer before he could kill her.

Medical people checked her out. No physical damage whatsoever they could find. Of course, the psychological toll on her must have been horrific. But that's not what I was worrying about now. I was still afraid of another attack on Doreen Trask. Someone still wanted her dead.

"We need to move you out of here to someplace more secure," I told her.

"Do you think someone else might try to kill me?"

"This guy was very likely hired by someone else to do the job. He failed with you and with us. We need to make sure there's not another attempt on your life."

"What about you? Aren't you in danger too? He tried to kill you too?"

"We get paid to risk our lives," I said.

We made arrangements to take her to a federal safe house in this area of Ohio. I could have put her in local police protection, but I wasn't sure who I could trust anymore. Munroe had died while he was in prison custody. And I wasn't sure whether Earnshaw was up to providing the protection she needed. Especially after eliminating the hit man sent to kill her. Someone might be looking for revenge.

But there was something important I needed to know before we moved her out of the house.

"The letter the gunman wanted. The one he said Munroe gave you in prison. Is there a letter?"

"Yes, it's in my office files here."

"What kind of a letter?"

"I'm not sure. It's in a sealed envelope. All I know is that David said I should give it to you if anything happened to him."

"Why me?"

"Because the letter is addressed to you."

Doreen reached into a drawer of the desk and took out a small white envelope. She handed it to me. The writing on it said: "For FBI Agent Nikki Cassidy. To Be Opened Only in the Event of My Death."

"I guess he meant it for when he died of cancer," she said. "Or maybe he knew he was in some kind of danger. But he wanted you to have this once he was dead. And now, well, now he is dead."

I wasn't sure what I was expecting when I opened up the envelope. A final confession from Munroe with specific details of my sister's murder like I'd asked him for every time I'd visited over the past fifteen years. The names of other people involved that I didn't know about. Or some other explosive evidence that would somehow answer all my questions and give me closure at last.

But there was nothing like that inside the envelope.

Just a single sheet of paper.

On it, Munroe had written three words: THE NOWHERE MEN.

Below that, there appeared to be the address of a website.

But with a bizarre website address.

It said... thenowheremen.in.onion.

"What is this website?" I asked Doreen Trask.

"I don't know. He never mentioned anything about it."

"What does 'nowhere men' mean?"

I remembered how had talked with me during that last visit at the prison about something he called the "nowhere world."

'I don't know that either."

"So what is this all about?"

"All I know is that David said to tell you when I gave you the envelope once he was dead—that all the answers you were looking for were right there. All you had to do was find them. He said the rest was up to you. He said you should be able to figure it out from this."

THIRTY-SEVEN

There was a computer in Doreen's home office. I asked her to power it up for me, and then I immediately tried to put in the website address and see where it would take me on the internet. But it took me nowhere. There was no such address.

I guess I kind of expected that. Because the website address for the "Nowhere Men" site—whatever the hell that was— didn't look like any other I'd ever seen. No www. No .com or something similar at the end. None of it made sense to me, and I soon found out why. It turned out this mysterious site was on the dark web.

Of course I knew about the dark web, but I hadn't ever been on it and neither had Alex or Girard.

That was confirmed by Ray Terlop, one of the FBI internet trackers back in Washington.

"Most people don't realize it, but there are three parts to the internet," Terlop explained. "First, there's the internet we all surf with Google Chrome or Firefox or whatever browser. That's the one everyone is familiar with.

"But there's also something called the deep web. That sounds more ominous than it really is. The deep web simply refers to content not accessible from a search engine like Google, but instead has a pay wall or other sign-in credentials. Things like Netflix are on the deep web, so it's not all that mysterious.

"Finally, we come to the dark web. This is the least known and the most mysterious part of the internet. Not everything on the dark web is bad, there are some legitimate things and people posting. But there is also plenty of scary, illegal and immoral stuff. Guns, drugs, false ID information, sex and more. Human trafficking, even sometimes selling women as slaves and that sort of thing. A lot of it is really sick, just like the people who troll through the sites for this kind of thing are sick."

"Like David Munroe," I said.

"Yes, like David Munroe."

I thought about how outrageous it seemed to me that someone like Munroe had access to this kind of thing—or was able to use a computer at all—while he was in prison for murdering my sister.

When I was a little girl growing up, I'd always imagined the bad guys my father arrested and sent to prison were working hard labor on a rock pile or something. Maybe it was more like that in the old days. But now prisoners had libraries with books to read, took college courses and were able to have free rein on a computer like Munroe. Hell, he even got his girlfriend/lawyer pregnant while in prison.

"The best part of the dark web though, for the people who use it," Terlop said, "is that it's completely anonymous. The encryption does not allow anyone—even law enforcement—to track a person's identity or location very easily. It's totally unregulated. It's like the Wild West or something on the dark web. Anything goes."

"Sounds delightful."

"Now you have to understand something," Terlop continued. "The dark web wasn't always a place for people to do bad things, illegal stuff. And it still isn't. In fact, the dark web was begun for a pretty noble reason. To allow people in countries where the government doesn't allow free speech to have a forum to communicate on the internet without the threat of official intervention.

"That's how it started anyway. The idea was to create something that would ensure anonymity, not for malicious content. And many reputable businesses still use it for legitimate reasons —as well as law enforcement and intelligence groups too who do not want their activities made public.

"And, yes, there is a lot of horrible, unspeakable stuff going on too when you search the dark web. Drugs, gun sales, money laundering, human trafficking, illicit sex involving minors, terrorist activities—you name it, you'll probably find it somewhere on the dark web. And, of course, bad people using it for these purposes and cloaking themselves in the anonymity it provides them."

"So how do we get on this dark web?" Alex asked. "Or can we?"

"Oh, we can. It just takes more effort."

"Every time I try to access the website I'm looking for, it just tells me I don't have access to go there," I told Terlop.

"You don't. Not with a normal browser. That's the key. You need a special browser to get on the dark web. You can download it. We have it here. It's called TOR. That stands for something called TOTAL ONION REPORT. It should be able to get us to that site. What's it called?"

I gave him the website and the address for it I'd gotten from Doreen Trask.

"The thing is we're still going to have a problem," Terlop said. "These sites on the dark web are different than anything else on the web. They use a scrambling service that changes the URL to avoid detection at various times. A lot of them don't end in .com or .co like other websites usually do. Instead, many dark web sites end with in.onion. That's where TOR gets its name from. And then they're heavily password protected. Do you have any information to access this site?"

"No," I said. "Munroe's girlfriend couldn't—or wouldn't—give that to me. But can't you guys in tech break into it somehow even without the password?"

"Hopefully. But it will take some time. Like I said, these sites are really well guarded and scrambled to maintain secrecy from the people running them and posting. They change stuff up a lot to avoid detection. It won't be easy. But if you could just figure out Munroe's password access—"

"Can't you run a series of password options through the computer?" I asked. "Let the computer do the work and find the right combination. Sooner or later, it would hit on the right password, wouldn't it?"

"That could work except for one problem. Most websites—even those not on the dark web, but certainly the ones that are—limit the number of times you can enter an incorrect password before shutting you out. Just like if you enter the wrong one on your bank or credit card site. That's what likely would happen here if we just let a computer keep putting up automated responses as a possible password. The site would stop letting us enter anything after a certain among of wrong tries."

I weighed up everything Ray had just told us. "That site holds the key to this case. We have to figure out a way in, and fast."

THIRTY-EIGHT

The dead guy who tried to kill us and Doreen Trask did not have any identification on him.

Which presumably was deliberate. He did have a wallet with several hundred dollars in cash, but no drivers' license or anything else telling us who he might be. I was kind of expecting that. If he really was hired as a professional killer, as I assumed was likely, he wouldn't be carrying around any of that kind of identification with him.

The SUV he had been driving had been stolen from a car dealership in a nearby town. Which wasn't surprising either. I didn't really expect to find his registration and insurance cards in the glove compartment.

We had coordinated with Chief Earnshaw back in Huntsdale and the local police. Everyone was there now, including a crime team. They dusted for fingerprints in the car, even though we already had the dead man's prints from the body. Still, I wanted to cover every base.

The most important thing was to figure out who he was working for. Someone had hired him to do all this. But who?

The vehicle had several dents on the side where he had hit

us on the road, but otherwise looked drivable. It had gotten him here after our encounter on the highway. He had probably picked the SUV to steal from the lot because it was so big and he knew it would withstand a collision with a normal car of the size we were driving.

Yes, he seemed to have planned it all out.

This was a professional job.

By a hired killer.

Except he hadn't been very good at his job.

He'd left the scene of our car crash before checking to make sure that we were all dead.

And he'd been overwhelmed and stabbed to death by the woman he was supposed to kill, Doreen Trask, even though he was armed with a gun and about twice her size.

The SUV did provide us with one item of interest. A cash receipt was found on the floor. It was from a motel. The receipt was for a payment of $161 for a three-night stay. The receipt said the recipient was still checked in through noon tomorrow. He must have paid in cash at the motel, gotten the receipt and then accidentally dropped it inside the car. Or maybe it fell out of his pocket or whatever during those collisions on the road with our car.

The name of the motel was the Strand, and it was located only about ten miles away. The four of us—Alex, Girard, Billy and me—drove over there. It was a nondescript, white building about fifteen minutes away, with a sign outside that said it had both daily and hourly rates. Just the kind of place for a hired gun to spend the night before going on the run again.

It didn't take much persuasion for the manager of the Strand Motel to recognize a description of the guy we found lying on the floor at Doreen Trask's place and take us to his room. He opened the door and let us in to search. It all seemed very routine for him. He'd probably had a lot of experience of visits from police or other law enforcement authorities before about his guests in a place like this.

Inside we found a suitcase with a few sets of underwear and an extra T-shirt. A razor too, along with toothpaste, an electric toothbrush and a pack of dental floss. I guess he took good care of his gums. The drawers in the dresser in the room were empty. He apparently liked to travel light.

But, when I opened the end table next to the bed, I found something that terrified me. Alongside a photo of Doreen Trask was a newspaper clipping of the Mattheu case. Alongside the story was a picture of me.

I was the target.

Earnshaw called us while we were still at the motel. He called Girard, interestingly enough, not me or Alex. I guess he still felt more comfortable talking with a man closer to his age instead of two young women agents like us.

"Wow, that was quick!" Girard said into his cell phone now. "Who is he?"

"They got an ID off the fingerprints?" I asked.

He nodded and listened some more to Earnshaw. Then he hung up and turned to Alex and me.

"Our boy's name is Miles Janos. Thirty-three years old, originally from Brockway, Pennsylvania, but he's drifted around a lot. Quite a criminal record for the departed Mr. Janos. Armed robbery, assault, and a few suspicion-of-murder charges along the way too that he somehow was able to evade conviction or jail time for."

Not surprising. But what Girard said next was.

"Janos had just recently been released from prison. Guess where? Dagmore State Prison in Columbus. He finished up a two-year stint there for grand larceny. He got out just a few days before the death of David Munroe in the same prison."

THIRTY-NINE

The Nowhere Men.

That was the message—the secret website—David Munroe wanted me to have.

It was buried somewhere deep online as part of the mysterious dark web.

Munroe told Doreen Trask it held the answers I was looking for.

But how did I get onto the damn website?

When we got back to Huntsdale, I checked again with Terlop in Washington. Nothing yet, he said. But they would keep trying and hoped to crack it at some point soon.

I didn't want to wait.

"I want to try from here too. Can you tell us how to set up that TOR network on our computer?"

"I suppose."

"Then let's get started."

Terlop gave us the instructions on the phone—and, sure enough, we were able to get on the TOR network.

Like he said, that part was pretty easy. Not much different

than downloading Firefox or Google Chrome or some other browser from the regular internet.

But the whole dark web experience was very confusing and hard to follow at first. There is no index or rankings list of topics on the dark web. No way to just google or search for anything very easily.

Of course, Terlop had warned us about this but it was still extremely frustrating for us to navigate.

Eventually I was able to figure out how to get to the Nowhere Men site.

There was a spot there to enter a screen name. I entered the name of David Munroe. I figured that made as much sense as anything else. It worked. The website accepted it as an approved name.

Then it asked for a password.

"'Nowhere Man' was a song by The Beatles, right?" Alex said.

"Yes," I agreed. "One of their earlier ones. I don't know much about it though. I mean I haven't even heard it in years."

"'Nowhere Man'," Phil Girard said. "Written by John Lennon/Paul McCartney recorded in 1965, but Lennon was the one who really wrote it. It appeared on their *Rubber Soul* album. It's about a man who has lost his way. "Doesn't know where he's going, a real nowhere man." Supposedly Lennon wrote the song about himself as he struggled to deal with all the overnight fame and fortune he'd suddenly become over-whelmed with when The Beatles hit it so big in America back then."

Girard then began to sing several verses of the song to us.

Alex and I just stared at him.

"I was a big Beatles fan growing up." He shrugged.

In the end, none of that helped. We tried Beatles as the password. Then Lennon's name. Both were rejected.

"Maybe it's someone close to Munroe—especially who played a big role recently in his life," I suggested.

I put in Doreen Trask's name as a password. First name, then last name—then both of them.

No good either.

"How about his victim?" Alex said.

"You mean...?"

"Yes, your sister. I could see him being sick enough to do something like that, couldn't you?"

I tried Caitlin's name.

Another rejection.

I was worried about what Terlop had told us about the possibility—a very good possibility—of the site having a limit on the number of times you could try to enter a password there.

I kept waiting for us to be shut out. But it didn't happen.

"Didn't Doreen Trask give you any hint at all when she gave you the website?" Girard asked.

"She just said he told her I should be able to figure out if I thought about everything he told me."

"So what did he say to you during that interview in prison that might give us some kind of a clue?" Alex asked.

"Nothing I can think of."

When I got back to the hotel, my phone buzzed. I looked at the screen and saw the call was from Greg. I let it go to voice mail. I'd left a message on his phone earlier to tell him about the incident on the highway and assure him I was all right. I didn't go into a lot of detail, but apparently it was enough to freak him out.

"My God, Nikki, you could have been killed!" I heard him screaming at me on the voice mail when I played it. "I can't believe you're still doing this. I can't believe you're still up there putting yourself in that kind of danger. You've got to get out of there and come home. I just want you to be safe. I'll do anything, whatever it takes, to keep you safe. Even if you aren't doing that for yourself. Call me as soon as you get this."

But I didn't want to call Greg back.

I had something more important on my mind right now.

Passwords.

Alex was right when she said Munroe might have given me some sort of a hint when I talked with him in prison.

But what did he say to me that day which could help me figure out the password?

I tried to remember it all from our conversation. Basically, he claimed he didn't kill my sister. And he said that he was there for the abduction and the murder—but someone else did it. Also, that my sister had been "targeted" as a victim—and it didn't matter whether I had left her alone that day at the carnival or not. She would still be dead, he said.

And then—when I tried to press him for more details—he said one other thing that was stranger than anything else.

He made that bizarre reference to my father that I didn't understand.

About how my father had known a lot of the answers.

My father.

That's when it hit me.

One password I hadn't tried.

I took out my laptop and turned it on again.

I logged on to the TOR browser.

Then I typed in Luke Cassidy.

And, just like that, the entire Nowhere Men website suddenly opened up for me.

FORTY

I wasn't sure exactly where I was at first. I mean I realized it was some kind of a room on the screen. A waiting room, I supposed. At least that's what it looked like to me. There was no one else in there that I could see except me.

Only I wasn't really me.

I was someone else.

Actually, an avatar.

David Munroe's avatar, since I had logged in as Munroe.

The Munroe avatar sure didn't look like David Munroe though. Munroe was a balding, average-looking middle-aged man. This David Munroe on the screen was handsome and big and had long flowing blonde hair, looking like some sort of fantasy Adonis instead of a real man.

Nope, not the real David Munroe. But David Munroe the way he imagined himself to be. In a fantasy world like I realized I was in. There was even a different name on the avatar. It was identified on the screen as Captain Courageous.

Second Life, I thought to myself.

I had a friend who was big on the whole Second Life thing when it was popular online a few years ago. You did it like that.

You created an avatar of yourself, generally more flattering than you were in real life. And you created a whole new identity for yourself. You could be an athlete, a movie star, a rock musician —whatever you wanted to be in the virtual world of Second Life.

I never really got into it that much.

But I knew people who had been obsessed with being in this fantasy world, sometimes preferring it to the real world they lived in, and spent many hours immersed as their avatar in this virtual universe.

Well, this seemed to be that kind of place.

But while Second Life had been mostly harmless fun, I knew that Nowhere Men was something more dark and sinister and evil than that.

It took me a while to figure out how to handle the avatar. It was a first person view I had of my surroundings, and I eventually learned—albeit a bit clumsily—how to move around and maneuver my avatar to a different spot in the room. I was able to sit down in a chair, move around the area and finally walk over to a door.

I stood, or my avatar stood, at that door for several seconds.

Once I opened that door, there was no going back for me.

I pushed my avatar to the door; it opened and went into a much larger area.

There were other people there. Or avatars. Milling around with no particular purpose, it seemed. I wasn't sure what to do so I stood still at first, then started milling around the group the same as the rest of them. But then one of the avatars—a long-haired young guy in a T-shirt and jeans who looked sort of like a surfer—approached me.

"Hey, haven't seen you around here in a while. What are you up to today, Captain Courageous, my friend?"

Why was he calling me Captain Courageous?

Then I remembered that was the name on my avatar.

The name David Munroe had given himself.

I'd been hoping I could continue to remain anonymous and just observe. But it clearly didn't work that way. Now I wasn't sure what to do. This guy might not have been a surfer in real life, but he was a man. You could tell that from his voice. If I answered him, I assumed it would come out in my voice.

A woman's voice.

Not David Munroe.

I wondered if there might be some way to communicate by typing or texting something into the system, and to just not speak at all. But I wasn't sure how to do that or even if it was possible on this site. And I had no idea how to even check for this information anywhere on the site.

I finally saw a graphic that might help. Some dots in a box that looked like the kind of thing you might see on a normal website. I clicked on that box and got a list of options. A lot of them didn't mean very much to me, but one was the kind of thing I could understand. It simply said:

DO YOU WANT TO RESUME YOUR SESSION AT THE SAME SPOT YOU WERE AT LAST TIME?

Okay, that made sense. I would go to whatever location and do whatever David Munroe was doing the last time he was here. But would that get me in some kind of trouble? I was just winging it here and wondered if I should take the chance to follow Munroe's footsteps that closely.

I read the option one more time.

DO YOU WANT TO RESUME YOUR SESSION AT THE SAME SPOT YOU WERE LAST TIME?

I took a deep breath, then clicked "yes."

The scene in front of me—and all of the other avatars—

disappeared. I was afraid at first I might have knocked myself off the site, but I hadn't. It was simply taking me to a different place. The last place David Munroe had visited when he was here. Before he died. I was about to get a first-person view of what Munroe saw that time on the site.

The screen came alive again and I was definitely in a different place.

Outside now.

In a wooded area.

There was someone else there. A different figure. This one was female. And she looked like a young girl. She was running through the woods. Some other avatars were chasing her. She ran as hard as she could, it looked like to me, but the others were too fast for her. They grabbed her and pushed her to the ground, then picked her up and pushed her against a tree.

I moved closer.

But they didn't see me, or they didn't care.

I was just steps away now from the girl being held captive against the tree.

And that's when the true horror of this place really hit me.

I knew who the girl was.

I recognized her right away now.

It was Caitlin.

I mean it couldn't really be Caitlin, I knew that. But it sure looked like her. The way she looked that last day when she was only twelve years old. She was even wearing the exact same clothes she was wearing that day when she went to the carnival. Tan slacks, a brown-and-white striped top and a Cincinnati Reds baseball cap.

How?

How could this be happening?

Then she began screaming, which was even crazier. Because it was Caitlin's voice that was screaming. Her voice just the way I remembered it. One of the avatars took out a gun now, pointed it at her and her screaming became even louder. Oh my God, I thought to myself, they're going to shoot her! They're about to shoot Caitlin! And I'm watching the whole thing right in front of me.

I didn't understand any of this, but I couldn't let it happen.

Even if it wasn't real.

I let out a scream myself, in my own voice, yelling: "Don't hurt her!"

I didn't know what else to do.

My voice—the voice coming from a character who was supposed to be David Munroe, not a woman, took everyone's attention away from Caitlin at that moment.

The avatars—there were three of them I could see now—began moving toward me.

"Who are you?" one of them said.

"What are you doing here?" said another.

"You have to leave!" the third one shouted.

Suddenly the screen went dark. I wasn't in the woods anymore. I was sitting in front of my computer, the images I'd just seen of my sister about to be murdered in those woods running through my mind.

My sister looked and sounded exactly like she did fifteen years ago.

But I just saw her again.

Right before they were going to kill her.

And it all looked so damn real to me!

FORTY-ONE

"Are you sure it was Caitlin?" Alex asked me.

"Couldn't it have been some image of a young girl your sister's age that made you think of her?" Girard said.

The three of us were back in the station house. We were on the phone to Washington, with Ray Terlop the computer expert I'd been talking to about the Nowhere Men site earlier.

I'd just finished telling them all about my trip into the site via the dark web.

"It certainly makes more sense that you could have simply jumped to that conclusion that it was your sister when you saw that she was the same age," Terlop agreed now. "I mean you were in a highly upset, highly emotional state when you saw the girl. You easily could have imagined the resemblance."

"I wasn't that emotional."

"Well, you said you suddenly started screaming at what you thought was Caitlin and at the avatars you saw on the screen, which alerted everyone there to your presence. So I assumed—"

"That was after everything else happened. After I saw the girl who looked like Caitlin for the first time. After I saw her running through the woods. After the other figures caught up with her. And after they pushed her up against a tree and pulled out a gun and seemed just about to shoot. That's when I started screaming, not when I first saw the Caitlin figure. I'm telling you it was Caitlin on that screen that I was seeing. I recognized my own sister. I recognized her voice. I knew it was her. Even in that crazy website world."

I went through it all again. Including the fact that she was wearing the exact same clothes in the Nowhere Men world that she'd been wearing on that last day I saw her at the carnival.

The tan pants.

The brown-and-white striped T-shirt.

And the Cincinnati Reds baseball cap she loved so much.

That image of the way she looked that day at the carnival before she disappeared forever is burned into my memory, and it had been for the past fifteen years. There was no mistake about it. And now I had just seen her again on this website, and she looked—she even sounded—just like I remembered my sister.

"There's something else," I said. "That whole scene at the end. Her running away from the others, them chasing her, finally catching up with her—and then that moment where they were about to shoot her. It all seemed real. Not like something someone had just faked with Photoshop or some other technical tricks for an on-screen showing. It was like I was actually watching Caitlin being murdered right in front of me. Everything seemed totally accurate. Like the real thing. Of course, that's impossible, but..."

"Maybe not," Ray Terlop said now.

"What are you saying?" Girard asked him. "Nikki's sister has been dead for fifteen years. So this has to be a trick, an illusion. It couldn't be real."

"Except all the details were totally accurate, as Nikki pointed out," Terlop said.

"So someone did a lot of research into the details, or already knew them—to somehow re-create her murder."

"That's a possibility."

"What else is there that could be possible?" I asked.

Terlop hesitated before answering. I think he was trying to decide whether or not to say what he was about to suggest. He was an FBI guy, and FBI guys customarily deal in hard facts. Not theories or conjecture or speculative scenarios. But Terlop went ahead and ran his theory past the rest of us anyway.

"This whole situation reminds me in some ways of a case I remember from the FBI files," he said. "It involved a cult. A group of scary cult members. They were a sick group of people who abducted—and then killed—girls for the thrill of it. No other reason, just thrill kills. Doesn't that sound like the same kind of people who could have been behind those avatars Nikki saw? There was something else from that case that sticks in my mind, too. They didn't just kill the girls. Many of the times they filmed the murders. That was part of the thrill of it for them. They set it up all in advance and captured all of the gruesome details on camera while it happened. And then it was there for them to watch on the video whenever they wanted."

"Jesus!" I blurted out.

"Like a snuff film," Alex said. "A real-life video of someone being murdered."

"Exactly," Terlop said. "So what if someone did that with your sister, Nikki? I know it's a horrific thing to imagine, but I think we have to consider the possibility. Based on what you've told me, and the details being so spot-on accurate about everything involving your sister, including her clothes, it makes sense that the people behind this took a video of her during those final moments."

"And they're playing it over and over as some sort of sick theater on this site," I said.

It was such a terrible thought.

My sister's death being exploited like that.

Caitlin had not only been murdered, but now someone was replaying that murder for their own fantasy out there on the dark web with this Nowhere Men website.

We talked about what to do next. I had been knocked off the site when they realized I wasn't who I was supposed to be, and the David Munroe login and password didn't work when I tried them again.

Obviously, the people on the site had figured out I was an intruder.

"Did you get a good look at the other avatars you saw?" Terlop asked me.

"Not really."

"Not sure it would have helped much anyway," Terlop said. "You told us the David Munroe avatar didn't look anything like Munroe. That it was handsome, probably the way Munroe fantasized himself instead of the way he actually looked. Everyone else on the site probably created their avatars the same way too. Only your sister was identifiable. And it had to be for the re-creation of the murder to work for them in this virtual world."

I told them I'd tried a number of other names and password combinations after I got shut out of the site, but with no success.

"At least we found out from that that the site has some flaws in its security options. It doesn't shut you out after just a single or a few incorrect entries. We may be able to run some more sophisticated efforts to get on the site with our computer analytics here. At least we can give it a try."

There was something else bothering me.

Yes, I had used David Munroe for my username.

That made sense.

But the password didn't. The password that got me entry into the Nowhere Men world was another name. My father's name. Why?

"Maybe Munroe just picked the name of the police officer who arrested him," Girard said.

"Maybe."

But then why not use Rudy Delgado's name? He was the Huntsdale police officer who actually arrested him?

Why did Munroe tell me too that my father knew more about Caitlin's murder than he had revealed before he died?

Why was there a wreath of roses on my father's grave?

So many questions about my father and this case now.

Was he hiding secrets about his own daughter's murder at the time of his death?

I didn't know the answer to that.

I did know someone who might.

But I sure as hell didn't want to have to question my own mother again.

FORTY-TWO

I had a new problem to deal with.

Phil Girard.

"I want out of this assignment," Girard announced to me at the station the next morning. "I almost got killed out there on the highway. I'm too old for this kind of crap anymore. I've only got a few months left until my retirement. Then I can go to my home in Florida and my boat and all the books I want to read and puzzles to solve all day."

I wasn't sure what to say. Despite my original misgivings to Polk about Girard being assigned here with Alex and me, he had been surprisingly helpful on several occasions. But now he wanted to back out on us.

"It's part of the job, Phil—" I started to say.

"Don't tell me what the job is all about! For God sakes, I've been doing this job since before you were born. Either of you," he said, looking over at Alex, who was watching this all unfold without saying anything.

Girard shook his head disgustedly. "You two think it's all fun and games, like you're a modern Cagney and Lacey running around catching bad guys and throwing them in jail. Except it's not like TV. This is real life. And I almost died out there in that car. All of us could have died."

He looked over at Alex now.

"What about you?" Girard asked. "You've got a family. A husband, a kid. Are you going to keep putting that all out there on the line—taking chances that you might not come home to them someday, all for some misguided devotion to duty with the FBI. Is the FBI more important than your family? What the hell are you looking to find out there every day carrying that badge? What are either of you looking for?"

"We're looking for a missing girl," I told him. "Natalie Jarvis. We still hope to get her back safely, Phil. That's our biggest priority right now. It should be your priority too."

"This isn't just about Natalie Jarvis for you," Girard said. "It's about your sister. You're looking for some kind of closure about your sister. Well, your sister died and she's not coming back. Nothing about the Natalie Jarvis case, even if you find her or confirm some sort of connection with your sister's abduction and death, is going to change that. You're chasing after ghosts. And that's getting damn dangerous. Whatever you're dealing with about your sister and the past is not about me. That's why I want out."

"Look, Phil," I said, trying my best to keep my emotions and anger too under control. "I know you're a short timer in the bureau now with retirement right around the corner. And I know that this assignment is turning out to be more than any of us expected. But I still want to do the job we came here to do."

"Fine but do it without me. I'm calling Polk and asking him to bring me back to Washington."

"Okay, that's your right. But have you ever quit on an assignment before, Phil? I don't think so. How is this going to look on your FBI record now?"

"In a few months, I won't care what my FBI record looks like. I'll be on my boat fishing in Florida."

"Just give it a little more time. The worst is over now after we survived that car crash unhurt."

"Is it over?"

"What do you mean?"

"If you're right—and I think you are—about that dead guy being a hired killer out to get you, whoever hired him is going to hire someone else to finish the job. I'm sure you must have thought about that. Both of you."

I looked over at Alex.

"How about you?" I asked her. "What do you think?"

"Like you said, Nikki, it's part of the job. My husband, my family, they knew what I signed up for with the bureau. So let's get back to work. We've got to find that missing girl."

My conversation with Greg about it all hadn't gone well either. He was as angry as I'd ever heard him when I called him back and told him the details.

"I warned you that this could happen," he yelled at me. "Now, you've got to get out of there. I don't want to take any chances leaving you up there even a second longer than I have to with some crazy killer after you."

I just let him go on ranting and raving like that for a while until he finally calmed down a bit. There was nothing I could say. We'd had this conversation before. No matter what I said, it wasn't going to change his mind about my job with the FBI. Especially after what had just happened.

Even Chief Earnshaw brought up the same concern that Girard had when I went to his office to talk to him about the latest developments. The threat of a new attack against me. Or any of us, I suppose. But, since my picture had been found in the dead man's motel room, it seemed that I was the most likely target for another attempt by a hired hit man.

Earnshaw offered to provide me with extra protection as best he could. I don't think he was enthusiastic about the idea of doing that, but he knew it was his responsibility as police chief to offer. I said thanks, but no thanks. I told him I couldn't do my job if I was constantly under police protection. Besides, I pointed out, I had Billy Weller from his force with me a lot of the time.

Later, when I went back into the war room, Girard and Alex were both gone. I wasn't sure where. Maybe they had gone outside to talk over the situation some more. Maybe Alex could convince Girard to stay. Or maybe Girard would convince Alex to get out of this, too. Either way, I knew what my job was. I was going to stay here until this all was finished.

Maybe Girard was right.

Maybe I was chasing ghosts.

I looked up at the picture of Natalie Jarvis on the wall in front of me.

Natalie was thirteen years old.

A pretty girl, with her entire life in front of her.

And then in an instant she was gone.

Where in the hell are you, Natalie?

FORTY-THREE

Greg called me every night at nine p.m. while I was in Huntsdale. Not at nine thirty or eight thirty. The call always came right on the dot at nine. He did this when I was out of town on the Julie Mattheu case too and when I was away on an FBI assignment of any kind. Most women would be happy to have that kind of devotion from a man. It's just that sometimes it became sort of overwhelming for me. And made me feel a bit trapped and a bit claustrophobic.

That was even more true now that Greg had become so obsessed about convincing me to leave Huntsdale. Especially after the scary attempt to kill me and the others on the highway. Most of our phone conversations were about that these days. And this ongoing back-and-forth with Greg every night over the issue of me still being here was really stressing me out, at the same time as I was stressed out over the cases of my sister and the other girls.

"Was that your boyfriend?" Billy Weller asked me after I hung up with Greg now.

I nodded.

"Problem?"

"You heard?"

"Well, you did sound kind of upset on the phone."

"Greg's just very concerned about my safety here."

"That's understandable."

"I guess."

We were sitting at a big table in the war room I'd set up in the Huntsdale station, munching on cheeseburgers, French fries and onion rings from the Burger King I'd gone to around the corner.

"When you asked me if I wanted to have dinner with you, I was thinking about going to a restaurant," Billy said. "Or even a diner. Not a takeout from Burger King."

"This is dinner. And, by the way, the onion rings are really good. I remember loving the onion rings when I was a kid growing up here. They still taste as good as ever."

"You realize, of course, Burger King is a chain with franchises all over the country. Even back in Washington where you live, there must be tons of them."

"Sometimes food just tastes better in a certain place. For me, well, the memory of eating onion rings at this same Burger King here in Huntsdale as a kid makes them taste even better."

"I thought your memories of Huntsdale from back then were bad ones, Nikki."

"Not all of them," I said.

Billy picked up one of the onion rings now and nibbled on it as he talked.

"So when are you and Greg getting married?'

"We don't have a specific date yet."

I bit into one of the cheeseburgers. I'd put a lot of ketchup and mayonnaise and relish on it, and some of the catsup squirted onto my face. Not a good look for me. But I grabbed a wad of napkins and managed to clean up most of the mess. Messy is usually good when it comes to hamburgers.

"How about you?" I asked.

"What about me?"

"Isn't there some woman for you out there in Huntsdale waiting for you to come home after work?"

"Not at the moment."

"But you used to be married?"

"Yeah, right."

"What was her name?"

"Who?"

"Your ex-wife."

"Why?"

"I'm curious."

"Karin. Karin Grieco. That's who I was married to."

"What happened?"

"Oh, I don't want to talk about my marriage. It's not very interesting."

"No, I'm interested in hearing more about you. Tell me about your marriage. What happened?"

He didn't answer right away. Instead, he grabbed another onion ring. I guess he liked them too.

"A lot of things didn't work for us. Mostly, she had very expensive tastes, and she pushed me into doing a lot of things with my life I didn't want to do—and wasn't very good at—so she had something to impress her friends with. I tried law school, learning to trade, real estate—you name it. By the time I discovered what I really wanted to do with my life, she was gone."

"Gone where?"

"She moved away from here. To a different city. Meanwhile, I'm still here working with Chief Frank Earnshaw and the Huntsdale Police Department. But, like I told you before, I've been going to night school. At Ohio State. Night-school classes. I'm studying for a Bachelor of Criminal Science degree."

"That sounds interesting."

"Yes. I figure I can leave Huntsdale then and get a real job in law enforcement. Like you have with the FBI."

"Sure, let me know if you want to find out more about how to apply," I said. "Maybe I can help."

"That would be great."

We ate in silence for a few minutes, finishing off the last of our meal.

"Back in high school, you know, I wanted to ask you to the senior prom," Billy Weller suddenly blurted out.

I wasn't quite sure how to respond.

"Why didn't you ask me?" I finally said.

"I never got the courage to do it."

"Why not?"

"C'mon, someone like you was never going to go to the prom with a guy like me."

I had a few guys who asked me, I was pretty popular that year—the last year before everything went wrong for me in Huntsdale. The guy I finally went with had been an All-State wrestler for Huntsdale High, and I wound up wrestling with him in the back seat of a car when I resisted his drunken advances. Finally, I managed to break away, get out of the car and race home. It was a moment that was not a highlight of my dating life.

"Who knows?" I laughed to Billy Weller now. "You should have tried. What if I had said yes? You and me might have wound up together."

I laughed then.

And he grinned and laughed back.

Still, it was an awkward moment.

There was a part of me that wondered even while I laughed with him at the idea: What if I had gone to the prom that senior year with Billy Weller? Would my life be different? Would other circumstances have changed? Would I have maybe been with him that summer a few weeks later instead of taking Caitlin along with me to the carnival with my girlfriends?

Billy was still grinning at me.

That damn infectious grin that made him so likable.

"That was a long time ago," he said.

"Yes, a long time ago." I pushed my food away and stood up from the table where we were sitting. "Okay, time to get back to work, Billy."

FORTY-FOUR

"You're absolutely convinced at this point that all three cases in Huntsdale are somehow connected?" Les Polk asked us.

"I am," I said.

"Probably," Alex said.

"Possibly," Girard told him. He was still with us. I wasn't sure what that meant, or if he had talked to Polk about returning to Washington yet.

We were on a Zoom session with Polk, updating him on Natalie Jarvis, Erica Kent and, of course, my strange experience involving my sister Caitlin on the Nowhere Men website. Behind us on his screen in Washington, Polk could see all of our wall in the Huntsdale police station filled with pictures, notes, evidence and pretty much everything else we'd been able to accumulate and find out about the three girls.

"Let's go through it from the start," Polk said. "What we *do* know. What are the most important reasons to indicate that all of these cases are connected?"

That was easy.

"The date," I said. "They all happened on the same date. July nineteenth. That's when my sister disappeared. And Erica

Kent and Natalie Jarvis after that. That's a pretty compelling fact. Not likely all occurred on the same date by coincidence. That date means something to someone. It's always been an anniversary for me. But it has to be some kind of an important anniversary for someone else too."

Polk nodded.

"What else?"

"All the girls have been approximately the same age," Alex said. "Nikki's sister was twelve, Erica Kent twelve and the Jarvis girl thirteen."

"And they all disappeared suddenly, the same way," I added.

"But not at the same kind of places," Girard jumped in to say. "One was at a carnival, another at a movie theater and the third from a bus."

"But they were all public locations," Alex said. "Okay, the circumstances of the three disappearances weren't exactly the same, but they are similar."

I got up and poured myself some coffee. There was an idea forming in my head, but I wasn't quite sure about it yet. Or when to bring it up with Polk. Maybe the caffeine could help clear my thoughts a bit more.

"There is one thing that's different," Polk said, and I could see him staring up at the pictures on the wall behind us from the Zoom screen. "The three girls don't look alike. Same general age, yes, but no real similarity in appearance beyond that."

He was right. I'd noticed it too. Caitlin was tall for her age and had long blonde hair; Natalie Jarvis was average size and had shorter dark hair; Erica Kent didn't look at all like either of them. We all knew that killers or kidnappers tended to target females with a special look that appealed to them. But that hadn't happened here. The ages of the victims were close, but not their looks.

"Anything else that might be a link between all three cases?" Polk asked.

'Yes," I said. "The roses."

I talked about the roses that had been found with my sister's body. And also about how someone had sent Natalie Jarvis a single rose before she disappeared, according to one of her friends. I also said to them that I had found roses placed on both my father's and Caitlin's grave recently.

Polk and Girard both looked at me with surprise when I said that last thing about the roses on the graves. I'd told Alex in one of our first telephone conversations, but I hadn't told them about it. Because I wasn't sure what it meant.

"Why would someone leave roses on their graves now?" Polk asked. "And why your father as well as your sister?"

"I don't know."

"How about the roses with the victims? Any theory on the significance of that?"

"No clue about that either."

Polk sighed.

"What else?"

"My sister was murdered days after she was abducted. We can't be sure about the Kent girl, but the ME and crime people estimate she could have been kept alive for a similar period of time before her death. So we have to assume that a similar pattern could be happening with the Jarvis girl right now. That means we still may have a window of opportunity to get to her while she's still alive. But that window is closing for Natalie Jarvis."

There was silence in the room for several seconds.

Everyone knew what I was saying.

And they knew I was right.

"So where do we go from here?" Polk asked.

I took a big gulp of the coffee and stood up. I walked over to the board on the wall and pointed to the pictures of the three girls—Caitlin, Erica Kent and Natalie Jarvis.

"Everyone disappeared on the same date of July nineteenth, right?"

"Yes, we know that," Girard said.

"So what's your idea?" Polk asked.

"What if there were more?"

"More victims?"

"Sure. I mean we know about these three. But young girls go missing all the time. Sometimes they turn up dead. What if there are more girls out there like this?"

It was the same question Billy Weller had asked.

But then it was just a possibility.

Now, after everything we'd found, it seemed much more likely.

"Damn, that does make sense," Alex said.

I turned back to Polk on the screen.

"How about this? We do a massive search with our FBI computer facilities of any teenage girl who's gone missing or died mysteriously in recent years. Not just here in Huntsdale, we'd know about that. But search databases for the rest of Ohio, and surrounding states, like Kentucky, where Erica Kent was from. If we do find more cases, then we will know we're dealing with a—"

"Yes, we will know," Polk said.

Neither of us said the words out loud.

We didn't have to.

We all knew what those words were.

Serial killer.

FORTY-FIVE

There were a number of cases we turned up that seemed to fit the general criteria. Not always exactly fit in terms of age, or date of disappearance and certainly not location. But we had no way of knowing for certain that every young victim—assuming there were other young girls who were victims—were specifically twelve or thirteen years old or had been abducted exactly on July 19th. That seemed a bit hard to believe.

So we expanded the search guidelines a bit.

Our targets were any young girl disappearances—or bodies found murdered—where the victims were between eleven and fifteen years old. I set the timing of the date for the entire month of July. I did ask the search team back in Washington to look for a mention—in any age or time period—of a rose or collection of roses. But I figured that would be a real long shot.

Phil Girard wanted to add one other element to our search.

"Natalie Jarvis and Erica Kent are both only children. Let's look for missing girls who share that characteristic—no brothers or sisters—as well."

"But my sister wasn't an only child," I said. "She had me."

"That was the first one. Or least that we know about. But

the two after that are both only children. That could mean something."

I was glad Phil Girard was still with us. He hadn't said anything more after his quitting rant. I wasn't sure if he had changed his mind or what, but right now he remained part of our team.

"It's only two cases of only children," Alex pointed out. "I'm not sure how significant that is."

"Do you know the percentage of families in this country that have only one child?" Girard said. "It's really low, like maybe one out of five. Here you have two more cases, both of them with only children. That doesn't line up with what the odds of that should be. So maybe that could play into the reason why someone is doing this. Focusing on families with only children after the first murder of your sister, Nikki."

"Okay," I said, "let's add only child to the list of things we're looking for in these cases."

We wound up pinpointing a number of similar cases of missing young girls. Including one case that was remarkably similar to what we were looking for.

On July 19th, 2013, a twelve-year-old girl named Kimberly Howell vanished from a shopping mall in Bedford, Ohio, about two hundred miles north of Huntsdale. She was with a group of other young girls when they realized she was gone. "It was like Kimberly just disappeared in an instant," one of the girls told police later.

The same as Natalie Jarvis. Erica Kent. And Caitlin. One minute they were there, then suddenly they were gone.

There was one more similarity too with the Kimberly Howell case. A rose. One of Kimberly's friends said someone had sent her a rose just before this happened. Her friends had joked with her that day about having a secret admirer. Kimberly said she didn't know who sent the rose, but she was very flattered. This sounded exactly the same as Natalie Jarvis.

"How come no one ever saw this rose connection before?" Alex asked. "Your sister, Natalie Jarvis, and now this girl."

"My sister's case involved a wreath of roses left with her body, completely different from Natalie or this girl. It would be easy for it to slip through the cracks, especially given the large amount of time between the cases. No reason to think about something like that unless you are specifically looking for the angle of roses, like we are."

Kimberly Howell's body had never been found, but law enforcement authorities in Cleveland assumed she was dead, according to the records.

And yes, she was an only child.

Another case that had some similarities, although not as many as Kimberly Howell, involved an eleven-year-old girl named Jessica Marrone. She went missing in the Oakmont suburb of Pittsburgh on July 15th, 2016, while selling Girl Scout cookies door to door. Her bag filled with boxes of cookies —along with some cash and checks she'd collected from her sales—was found in a field nearby. But the girl was nowhere around. According to records from Pittsburgh authorities, the disappearance of Jessica Marrone was still an open cold case.

And then there was the case of Nancy Barstow. She fit in as a possible related case too. She was twelve years old and she went missing on July 18th, 2017 just a day before the July 19th date we were looking for. She had disappeared after going out on a bike ride. The problem with this one though was the location. It happened in Palo Alto, California, across the country from Huntsdale. But that didn't mean someone couldn't have jumped on a plane to Palo Alto to abduct her. Or been in Palo Alto for some other reason—business or vacation or something else—and seen the opportunity to grab the Barstow girl.

There were a number of other cases too that might fit the pattern we were looking for to tie them to Caitlin, Natalie and Erica.

I posted all the new cases, along with pictures of the girls, on the bulletin board.

"Thoughts?" I asked Alex, Girard and Billy, who was there too. He wasn't officially working with us, but he hung around a lot so I included him. Maybe he really was interested in learning more about how the FBI worked, like he said. Or maybe he was interested in me. Either way, I was still glad to have him around.

"There were no bodies ever found with any of these cases," Alex said. "They disappeared but were never found dead or alive. Nikki's sister Caitlin was buried here, and Erica Kent too—even if she was most likely killed somewhere else. So why are there no bodies on these other cases, if they are connected?"

"Maybe the bodies are in Grant Woods where the other two remains were discovered," I said.

"All of them?" Girard asked.

"Why not? There could be more bodies out there. A lot more."

"Are you saying that place could be a graveyard of murder victims?" Billy asked. "Is that really possible?"

"We won't know unless we do a complete search of the entire Grant Woods area."

"There's miles and miles of woods there," Billy said. "Covered with trees and bushes and plants that would have to be dug up."

"Sounds like a perfect place to bury bodies."

"Damn, if this is true, someone is really playing a very sick game here, people," Alex said.

"What about digging it all up and searching the area?" I asked Billy now. "Is that possible? What kind of resources would the city of Huntsdale have to do that?"

"I'd have to ask Chief Earnshaw."

"That should be an interesting conversation." Girard

laughed. "You know that crazy FBI lady? She wants to dig up the whole damn town now."

Billy shrugged. "Like I said, that's a lot of area out there. It would be a huge undertaking."

"Hey, look at this!" Alex suddenly yelled as another case popped up on her computer screen that had been sent by the people searching through crimes files for us in Washington. "This one is different."

"The girl's name is Susan Cabot. Thirteen years old. From Troy, Ohio—a small town near Dayton, about a hundred miles west of us here in Huntsdale. She didn't show up for school on the date of July nineteenth, 2015. She seems like a perfect young missing girl case for us—like we were looking for—almost as good as Kimberly Howell."

"Okay, so what's different about this young missing girl?"

"She's not missing anymore," Alex said.

"What?"

"Susan Cabot was discovered at a truck stop on the Ohio Turnpike, just outside of Columbus, about ten days after she disappeared. Police said Susan Cabot had been a troubled kid with a history of run-ins with the law and school officials for drinking, taking drugs and several incidents of petty theft. They concluded that she had simply run away on her own. And then, when she was identified at the truck stop and brought back to Troy, she made up an unbelievable story about what happened to her. So unbelievable that everyone just assumed she was lying so she wouldn't get in trouble for running off like that."

"What was the story?" I asked.

"She claimed someone had tried to kill her and film it for some kind of a snuff film."

FORTY-SIX

We managed to track Susan Cabot down.

She was still living in the Dayton area. I drove there the next morning. I left Alex and Girard behind to keep working on Natalie Jarvis and the other angles of the case in Huntsdale. Alex wanted to come with me, but I think Girard was just as happy to stay there. I knew he was still jittery after that last trip in the car with me. I'd been able to talk him into staying on in the end. But I didn't want to do anything that might change his mind again.

And he was right about one thing. I was a potential target. No reason to put him or Alex or Billy or anyone else in danger again by riding in the same car with me, just in case someone else tried to run me off the road.

But nothing happened.

I made it to Dayton without incident.

And I was soon talking with Susan Cabot.

She had been a runaway and in constant trouble with the law and other authorities at the age of twelve back in 2015 when the incident we'd found in the nationwide crime files had occurred. That was eight years ago. I wasn't even sure she'd be alive now when we started looking for her. I mean she seemed like a girl on her way to tragedy, one way or another.

But it turned out she was very much alive.

And not what I expected at all.

She was a student these days at the University of Dayton.

Studying in the education department and working to get a teacher's degree.

I thought at first that maybe I'd found the wrong Susan Cabot. But it was her. The same girl who'd disappeared back in 2015 and turned up days later at a truck stop near the Ohio Turnpike with a hard-to-believe story about where she'd been and what happened to her during that missing time.

She met with me in the student union of the University of Dayton campus. She was a pretty young woman, with glistening blonde air and dressed immaculately in a fashionable skirt, blouse and shoes. I remembered the picture of her I'd see in the old files we'd read. Gaunt, stringy hair, a crazy look on her face. Yes, this was the same Susan Cabot—but she seemed to be completely different now as a young woman.

She talked about the changes that had taken place in her life with me as we drank coffee together.

"My mother died when I was six. Leukemia. She was barely thirty. My father... well, he started drinking a lot after that and he pretty much stopped acting like a father. He didn't want me around anymore, I was only a reminder for him of the wife he'd lost. He wasn't actually abusive to me or anything, he just ignored me. And so I had to grow up on my own. Lots of it took place on the street. And, as you probably saw from reading about me before you came here, I got myself into plenty of trouble.

"Then, after the police picked me up and didn't believe my story about what happened to me when I went missing, my father gave up on me, too. He said I was too much trouble for him to deal with anymore. I wound up going to child services, and eventually got placed with a foster family.

"I wasn't happy about that at the time, but the family I went to turned out to be wonderful. They gave me love and affection and guidance that I'd never gotten from my father after my mother was gone. They changed my life. I started to get good grades in school, I stopped getting in trouble, and here I am now. I'm in college.

"I made the dean's list last semester, and I hope to be teaching in another year or so. My major is in English. I'd like to be an English teacher and teach young people all about great books to read. I want the students I work with to have a better life than I had when I was growing up. Being a teacher is a way for me to accomplish that."

It was a nice story.

An uplifting one.

A woman who didn't let a tragic incident defeat her, but used it to build a better life for herself.

But that wasn't what I came all this way to talk to her about.

"Tell me everything you can about what happened back in 2015 when you disappeared," I said to her.

"Sure. But why is the FBI interested now?"

I told her there were several other possibly related cases that had emerged recently and we were investigating.

"I heard about that. In Huntsdale, Ohio. I wondered... I wondered if there could be some sort of connection."

"Talk to me about your case, Susan."

"I don't remember a lot about it. I was drinking a lot and smoking pot and I guess I was pretty wasted. That's why the police found it so easy to not believe me when I told them my story.

"Anyway, I was looking for some cigarettes, a bottle of vodka and maybe some pot too. I was only twelve years old, but I'd figured out how to score that stuff. What I would do is stand outside some liquor store or convenience place and try to convince a guy to buy all that for me. Sometimes I would have to have sex with them as payment, but that didn't really bother me. I just wanted to smoke and drink and get high.

"This time the man who offered to buy me stuff was older than usual. At least I thought he was at the time. Probably in his forties, I guess, but he seemed old to me as a twelve-year-old girl. Still, he was going to help me score what I needed, so I let him do it.

"Afterward, he wanted me to share a drink with him in his car. I figured he might try to hit on me, but I was okay with that. I knew how to get out of trouble with a horny guy. I'd done it before. I'd drink with him, smoke a bit and then get the hell out of there. Except it didn't work out that way."

"Why not?"

"I was never sure. All I knew is that I lost consciousness for a while. And, when I woke up, I was somewhere else. Somewhere in a bunch of woods. I guess the guy must have put something in my drink, a knockout drug to make sure I didn't leave while he brought me to this place.

"I was still dressed and there was no sign I'd been sexually attacked yet. I thought I was okay. But then I saw the man—the one from the store—again. He had a gun in his hand now. He was pointing it at me. And he had other men with him. There were three more men. They were younger, but still scary looking even before they began to talk. And then it really got bad. Really weird. He told me I should call him The Black Knight."

"The Black Knight?"

"That's what he said."

She stared down at the coffee in front of her. Still in a state of shock after all this time talking about it. I felt a bit badly about making her relive all this over again. But I also knew that I needed to do it to make sure we caught whoever might have done this, and prevent any more young girls from enduring this kind of a nightmare.

"He said they were going to kill me. They all laughed when he said it. Him and the others there. But first he said they would play a game with me. One of them had a camera, and he started filming me. I said I was terrified and pleaded with them to let me go, but they kept laughing. One of them said it would be better for the film the more I pleaded for my life like that.

"They said they were making a snuff film. The older man told me: 'That's a film of someone being killed. You're going to be the victim. But first let's make it more interesting. Keep pleading. Keep crying. Try to get away if you want. We'll chase you down and drag you back for the grand finale. We want to make this as dramatic as we can.'

"They all started to laugh even more. They were laughing so hard they weren't looking directly at me.

"I figured this was my only chance. I couldn't just run, they would catch me. Or shoot me down as I ran. I had to do something else. I saw a tree limb lying next to me. While they were all distracted laughing about what they were going to do to me, I picked it up and swung it at the man with the gun. I hit him flush in the head, and blood began spurting out. He dropped the gun.

"That's when I ran, as fast as I could.

"I'm not sure how far I ran. I thought some of the others would chase after and catch up with me. But no one ever did. I finally reached a highway and hitched a ride with a trucker. I told him everything that had happened. He pulled into that truck stop and called the police. That's how they found me there. I told them my story, but no one believed me. They thought I made it up. Or I was just high and hallucinating."

I wasn't sure what to say to Susan Cabot when she was finished.

It was a pretty unbelievable story.

So why did I believe it?

"What do you think after all this time?" I asked her. "Do you think you might have hallucinated it all?"

She shrugged.

"I suppose it's possible. Hell, I probably wouldn't believe my story if someone else told it to me. But it was—and still is—very real to me. If I simply imagined it all in some drug or alcohol haze, would the nightmare still seem so real and so terrifying to me after all these years?"

"Do you have any idea who this man who did this to you might have been? Or any of the other men you saw with him in those woods?"

"Nope. No idea at all."

I took out a picture of David Munroe and showed it to her, even though I knew he had been in prison for my sister's murder at the time.

"Could it possibly be this man?"

She looked at the picture of Munroe and shook her head no. Of course, that didn't surprise me. But I was simply trying to see if this might spark some kind of memory or lead from Susan Cabot.

"Do you think you would recognize the man if you saw him now?"

"Yes, I could."

"You're sure about that?"

"I could never forget him."

FORTY-SEVEN

"I just received a request from the Justice Department to consider pulling you out of there," Les Polk said to me on the phone when I got back to Huntsdale.

"What?"

"They want me to recall you back to Washington."

"Why would they do that?"

"They say you're a target of a killer there and we might be endangering your life irresponsibly by keeping you in Huntsdale."

"Can the Justice Department tell you to do that?"

"Oh, they can tell me to do it. But they can't make me do it. And I'm not going to do it. We make our own decisions here at the bureau, no matter how big someone is at Justice trying to pull our strings. I told them no. I want you to be careful up there. But you're still assigned to this case or these cases or whatever the hell is going on up there."

"Why would anyone that important at Justice even care so much about getting me to leave Huntsdale?"

"You might ask your boyfriend."

"Greg Ellroy?"

"Uh, huh. His law firm represents some pretty important cases involving the Justice Department. So when the law firm makes a request, the Justice Department listens. This is Washington, and everything is about connections and politics."

Greg.

He said he'd do anything to make sure I was safe.

I guess he really meant it.

"I just thought you should know," Polk said.

"I know you're angry," Greg said. "But I was so worried about you after what happened with your car and all the rest. So I asked the top people at my firm to reach out to the Justice Department about you. I'm afraid you're in real danger there. I had to do something to protect you. I just want to see you, I want to be with you here again, I want us to get married. Is that such a terrible thing?"

"Greg, I can't be the wife I think you want me to be. I can't fit into some cookie cutter image for you. This is me. Nikki Cassidy. This is what I do."

"You still want to marry me, don't you?" Greg asked.

"Of course."

"I love you, Nikki."

There were a lot of things I could have said to him at that moment. Various responses went through my mind. But I picked the simplest one.

'I love you too," I said.

The worst part of all this was it was taking time away from what I really wanted to be doing. Working on the damn case. Because I still didn't have any answers about all the girls we knew about now who had been victims of these mysterious people from the Nowhere Men site.

Whenever I'm stuck on a case, I try to go back to the beginning and start all over on it again.

The beginning of this case was my sister Caitlin's murder.

What was I still missing?

I went back and started reading through the police report again on my sister's disappearance and murder. The one put together fifteen years ago by my father. I was looking for anything that I might have missed when I first read it that could give me a lead on where to go next.

I mean my father had written the damn report a long time ago—maybe he left me some kind of clue in there that I'd missed.

When I was a little girl in Huntsdale, my father used to play a Who Done It? game with me. It was sort of like Clue, but he'd made it up himself. He'd create an imaginary case, imaginary suspects, imaginary evidence and clues, then ask me to solve it.

I'm not sure if he ever played the game with Caitlin. Or if it was just with me. Maybe Caitlin was too young. Or maybe he thought even then that I was somehow going to follow in his footsteps by pursuing a career in law enforcement.

But the game was one of the memories that always came rushing back to me whenever I thought about how much I missed him and how much I loved him.

Sometimes I would get the correct answer—the identity of the killer and the motive and all the rest—in the game. But other times I didn't. And, when that happened, I pleaded with my father to give me another clue. "Just one more clue, Dad" I would say. "If I had one more clue, I could figure out who the murderer was. I could solve the case."

Usually, he would give me the clue.

And then I'd figure out the case.

Or, if I was really stuck, my father would tell me how to find the answers that I was looking for.

I sure wished I could ask him to do that now.

"Dad, wherever you are, give me another clue," I mumbled as I paged through the police report he'd put together about my sister's murder case. "Just one more clue, and I can do it. I promise. But I need your help, Dad."

There was no answer, of course. All I had from him was this damn report. If there were any answers my father was going to give me about my sister's death, they were in this police report. I read through it all again. Skipping some of the routine stuff and focusing on whatever I thought might be important. It still all looked the same to me.

The initial report of my sister's disappearance—from me and my friends at the carnival; the arrival of Police Officer Gary Lawton at the scene; the search of the entire carnival area and surrounding streets; the desperate efforts over the next six days to try to find Caitlin; the discovery of the body in Grant Woods at the burial site with the roses; and, after that, the arrest by Officer Rudy Delgado of David Munroe at his house with the evidence from Caitlin's body inside.

It was all there in the police report.

But I was still missing something.

It took me a while, but I finally stumbled across something strange. I was reading one of the passages toward the end of the report, and I realized it kind of ended in mid-sentence at the end of a paragraph. And the sentence that began the following page didn't seem to be related to the previous sentence fragment.

I checked the report again. There was a total of 102 pages in it, according to the summary at the end. Or at least there were supposed to be 102 pages. But, when I went back and counted, I could only find 95 pages. I did it again. Still only 95 pages in the report. Even though there were supposed to be 102 pages here.

I didn't have to be a genius investigator to figure out what that meant.

Seven pages of this report were missing.

But what did these missing pages say and who removed them?

Chief Earnshaw wasn't of much help. "I have absolutely no idea," he said, when I asked him about the missing pages. "I didn't work here then when your father wrote that report. No one here was around back then."

Billy Weller told me pretty much the same thing.

"I imagine you're probably the first person to go back and read that report in years. No one else would have any reason to do it. So it's just been sitting there all this time. The case was closed once David Munroe was arrested and convicted and went to prison for the rest of his life."

"And there's nobody around still working here that I might be able to talk to about this, Billy?"

"Nope, no one I can think of on the Huntsdale force now."

No there wasn't, not on the force.

But there was someone in town who might know something.

Tommy Thompson, the D.A. who'd prosecuted David Munroe.

"I do think I know what's missing here," Thompson said to me when I showed him the report. "Your father always liked to put in a personal section to a police report like this. His own insight into the case, not simply the basic facts and evidence that had been uncovered. I don't see that anywhere in this report. So that's very likely what was on those missing pages."

"Do you have another copy anywhere in your files?"

"No. I mean we have our own files on the case. But this report was only for police use. That's why it was kept at the police station and not here with us."

"What about a digital version? Would it be online anywhere in town files?"

Thompson shook his head no.

"We didn't really convert our files in Huntsdale until a year or two later. I know that seems hard to believe in this day and age when everything is up there in the cloud or somewhere, but it cost a lot of money to automate the whole system. And Huntsdale is a small town, working on a small budget. We only have computer files for recent years since after your sister's murder."

"Then this police report here is the only copy of it you have?"

"I'm afraid so."

"And someone removed pages from it. Some personal opinions you think my father might have written about the case. About his daughter, about my sister, about her murder. Why would that have happened?"

"Well, there are only two reasons that I can think of. One, someone didn't want anyone to see what your father thought about the case and about David Munroe back then. Or two, well..."

I knew what Thompson was going to say even before the words came out of his mouth.

There was only one other option.

"Or your father took out the pages himself," Thompson said.

"Why would he do that?" I asked.

"I have no idea."

"Who else might know what he might have been thinking about the case before he died?"

"What about asking your mother?"

FORTY-EIGHT

"What are you doing here?" my mother asked as I showed up at her door. "I thought you were just here for a day and then going back to Washington."

Unbelievable. I've been here for days, I've been on national television and I almost got killed in a car crash—but my mother didn't seem to know anything about it. Some of that was my fault, I guess. I mean I thought about calling her after what happened on the highway to let her know I was all right, but I didn't. Probably because I was upset she hadn't reached out to me when she heard about it.

But now it seemed as if she didn't know about any of the things I'd been involved with in Huntsdale, which was strange. Did she not hear about me on TV news or somewhere else? That's when I realized I hadn't seen any TV in her house. Or computer either. It was as if she had shut herself off from the world in this house, alone with her memories of my father and Caitlin and the life she used to live before it was taken away from her.

"I'm here investigating the disappearance of a girl from Huntsdale," I said, once we were sitting together in the living room. "The girl is a thirteen-year-old named Natalie Jarvis who went missing a few days ago at a movie theater."

"That's terrible," my mother said. "I feel so badly for her family."

She seemed to mean it. Like she was feeling the pain of Natalie Jarvis' mother at that moment, and reliving her own pain at the same time.

"Do you know anything about what happened to her?"

"We're investigating several potential leads," I said, realizing as I did so that I was pretty much mouthing the same words FBI and law enforcement groups put out when they had nothing else to say.

We sat in an uncomfortable silence looking at each other.

"There's more, Mom," I said finally.

"All right."

"Did you see my press conference on TV?"

"No, I don't watch television news. Or any kind of news. It's too upsetting."

So what I was about to tell her was going to be very new and very shocking to her. I took a deep breath and plunged ahead.

"I know you don't want to hear this, but I strongly suspect that there is some sort of a link between Natalie Jarvis' disappearance and the finding of another young girl's body in Huntsdale to what happened to Caitlin."

I told her about finding and digging up Erica Kent's body at the same spot in Grant Woods where Caitlin had been found.

She looked shocked, but angry too. Angry at me.

"Oh, Nikki, don't do this. Please don't do this again..."

"I want to ask you some questions about Dad and what you remember him doing during that period after Caitlin disappeared at the carnival."

"There's nothing to tell. He found the man who did it and put him in jail."

"I'm not so sure about that anymore."

"Is this about what you told me last time? How that horrible monster your father put in prison claims now he is innocent? Even worse, you believe him over your own father?"

"It's just that new information has come out that raises some questions for me about what Dad did or didn't do back then."

"Like what?"

"Well, for one thing, a witness at the carnival saw Caitlin talking to a man right before we got on the Tilt-A-Whirl. Dad never said anything about that. Not to other officers at the scene. Not in the official police report. Not to anyone. I'm hoping he might have said something to you that would explain why. Do you remember anything at all like that?"

"I'll tell you what I remember," she yelled at me now. "I remember your father working day and night on this case. First to try and find Caitlin. Then, once she was dead, to catch the man who did it. That was all that mattered to him. He put his heart and his soul and every part of his being into that investigation. It wound up costing him his life. So don't you dare question anything your father did or didn't do for Caitlin. Don't denigrate his memory like that, for God's sakes. Caitlin is dead, he's dead—the past is dead. I hope you find Natalie Jarvis, and she gets home safely to her family. But the man who killed Caitlin didn't do this; he's been in jail for fifteen years. Your father put him there. So just leave it all alone!"

"I'm not going to leave it all alone. I'm sorry if what I'm doing opens up old wounds for you. But I'm going to do whatever I have to do to find out the truth."

My mother shook her head sadly. "You never did listen to me, Nikki. You always just did what you wanted. No matter what the consequences. Like…"

She didn't finish that thought, but she didn't have to.

Just like the time I didn't listen to her and took my sister to the carnival.

And Caitlin wound up dead.

"What do you want from me?" she asked.

I'd come up with a plan originally not to tell her the real reason I was there. I was going to say I'd been thinking about my father since being back in Huntsdale and how I used to sit with him at the old house going through some of his cases with him. That I just wanted to relive that memory a bit. Going through his old records and papers might help me do that.

It wasn't a very plausible story, and I knew it wasn't going to work now.

So I came right out and asked her.

"I know Dad always kept his own files in the house. Are they still here with you? If so, I want to see them. There might be something about Caitlin's case that could help me now."

I thought maybe she'd tell me she'd thrown them all away.

Or refuse to let me see them, even if I was her own daughter.

But, for whatever the reason, she led me down to the basement where all my father's old papers and belongings were still stored.

"This is everything," she said. "I've never really gone through it in all the years since he died."

She turned abruptly and began walking away from me, on her way back upstairs.

"Will you ever forgive me, Mom?" I called out to her. "I know I made a mistake. But I didn't kill Caitlin. I didn't kill Dad. Now I just want to find out the truth about what really happened. Is that such a terrible thing for your daughter to do?"

"Just put everything back the way you found it," she said, before leaving me alone in the basement with all my father's things.

It was a lot of stuff. Awards, trophies, pictures of him on the job. And lots of documents—paperwork from so many Huntsdale cases that he'd worked on and kept the records at home for himself. Finally, I found the one thing I was really looking for.

The police report on my sister's case.

My father kept a copy for himself.

Which was just like him. He was so careful and organized about his police records. Now I'd finally get a chance to see what was on those pages that had been removed from the official police report I found in the Huntsdale police files. Or so I thought...

But when I turned to the section of the report I was looking to read—the part that was missing—I discovered something even more shocking.

The pages were missing from this one too.

Which meant only one thing to me.

My father was the one who must have removed the pages.

There was something in there he didn't want anyone to ever see.

But I did get one clue from looking through my father's version of the report. Not all of the pages were gone from this one, there was enough left on one partial page so that I could figure out what the part of the missing section was. It was my father's description and conclusions on the medical report about Caitlin's remains, the autopsy filed by the ME Michael Franze.

So what was in Michael Franze's autopsy report that my father didn't want anyone to see?

It was time to go talk to Franze again.

FORTY-NINE

Michael (Big Mickey) Franze wasn't as happy to see me this time as he'd been on my first visit to the medical examiner's office. Especially when I told him what this visit was about. No, he wasn't happy at all.

"Why do you care about whatever I put in the police report about your sister after all this time?" Franze asked me. "Why do you want to read that police report? Why is it so important to you to read the damn police report?"

"I've already read the police report."

"Then why are you asking me about it?"

"There's a section missing."

"What is it you think is missing?"

"My father's observations and conclusions on the medical examiner's findings. His reaction to whatever you submitted to my father for that report. It's gone."

"Maybe it just got misplaced."

"From two versions of the report?"

"Two?"

"Yes. Once from the official report stored at police head-quarters. And also from a second report—a copy of the original

—that I found among my father's belongings at my mother's place. Doesn't seem very likely it was 'misplaced' twice. Someone removed those pages from that report for a reason."

Franze glared at me. No, he definitely was not happy to see me here in his office this time.

"What is it you want from me?" he finally asked.

"A copy of your findings that you submitted for that report. The findings my father would have commented on in his own notes. The ones that are missing."

"I don't know if I have something like that readily available."

"You don't have copies?"

"This was fifteen years ago."

"There were computers fifteen years ago. File cabinets too to keep hard copies. I can't believe the medical examiner's office wouldn't have some record like that of past cases. Especially one of the few high-profile crimes to ever take place in Huntsdale. At least until recently."

Franze shrugged. "I'll take a look and see what I can find. Okay?"

"Fine. In the meantime, do you remember what you wrote in the report? If you tell me that, as best you can recall, it might help me figure out why someone would want to remove it from the report."

"It was all pretty straight-forward. Nothing too significant in there. Your sister Caitlin died from a gunshot wound to the head. It was delivered at close range. I also noted that marks on her wrists and ankles indicated she'd been restrained with rope or something else at some point. The time of death was relatively recent from when the body was found. Most likely only a matter of hours prior to her discovery in the woods by a dog walker."

"Was it the dog walker who first noticed the wreath of roses placed where her body lay?"

"I guess."

"And then saw the roses had been placed prominently on her body? Actually, the roses were placed on top of her head."

"That's right."

"Almost like whoever did it wanted her to be found quickly."

"Possibly."

"How similar was it to the remains of Erica Kent which were found in the same woods?"

"You know the answer to that. I told you last time you were here. Erica Kent also was killed by a gunshot. And, yes, it was a .45 weapon that fired the fatal shot into her. A .45 is a pretty common firearm, I should point out."

"But both Erica Kent and my sister Caitlin were killed the same way, and their bodies found in the same location, which is why I want to read every detail of what you determined about my sister and compare it more closely with the results on Erica Kent."

"What is it you're trying to prove here, Nikki?"

"I believe that there may have been other people involved with Caitlin's death. That David Munroe was a patsy who wound up taking the blame for it. And, for whatever reason, maybe fear for his own safety, he kept his mouth shut all this time. But now, staring death in the face from cancer and about to become a father—as crazy as that might seem—David Munroe finally told me the truth. Or at least part of the truth. That's why he is dead. I think he was murdered in prison because he talked to me, and Munroe might have told me even more if he stayed alive. He was murdered by someone who wants to cover up the truth about what really happened to Caitlin."

Franze stared at me in amazement.

"Are you suggesting that I might somehow be part of this cover-up?"

"All I'm saying is that it's strange some of your findings, along with my father's, are missing from the official police report about Caitlin's murder."

"I didn't do the police report, Nikki. Your father did. Your father was supposed to have included my findings in that report. I have no idea why everything is not there. But your father would have been responsible for the report. And responsible for anything that might or might not have been missing from it."

"So maybe my father was part of this cover-up, too."

"What are you saying?"

"I've uncovered a lot of questionable actions by my father in his investigation."

"Why would your father cover up anything about his own daughter?"

"That's what I need to find out."

"And you think that whatever I wrote in my medical report on Caitlin's murder will somehow help you do that?"

"I won't know until I read it."

"Jesus!"

"Can you look for it now?"

"I'll see what I can find and then get back to you."

"Thank you," I said.

But I was pretty sure the missing medical findings from the report would never be found.

Big Mickey Franze wasn't going to help me get the answers I needed.

My father couldn't help me anymore.

And now it was up to me to figure out what everyone was hiding in Huntsdale from fifteen years ago.

FIFTY

"Where did you live when you were growing up in Huntsdale?"
Billy Weller asked.

"See, if you'd played your cards right in high school, you'd
know the answer to that."

"Huh?"

"All you had to do was ask me to the prom, like you say you
wanted to, and you'd have picked me up there at my house."

He laughed, and so did I. There was definitely a lot of
flirting going on between Billy Weller and me, no question
about it. It was all harmless fun, of course. At least, so far it was.

"Would you have gone to the prom with me?" he asked.

"We'll never know the answer to that question, will we?"

"Who did you go with?"

I told him about my disastrous prom date with the star
wrestler and the grappling between us in the back seat of his car
and all the rest of what happened.

"I would have been a better date for you than that if I
showed up at your door that night instead of the wrestler," Billy
said.

"Wouldn't have been hard to beat."

"Can I see it with you now?"

"See what?"

"Your old house."

"Why?"

"I'm curious."

"Sure. Why not? It's just a short walk away from the station."

I told him about going back and forth all the time from my house to the police station to see and hang out with my father, the police chief then.

A few minutes later, we were standing in front of the white, two-story house with the big porch out front, just like I'd done when I first came to Huntsdale this time and on all of my previous visits back here too.

"Who lives here now?" Billy asked.

"I have no idea."

"You know you could go inside and look at the place. People do that. They knock on someone's door and say they grew up in the house and would love to come in to see it again."

"Uh-huh."

I kept staring at the house.

"Do you want to do that?"

"Do what?"

"Ask the people who live there now if you can look inside."

"I don't think so."

"Maybe there's some more memories for you inside."

"Not any memories I want to remember."

We did walk up onto the front porch though. The front porch where I used to sit with my father and listen to his stories about being the police chief and dream of catching criminals one day too, just like my father did.

"You know, I never would have hurt you, if you'd gone to the prom with me."

"Good to know."

"I would have been the perfect gentleman. Bought you a corsage; danced with you and brought you punch and refreshments at the prom; taken you out to eat at a nice restaurant afterward; and then brought you right back here. If that happened, we might have been standing on this exact porch back then on that prom night. And... well, I probably would have kissed you goodnight."

I felt like this was a repeat of the scene outside my hotel door the other night. Billy wanted to kiss me then, all I had to do was say yes—and it would have happened. Except that was at night and after we'd drunk a lot of beer. This was in broad daylight, on the porch of the house where I grew up and when we were supposed to be working.

Of course, I still could have done it.

Kissed him right here now like I guess I wanted to.

But, if I did that, I would be opening up a door that might take my life in a totally different direction.

And I wasn't sure I wanted to go through that door.

"I'm finished here," I said to Billy Weller. "Like I said, too many memories."

Before we left though, I stopped on the sidewalk and took one more look back at the house.

"Everything started happening at the same time I came back to Huntsdale to interview Munroe about my sister's murder," I said to Billy. "Natalie Jarvis. The body in the woods. Even the roses I found on my father and sister's graves after I went to see Munroe in prison. Everything since I came back here to Huntsdale. That can't all be coincidence."

"So who would do something like that? The roses and all the rest, just to get your attention?"

"A killer would."

"You mean David Munroe?"

"He was in jail. But he liked to play games. Mind games. He did that for fifteen years with me all those times I visited him in jail. And I think he was playing some kind of game with me before he died. With the stuff about the Nowhere Men and all the rest. But he couldn't do all this from behind bars by himself. There must have someone helping him even while he was in jail."

"Who?"

"There's only one person that makes sense."

Billy thought about it for a second, then realized what I was saying.

"Doreen Trask?"

"Doreen Trask," I said.

FIFTY-ONE

"Did you put wreaths of roses on the graves of my sister and my father?" I asked Doreen Trask.

"Why would you say that?"

"Because it's the only thing that makes sense."

"What are you talking about?" she asked, but I could see she was unnerved by the question.

"Let's discuss you and David Munroe and your entire relationship a bit more, Doreen," I said.

We were sitting in the safe house where we'd stashed Doreen Trask after the attack on her life by the gunman that she managed to kill first. We'd gotten some state troopers to guard the place, so I knew she was pretty safe. Now I just had to figure out how to get the secrets about her and Munroe that I believed she was still hiding.

"I want the truth. About everything. Tell me again exactly how you connected with a convicted murderer like Munroe."

"I told you. I wrote to him in prison. And, yes, like I said before, I've done that in the past with other prisoners too. Some of them convicted for murder like David was. Even a few on Death Row. I've just always found it a turn-on to connect with men like that. I'm not sure why. I guess I want to be wanted. To be needed by someone. To be important in their life, or something like that. And these men, who had almost nothing to live for, well, they wanted me. That's the thrill of it. Whatever you think of me, that's the truth. The truth about what me and David had together.

"The relationships never went so far with any of the others though as it did with David. With them, we emailed, texted, sent pictures, I visited a few. But with David... David was different. This was a real relationship. We were soulmates. That's why we got married. Or at least in our minds we were married."

"Okay, that stuff is true. Let's talk now about the parts of your story that aren't true," I said.

"Such as?"

"You telling me that you were his lawyer."

"I represented him as his lawyer in prison, like I said."

"Except for one thing, Doreen. You're not his lawyer."

"Of course, I am."

"Actually, you're not anyone's lawyer. Because you're not a lawyer at all."

She started to answer me, but then stopped. She knew what was coming.

"I checked. You have never passed any bar exam in the state of Ohio or anywhere else. You don't have a law degree from any accredited law school. And, as far as I can tell, you never even attended a law school. Also, the prison doesn't list you anywhere as Munroe's legal representative. He doesn't have any lawyer, he hasn't had one in years. So how about you tell me the truth about that?"

"I was still functioning as David's lawyer no matter what you say."

"How can you do that without a law degree or a license to practice law?"

"I took a bunch of correspondence courses on law. I learned

some things to help David. That part is true. And so I represented him as best I could. It's the same as our marriage was. We didn't need to get some kind of government or official approval to make it legal. David told me I was his lawyer, he accepted me as his lawyer and as his wife—that's all I needed. You can understand that, right?"

Jesus, this woman was even wackier than I thought.

"And the other thing you told me—that you were pregnant with David Munroe's baby—that was true too?"

"Of course, it's true."

"What was his reaction to that?"

"He was happy."

"You're certain about that?"

"Why wouldn't he be happy?"

"Because I don't think he wanted you as his soulmate, the way you felt about him, Doreen. Or at least he didn't want you as much as you wanted him. He was using you. Right up until he died. And that's what almost got you killed. Which means someone could still be after you. Me too. That's why I need to know the truth about everything from you. So let's start by you telling me about the roses."

"Why do you keep asking me about roses?"

That was the real reason I'd come to talk with her again.

Not to question her story on how she met with Munroe.

The connection with the roses I'd found on my sister and my father's graves when I first came back to Huntsdale had been bothering me ever since.

Now I believed I'd figured out the answer.

"David Munroe knew better than anyone about that first wreath of roses on my sister's head when her body was found. That means he would understand the significance of placing roses now on my father and my sister's graves. Except he couldn't have done that because he was in jail. He must have told someone else to do it. Someone he knew would do whatever he said. Someone like his 'soulmate,' as you described your relationship. So why don't you tell me the rest about the roses now? I know you did it for him. But why? Why did he want to put those roses there for me to see after I interviewed him in prison, Doreen?"

She didn't deny it again.

"He never told me why," she said. "He just said that day, the day you came to see him, that I should place those roses there. I didn't think it was any big deal. They were only flowers. He said it was important that I do this for him. Important for you to find those roses there in the graveyard. I guess he assumed you would go there to visit the graves once you went back to Huntsdale after talking to him."

"But did he say why it was important for me to see the roses?"

She sighed.

"He said it was a game. A game with you. That's what he was doing. Playing a game. And he needed you to see the roses to keep the game going."

I realized now that I had been wrong about David Munroe.

Again.

First, I had assumed for years that Munroe was the sick killer who had murdered my sister Caitlin for some senseless reason.

Then, after meeting with him in the prison and hearing what he finally had to say about Caitlin's death, I began to think that maybe he was feeling remorseful and trying to do the right thing because of his terminal cancer diagnosis by saying he wasn't the killer, that someone else had done it and gotten away with the crime. Someone else that I needed to track down now after all these years and finally bring to justice before I could find closure for Caitlin's death and everything that followed after that. I thought it was the cancer that had turned him into a better human being at the end. That maybe he wasn't as evil as I always thought.

But now I knew the truth. David Munroe was evil. Always had been, always would be. Maybe he didn't actually kill Caitlin, like he insisted to me that last day. But he was involved in her abduction and murder. He didn't deny that.

And he'd been playing games with me right up until his death.

Just like he'd played games with me for all those years before when I went to the prison and tried to find out the secrets he still held about my sister and her murder.

The prison meetings where he wouldn't speak.

The time he finally did talk to me.

The roses on Caitlin and my father's graves.

They were all games for him.

But now David Munroe was dead, and someone else was involved in the game.

It wasn't just Doreen Trask.

No, she was just a small part—a bit player—in the sick game David Munroe was still playing with me even from beyond the grave.

FIFTY-TWO

I needed to find out more about David Munroe. Oh, I knew a lot about him. I'd been obsessed with Munroe for fifteen years. I'd hated him for fifteen years. But I didn't really know a lot of details about his previous life. Maybe there was something there that could help me understand the man better, and why he'd been doing everything he'd been doing. So I decided to go back to the town of Cloverfield where he had grown up and gone to high school.

Cloverfield was only about thirty miles from Huntsdale. But it was a dramatically different place than my hometown. And not in a good way either. Huntsdale had managed to revitalize itself in recent years with new businesses and new housing which helped attract more people to the town.

Cloverfield, on the other hand, looked like it had stood still in time. Older buildings in disrepair; shops and stores boarded up and closed; only a few people, mostly elderly, that I could see on the street.

Cloverfield High School, which David Munroe had attended, looked like it had seen better days, too. Same as the town. It was an old building, with faded tan bricks and dirty windows that seemed like they hadn't been washed since Munroe went to school here. I went inside, showed my FBI credentials to a security guard at the door and asked him to direct me to the principal's office.

The principal's name was Lester Gruber, and he seemed like the perfect fit for this high school. Gruber was a small man, dressed in a drab gray suit and maybe in his forties, although he looked older. He seemed nervous about being questioned by the FBI. Or maybe he was the nervous type all of the time.

He said he had been principal here for only two years, so he had no real knowledge of Munroe. He said it as if he was trying to justify why he'd be at a school like Cloverfield High. He even made it clear to me he was hoping to move on to a bigger job soon.

"Even though you weren't here, you're obviously aware of some of the facts about David Munroe's attendance at this high school," I said, when he stopped talking.

"Of course, I know about him."

"He is your most famous graduate."

"Infamous." He frowned. "We've had many outstanding graduates from our high school who've gone on to become productive members of society. It's a shame that all this attention is given to someone like Munroe just because he attended school here a long time ago. His crimes have nothing to do with us."

Gruber obviously didn't know who Caitlin was or her relationship to me. But I didn't say anything. It didn't really matter for what I was trying to get from him. Probably made it easier for me if he didn't know Caitlin was my sister.

"Mr. Gruber, some new questions have emerged recently about David Munroe and his role in the killing of this girl. Also whether it might be linked to some new crimes that have occurred in Huntsdale. I'm trying to find out everything I can about his past in hopes of gaining more insight about him and his possible motivations. And a big part of his past is his time right here at Cloverfield High."

"How can I help?"

"Are there any teachers here who might have been here when Munroe was a student?"

"Hardly any of them would still be at the school. As you might expect, at a small place like this, we have a lot of turnover."

"You said 'hardly any.' Does this mean that there might be someone here who was a teacher while Munroe attended Cloverfield High?"

Gruber thought about it for a minute.

"Well, there is Martin Udall. Udall has been here for many years. He's a fixture at this school. Teaches history and government and social studies to juniors and seniors. I assume that would have included David Munroe. Maybe Udall can help you."

"Can you arrange for me to meet with him?"

"Of course."

He made a phone call, explained who I was and what I was doing and then told me the classroom number where Udall would be waiting for me.

"Anything else I can do to help?" Gruber asked.

"I'd love to get copies of any paperwork you have on Munroe. Grades, evaluations, disciplinary actions, yearbook pictures, anything you can find for me."

"Sure. I'll get my secretary to do that right now and get it ready for you."

"How long will that take?"

"Not long. She should be able to have those copies of whatever we have in the files ready for you by the time you finish talking to Udall."

Martin Udall turned out to be a lot more interesting than I thought he would be. He was up in years now, probably at least sixty. But he still had a real vitality about him, especially when he talked about his students. He seemed like the kind of person who really cared about the kids he taught.

I wondered why he had stayed at a small high school like Cloverfield and never moved on like Gruber said so many teachers here did. There was probably an interesting story there, but it had nothing to do with me.

I was only interested in asking him about Munroe.

"People always say that it's always a surprise when a person they know does something terrible," Udall said. "How he seemed like a quiet, nice person until then. Well, David Munroe was quiet. But when I heard about what he did, I wasn't surprised. He always seemed strange to me."

"What kind of student was he?"

"Pretty average. Pretty much a C average. Not terrible, but nothing special either."

"So he wasn't that intelligent?"

"On the contrary, I thought he was extremely smart. He simply wasn't motivated. At least in the classes he had with me. He always seemed to do the minimum amount of work. I had a few discussions with him about his academic potential, if he wanted to pursue it. But he didn't follow up on any of it."

"He never went to college," I said. "He took a job with the post office after gradation here, from what I understand. That's where he worked—as a postal clerk—until he was arrested. Why do you think he wouldn't have tried to get a better job if he was that intelligent?"

Udall shrugged. "Like I said, he wasn't motivated to do things like that. He had other priorities, I guess. I never understood what they were though. Clearly, he was a troubled young man. Which is why he committed such a horrible act in murdering your sister."

I looked at Udall with surprise.

"You know who I am?"

"Of course. I followed all the news about David Munroe from the beginning. Not too many of my former students are convicted of murder. And you, you're famous, Agent Cassidy. I understand why you're so interested in Munroe. Although I'm not sure I know why it's coming up again after all this time. Does this have to do with the other girl that's missing in Huntsdale and the body found there?"

"You do follow the news."

"But what would any of that have to do with David Munroe who was in jail for the past fifteen years?"

"That's what I'm trying to figure out, Mr. Udall."

I asked him if he'd had any other interactions with Munroe outside of his classes.

"Yes, he was in the chess club. I was the facility adviser to the club. We don't have a lot of students here interested in chess, and it eventually disbanded. But back then, there were a few chess players at Cloverfield, including Munroe."

"He played chess? I never would have thought he was a chess player."

"He was very good, a very smart player. But again, he didn't stay in the chess club for very long, less than a year or so. I guess he just..."

"Wasn't motivated?" I said.

"Something like that." Udall smiled.

On my way out, I stopped by Principal Lester Gruber's office again to pick up the copies of Munroe's records he had waiting for me. I thought about reading them there, but instead I carried them to my car and drove back to the Huntsdale station house. I plopped them down on a desk in the war room, got myself a big cup of coffee and began to read through it all.

They weren't extensive and there wasn't anything mind-boggling there that I saw at first glance.

Like Gruber and Udall had said, Munroe appeared to have been an average student and a quiet guy who didn't make too much of an impact in high school. There were a few reprimands and detentions along the way, but not for anything too significant. Just some lateness, incomplete assignments and routine school issues like that.

It all seemed like a wasted effort on my part.

At the end of the file, I saw some of the material relating to Munroe's time in the chess club. I still found it difficult that a kid like him—with his non-distinguished academic record—had been interested in an intellectual pursuit like chess.

But there was his name on the list of participants in one of the school yearbooks from his time at Cloverfield. There was a picture too of the chess club. I looked at it now. Only five people in the picture. Martin Udall and four students. I looked at the picture of Udall and nearly didn't recognize him at first—the years since must have worn him down at Cloverfield.

David Munroe looked younger too in the picture, of course. He wasn't a bad-looking kid in high school. Average height, but more weight on him than now since the cancer had been eating away on him. No way to look at this old high school picture though and predict that one day this kid would turn into a vicious murderer.

I was just about to close the file when I noticed something else. One of the other kids in the chess club picture. A student behind Munroe. He looked different at first to me now too, which is why it took me so long to make the connection. But it was the smile that did it.

He was smiling at the camera.

It was a friendly, infectious-looking smile.

I knew that smile.

It was Billy Weller.

FIFTY-THREE

Billy Weller went to high school with David Munroe. They were in the chess club together. Hell, they might have been good friends.

But how could this be?

Billy Weller went to Huntsdale High, the same high school as I did. Graduated the same year as me. He admired me from afar there and even wanted to ask me to the senior prom.

How do I know all this?

Because Billy Weller told me.

And I believed him.

But now...

There had always been something a bit off about Billy's story, now that I thought about it some more. How he remembered me so well from high school, even though I couldn't really remember anything about him.

At the time, I just put it down to this all being a long time ago, and I'd probably forgotten about other classmates too. Except it wasn't that big a high school and you'd think that connection with Billy and my high school days would have popped into my memory after all the time I'd spent with him recently.

Sure, he explained that he was quiet and didn't have many friends or take part in activities in high school. In other words, we didn't run in the same circles then. I accepted that at the time he told me. But maybe there was another reason I didn't remember him.

Because he was in another high school in another town.

Hanging out with future killer David Munroe.

So what did this mean? Maybe nothing. But I knew now he lied to me about this. Maybe he lied to me about other things too. Like his marriage. His previous efforts to be an attorney or a stockbroker. Even the night courses in criminal justice he was taking at Ohio State.

Why would he lie to me?

There were a number of possible answers to that question.

None of them good ones.

I remembered that Billy told me his ex-wife's name was Karin Grieco. Not sure why I remembered the name so specifically. But I did. Maybe I wondered what she was like and why she'd left a seemingly good guy like Billy Weller.

There was only one Grieco I could find in the phone listings for the Huntsdale area. I went to the address listed with the number instead of calling, and I knocked on the door. It turned out to be Karin Grieco's parents' home. I showed them my FBI credentials and said I wanted to talk to their daughter about someone we were doing a background check on as a potential FBI job candidate.

It seemed as plausible a story as any, since Billy had talked to me about one day maybe wanting to join the FBI. Anyway, the Grieco family bought it, which was all that mattered. Mrs. Grieco said her daughter had moved to Cleveland. She gave me a contact number for her there.

I went back to the station and called it from there. Karin

Grieco was surprised when I told her who I was and why I was calling, but also seemed to have no problem cooperating in what she presumably assumed was simply a routine background check on her former husband. She actually seemed happy about it.

"The FBI, huh? Well, that's good for Billy."

"Do you think he'd be a good FBI agent?"

"Of course. And I know it's something he's always dreamed about. He likes being a cop. But he always wanted something bigger than Huntsdale. The FBI and he would be a great fit."

Okay. So far Karin Grieco was backing up everything Billy had told me.

Except when I asked the next question and it all fell apart.

"How long were you and Billy married?"

"What?"

"Your marriage? How many years? Tell me a little bit about that and why it didn't work out."

"I was never married to Billy."

"I thought..."

"Who told you that?"

"I must have gotten some erroneous information," I said.

"You sure did. I'm happily married here in Cleveland. I have two terrific sons and a wonderful husband."

"I understand," I said.

Even though I didn't really understand.

"So did you just date Billy for a while before your marriage?"

"No!"

"Okay, the two of you were friends who—"

"What are you talking about?"

"I'm simply trying to understand your relationship with Billy Weller."

"These seem like very strange questions for an FBI interview about a job applicant."

"I'm only trying to find out as much background information as I can about Billy. I was told you were an important part of that background. So if you weren't his wife, you didn't date him and you weren't really his friend, then what was your relationship with him?"

"I was his therapist."

I talked to Karin Grieco for a while longer. She wouldn't tell me anymore about the specific issues Billy was being treated her for, citing patient-doctor confidentiality. But I was able to ascertain that Billy Weller had been seeing Dr. Karin Grieco, PhD for psychological counseling sessions until her husband got a new job in Cleveland and she moved there with her family.

I had just hung up when Billy came into the station house and walked into the war room where I was still sitting.

"Anything new going on?" he asked, flashing me that friendly smile again.

"Not really," I said.

I quietly slid the file folder I'd taken from Cloverfield High —the one with the picture from the chess club of Billy standing next to David Munroe—into a drawer next to where I was sitting.

I wasn't ready to confront him about this yet.

I wanted to find out more first.

"Let me know if anything breaks," he said.

"You'll be the first to know."

"Great, Nikki."

Another big smile from Billy Weller.

He sure did have a great smile.

But now I just kept wondering what other secrets Billy Weller was hiding behind his smile.

FIFTY-FOUR

It got worse after that.

A lot worse.

I told Alex and Girard what I'd found out about Billy Weller, and I said we needed to do a deep dive investigation as quickly as we could to find anything else he'd been keeping from us—or outright lying about.

"In the meantime, we have to figure out some way to keep him away from anything we're working on. He's found out a lot so far, we have to make sure he doesn't have access to anything else. At least until we check him out further. Any ideas on how to keep him busy and away from what we're doing?"

"You shouldn't have any trouble doing that," Girard said to me.

"What do you mean?"

"Weller seems to be smitten with you. So keep on flirting with him—like you've been doing—for a while longer and let Alex and me do the investigative work."

I glared at Girard.

"That's a totally inappropriate thing to say to me, Phil."

"Hey, I'm only telling you what I've been seeing." He looked over at Alex. "What everyone has been seeing."

I turned to Alex for support, but she just shrugged.

"It has been pretty obvious that he has a thing for you," she said.

I wanted to make some sort of snappy comeback, but I didn't. There wasn't much I could say.

I took out the picture of Billy Weller and David Munroe I'd gotten from Cloverfield High and put it down on the table where we were sitting in the war room.

"Look," I said, "I'll come up with some assignments for Weller. Interviews with people. Doesn't matter who they're with. I'll make up some reason we want him to talk to all of them. That ought to keep him busy and away from us so he won't be able to know what we're really doing here right now."

"And what are we doing?" Girard asked.

"Finding out the truth about Billy Weller."

It didn't take too long for Alex and Phil Girard to get back to me with some information.

All of it was bad.

"There's no record of him ever being in the army or with any kind of military branch," Alex said. "He also is not currently taking any classes in criminal justice or law enforcement at Ohio State or any other night school in the area that I could find. Like he claimed to you he was. And, as you found out from the psychiatrist, Billy Weller is not now and never has been married to anybody."

"When did he join the Huntsdale police force?"

"About three years ago."

"Well, at least he told me the truth about that."

"He didn't mention anything about the military on his application for the force. I guess he knew that would be checked out pretty easily. His background included a series of other jobs, none of which he stayed at for very long."

"It makes you wonder how a guy like that would get hired here for the police force," I said.

"Probably their standards for new recruits are a lot lower than ours at the bureau," Girard grunted. "I mean I don't think people are lining up to join the Huntsdale police force to fight crime here."

"Does it say why he did get hired?"

"No, only the person who did the hiring."

"Who was that?"

"Chief Frank Earnshaw. Who also wrote a glowing recommendation about him during the hiring process."

"Whoa!" I said. "I thought Billy Weller and Chief Earnshaw didn't get along very well. That's what he always told me."

"He told you a lot of things," Girard said. "Doesn't mean any of them are true."

It was Phil Girard who later came up with the most disturbing news. He joined Alex and me later with a stack of files and paperwork he'd downloaded. He said they came from the Ohio State Correction Department.

"It turns out that Miles Janos—the ex-con who tried to run us off the road before the Trask woman killed him—had a cellmate in prison named Jerry Butcher. Butcher was arrested for robbery when he tried to hold up a convenience store. Guess where the arrest happened? Right here in Huntsdale. And the arresting officer was..."

"Billy Weller," Alex said.

"Bingo."

"Jesus," I said.

"So Janos and Butcher are cellmates," Girard continued. "Janos gets out of prison in time to try to kill us and Doreen

Trask. Butcher is still in jail with David Munroe. Want to bet Butcher was in the shower when Munroe had his fatal fall? And so Weller was connected with both Butcher and Munroe. It's not hard to put the pieces together..."

"But Weller was in the car with us when Janos tried to run us off the road," I pointed out.

"Maybe Janos didn't know that."

"Right," Alex said. "Weller wasn't originally supposed to be with us that day when we were driving to the prison. He asked to come along at the last minute. Maybe, even if he was involved with Butcher and Janos, he didn't know something was going to happen to our car."

"Or maybe someone decided to eliminate him too to keep him quiet about what he knew, just like with Munroe," Girard said.

I was going to have to confront Billy Weller about all of this, I realized that.

But I wanted to be absolutely sure.

I needed to gather as many facts as I could before I did that.

"Where's Butcher now?" I asked.

"Gone."

"What do you mean?"

"He was released from prison. Right after Munroe's death. For good behavior, believe it or not. Supposedly supported by someone in law enforcement from the area where he committed the crime for his parole. That means someone in law enforcement here in Huntsdale. Don't know who it was yet. But not a lot of candidates here who might have done it. Leading candidate would be our boy Billy Weller."

"Or maybe even Chief Earnshaw," Alex said. "I sure don't trust him either."

"He did write that glowing recommendation for Weller to get the job on the force. Maybe the two of them are working together and—"

"This is all speculation at the moment," I told them.

"Maybe, but we can't be sure who we can trust in this town right now, Nikki," Alex said.

She was right.

Billy Weller.

Chief Frank Earnshaw.

Medical Examiner Michael Franze.

Even my own dead father.

Who was there to trust in Huntsdale?

Well, maybe one person.

I'd only met her once.

I just hoped I was right in thinking I could trust her.

I put in a call to the Huntsdale Town Hall and asked for an urgent meeting with Mayor Stacy Harris.

FIFTY-FIVE

I had a surprise waiting for me when I got back to the hotel where I was staying. Greg Ellroy. He was right here in Huntsdale, standing in front of my room door and waiting for me with a big smile.

"Surprise!" he said.

"My God, what are you doing here?"

"I figured if I can't convince you to come back to Washington to be with me, I'll come here to be with you."

"What about your job at the law firm?"

"I took a day off. I'll fly back tomorrow morning. I was going to take like three weeks off in the fall for our honeymoon. Let's pretend this is part of the honeymoon. A little advance honeymoon for us. Sounds great, doesn't it, Nikki? And I promise you I won't keep pestering you about quitting this case. We'll just enjoy being together for a night."

Greg stepped close, leaned down and kissed me. It was a passionate kiss. I kissed him back. I guess I didn't show as much passion as he did in my return kiss. Greg looked disappointed.

"Aren't you happy to see me?" he asked.

"Of course, I am."

"You're not acting like it."

"I just wasn't expecting to see you, Greg."

"That's why I made it a surprise. I thought that would be fun."

"I wish you'd have let me know beforehand."

"That would have ruined the surprise." He smiled.

"I'm not big on surprises right now, Greg. I'm busy here. Really busy. I'm working hard on these cases."

"That's why a bit of relaxation will be good for you. I reserved a table for us at what I'm told is the best restaurant in Huntsdale. Let's go there now and you can begin unwinding a bit. Forget for a little while about missing girls and murders and all those other unpleasant things you have to deal with in your job."

"I need to work tonight."

"C'mon, you can take a night off to have dinner with me. I traveled three hundred plus miles here to see you. Is it too much to ask for you to walk a few minutes with me to an elegant restaurant where I can wine and dine you?"

Greg was right, of course.

No reason I couldn't go to dinner with him.

No reason at all.

"Let me call Alex and tell her what I'm doing," I said.

A short time later, we were at a place called The Golden Duck. I didn't remember it from my old days in Huntsdale, it must be relatively new. But it was very nice and very expensive looking. All you had to do was look at the menu to check that out.

There were candles lit up brightly on our table.

A bottle of champagne Greg had ordered ahead was waiting there for us.

Romantic music was playing from a small group of musicians that Greg told me he had paid to play for us too.

He had really gone all out to make this a wonderful evening.

So why did I wish I was back eating Burger King burgers and fries or tuna salad sandwiches at the Huntsdale diner again?

I told Greg about everything that had been happening here since we last talked. The links to the new missing girls. The one we'd found alive with the unbelievable story. The continuing efforts to crack into the Nowhere Men website and find out what other secrets it held there. The questions I had about who I could trust in Huntsdale.

I told him about my latest meeting with my mother too, and about the continuing questions I kept having about my father after the time of Caitlin's murder until he died several weeks later.

Greg listened patiently to it all, I'll give him that. I guess he finally understood how important this all was to me. Or at least he pretended to care about it all. Because he wanted to make me happy.

We'd drunk about half a bottle of champagne and finished our salads and we were working on the entrées when he brought up the topic he really wanted to discuss: our wedding.

"I found a church that says now we can probably get two hundred people in there for the ceremony. That means we can send out more invitations than we expected. I've got a lot of people who will be coming from my law firm. I'm sure you'll want to invite a lot of FBI people too. What about relatives? Who besides your mother will you invite?"

My mother.

Would my mother even come to my wedding?

And, if she did, how would she react to her daughter making her wedding vows?

I didn't want to think about it. I didn't want to think about the wedding either. I didn't want to think about any of it.

"No," I said to Greg.

"Huh?"

"Don't do this now."

"Don't do what?"

"Don't talk any more about wedding plans."

"What's wrong, Nikki?"

I didn't say anything. I didn't really have to say anything more. I mean I could have just laughed and told him to go on about our wedding plans and looked happy and reassured him that I was just as excited as he was about living happily ever after with Greg Ellroy. It would have been so easy to just do that. But I'd been doing that for a long time, and I was tired of it.

"Is there some problem?" he asked.

"Yes."

"Did I do something wrong?"

"No, you didn't do anything wrong, Greg. You never do anything wrong. You're perfect. Or damn close to it anyway. Any woman would love to have a man like you. People tell me that all the time. And they're right. In many ways, you are the perfect man."

"Then what?"

"That's the problem."

He still didn't understand what I was saying.

"You're too perfect."

I shook my head sadly.

"I don't think I can be with someone as perfect as you."

"What?"

"I'm not perfect. I think I need to be with someone... well, someone who is not so perfect."

"What are you saying?"

I didn't answer him.

"Don't you love me, Nikki? The way I love you?"

I didn't answer him.

"Nikki?

"I tried, Greg," I said finally. "I really tried. I'm sorry."

Greg Ellroy sat there with a look of shock on his face.

"I don't understand," he said.

"I don't really understand it either."

"Where did this all come from?"

"These things just happen sometimes."

"Is there someone else you met up here?"

I thought about Billy Weller.

Billy and his infectious grin.

Billy who once knew David Munroe and didn't tell me that and also lied about his marriage to me.

Maybe lied about a lot of other things too.

"Yes, I did meet someone," I said.

"Are you in love with him?"

"No. I'm not in love with him. Or in any kind of a relationship with him. To be honest, I don't want to be. He lied to me. And I think he might still be lying to me."

"Then why are you doing this?"

"Because he made me realize I was lying too. Lying to you. Lying to myself. About you and me. Pretending that we were something that we really weren't. You're a great guy, Greg. You really are. You're just not the great guy for me. I know that now. And I'm sorry. Sorry I waited so long to tell you that. I really am sorry."

FIFTY-SIX

Mayor Stacy Harris was happy to see me. Until I told her that Billy Weller had lied to me and might not be what he seemed on the Huntsdale police force. About how he knew David Munroe in high school—and even been in a chess club with him. About how I'd found out Weller had arrested Jerry Butcher, the man we believed killed Munroe in prison to keep him quiet and not reveal names of other people that he was involved with in the murder. About Billy Weller's other lies too.

I revealed my concerns that I had also about Police Chief Frank Earnshaw and Medical Examiner Michael Franze.

Once I did that, she wasn't so happy that I was there.

"I'm not sure who I can trust anymore," I said to her. "That's why I came here to see you today, Mayor."

"Why do you think you can trust me?" she asked.

That was a good point.

"I mean I only met you for like five minutes in a bar the other night. You don't really know very much about me. I could be lying to you about me and my motives in the same way that you seem to think these other people might be."

"I have a good instinct about people."

"And your instinct tells you that I'm trustworthy?"

"It does."

"That's quite a leap of faith, isn't it?"

"Well, Tommy Thompson spoke well of you to me that night. So that's in your favor."

"What about Thompson? Why not go to him? Do you trust Tommy?"

"I do. He was a friend of my father for a long time, and he's been in that D.A.'s job forever. But maybe that's a problem. He's too set in his ways. He's convinced that David Munroe— and no one else—murdered my sister. Maybe he really does believe that. But I think a lot of it may have to do with him protecting his reputation."

I explained to her my theory about how since this was the biggest case of Tommy Thompson's career, and that he had personally prosecuted Munroe for the conviction, he was very defensive about the idea that other people might have been involved that he missed or was unaware of at the time.

"Admitting that now would create a very awkward situation for him," I said.

"But not for me and the town of Huntsdale?"

"You're new to the job. You haven't been here for twenty years like Thompson. If I find out Huntsdale was wrong about who killed my sister, you can blame it all on a lot of other people who were here back then. Even my own father. So I'm trusting you to do the right thing here no matter how it turns out."

We talked a bit more. The more we talked, the more I felt like I was winning her onto my side. In the end, she agreed to do what she could to help.

"What is it you want me to do?" she asked.

Mostly, I told her, I just wanted to know I could come to her with whatever damning information I turned up. About Weller. About Earnshaw. About Franze. Whatever that information might be. I said I would alert my boss in Washington that I was in direct communication with her now, and not Huntsdale Police Chief Frank Earnshaw or anyone else in town.

"I'd also like you to see what other background information —public or not so public—you can find on Weller, Earnshaw and Franze. I've done some checking on my own, but you might have better success using your authority and powers of the mayor's office."

"What exactly are you searching for?"

"I'm not sure."

"Then what...?"

"I'm looking for something about one of them that doesn't seem right, doesn't make sense for whatever reason. That would show they aren't telling me the truth about everything they know. That they are hiding something about this investigation. And why they're doing it."

"Obviously, you don't want any of them to know that we are doing this."

"Not Earnshaw or Franze. I don't want them to know I suspect anything about either one of them yet. Not until I find out more."

"What about Weller?"

"I already have enough evidence to confront Billy Weller myself."

When I left Stacy Harris, I reached out to both Katie Gompers, the friend who had been with me that day at the carnival with Caitlin, and Susan Cabot, the girl who had survived an abduction and effort to kill her as part of a "snuff film."

Both of them had talked about seeing someone significant: Gompers the man talking to my sister Caitlin outside the Tilt-A-Whirl just before she disappeared, and Cabot the man who kidnapped her outside a convenience store in Cleveland.

I told them both I was going to email them pictures of three people to see if they recognized any of the three from those incidents.

The three pictures, of course, were of:

Billy Weller.

Frank Earnshaw.

Michael Franze.

It was a long shot, I knew that. But worth a try because one of them might make a connection to one of the three.

Then I went looking for Billy Weller...

FIFTY-SEVEN

I decided to confront Billy Weller myself, one-on-one, without Alex or Girard there with me.

I felt like I owed him that much.

And maybe he'd find it easier to tell me the truth about himself in that kind of situation.

We went back to the diner we'd been at before. Billy seemed happy when I suggested us going there. I guess he figured it was going to be another personal conversation between him and me.

"I wanted to talk to you outside the station house," I said to him once we got seated at one of the booths.

"Sure, what's going on?"

"A lot, actually."

"Tell me."

"I don't think you're going to want to hear what I'm about to say."

"Always happy to talk to you about anything, Nikki."

I took out the photo from the Cloverfield High chess club and put it down on the table in front of us.

"Let's talk about this," I said.

He stared at me without speaking for a long time once he saw that. At first, I thought he wasn't going to answer me at all.

"What do you want me to say?" Billy Weller finally asked.

"I want you to tell me why you lied to me."

"I didn't lie."

"Billy, the first time we met, you announced to me that you and I went to high school together at Huntsdale High. Later, you said you had a crush on me and wanted to invite me to the senior prom, but never had the nerve to ask me out on a date. I didn't question any of that at the time. I mean I didn't really remember you, but who would make up a story like that? And why? Except now I find out you didn't go to Huntsdale High. You went to Cloverfield, the same school as David Munroe. And you knew Munroe."

"I didn't lie to you about that," he said.

Billy Weller looked down again at the picture I'd placed in front of him. The one of him and David Munroe standing next to each other as members of the chess club at Cloverfield High School.

"I did go to Huntsdale High School. I did have a crush on you there. And I did want to ask you to the senior prom at Huntsdale. My family moved from Cloverfield to Huntsdale right before my senior year. So I spent my first three years of high school at Cloverfield. That's probably why you didn't remember me. I was only at Huntsdale for one year. And I never got to know many people there because I was new. But I graduated from Huntsdale High. You can check that out if you want.

"And yes, I did attend Cloverfield High at the same time as David Munroe. But I barely knew him. This picture from the chess club was taken when I was a freshman and he was a senior. He was three years ahead of me. I must have had a brief conversation or two with him, maybe even played a bit of chess with him. But that's all. It's the only relationship I ever had with David Munroe."

"And you didn't think that was worth mentioning?"

"Why would I?"

"Our investigation into Munroe—"

"C'mon, Nikki, Munroe killed your sister fifteen years ago. He's been in jail since then. I had no reason to tell you about being in a chess club with the guy when I was a high school freshman. I'm focused on the Natalie Jarvis case. Finding her and also finding out how the body of Erica Kent got left here in Huntsdale. I simply didn't see any point in bringing up the fact that I'd met Munroe a long time ago when we were kids. It wasn't relevant to what we're working on now. If you calm down and think about it for a second instead of making accusations against me for hiding secrets, you'd realize that too."

He was right.

Well, sort of right, I guess.

Still, it would have been nice to know.

"Okay, maybe you weren't actually lying—maybe it was more of a sin of omission than a lie. But you did lie to me about your marriage. You were not married, at least not to the woman you said was your wife. She wasn't even your girlfriend, she was your therapist. I talked with Karin Grieco. She told me about your real relationship. Why did you make up the marriage story to me? Because I gotta tell you, a person who lies about something like that, probably lies about other stuff too. Why? Why the claim to have been married to Karin Grieco? Why did you do that?"

Billy looked uncomfortable. I sensed that the answer to this was going to be more difficult for him to deal with than the questions about him and Munroe. I was right.

"It was stupid," he said. "I'm not sure why I did it. But when I was talking to you then, you still seemed like the girl in high school who was so popular. You have a great job now, a great boyfriend, you're about to be married to him. I didn't want you think of me as some loser guy who couldn't get up the courage to ask you for a date. So I told you I was married. Like I said, it was stupid. I wish I hadn't done it. But it has nothing to do with any of the rest of the stuff we're working on. It was just a personal mess up on my part."

"But why did you use your therapist's name?"

"You asked for the name of my ex-wife. It was the first name I could come up with."

"Couldn't you have used some other woman instead? Why Karin?"

"I'm in love with her. Or at least I was, until she left town."

"Your therapist?"

"Yes."

'You were having an affair with her?"

"No, nothing happened. It was a fantasy of mine. She's a very attractive woman, very brilliant, very charming. I began to imagine what it was like to be in real relationship with her. Sometimes it almost seemed real to me. And when you asked me the name of the woman I was married to, all I could think of was Karin. Then, when you pressed me on the name, her name just came out of my mouth."

"How long have you been seeing a therapist, Billy?"

"Several years."

"For what?"

"Look, I don't want to talk about it really. And don't think like I haven't been with other desirable women. I've dated a bit since I've been in Huntsdale. But I was really head over heels for Karin. Even though I knew she was married. And she had a family. And she was my therapist. She was aware of my feelings, and I guess it made her uncomfortable. Anyway, her husband got the job in Cleveland and she moved away. I haven't really been serious about anyone since. And then you came to Huntsdale—the girl I had a crush on in high school—and I guess I wanted to impress you. So I made up the story about being married to a woman like Karin Grieco. And I told you I was an MP in the army too before I joined the force. You've probably found out that's not true either. But I thought it made me sound better, seem more interesting to you. Stupid, huh? So stupid of me to make up lies like that."

"What about all the other stuff you told me? Trying to be a stockbroker and applying to law schools and taking criminal justice courses at night at Ohio State?"

"That's true. I tried those other things. In fact, Karin pushed me in our sessions to give them a shot. Just like I told you she did when I pretended she was my wife. She thought it would be good for me. And I am taking criminal justice courses at night. I go to a community college now near here. It's very small and you wouldn't have looked there to check it out. I guess I said I was going to Ohio State for the same reason I claimed to have been married. I wanted to impress you. I wanted to seem important to you."

Finally, I brought up the fact that he had arrested Jerry Butcher, the cellmate of the man who'd tried to kill us and Doreen Trask.

This time he looked really shocked.

"Yes, I was the one who arrested Butcher for that robbery. It was at a convenience store outside of town. He tried to hold it up. I got the call a robbery was in progress, and I stopped it. But that's all that happened. I thought I did a good thing by arresting Butcher. A heroic thing."

"You mean you never knew he wound up as this guy Janos' cellmate at Dagmore?"

"Of course not. How would I know something like that?"

"It seems like a pretty big coincidence."

"Well, that has nothing to do with me. I arrested Butcher. That's all I did."

"And you never did anything to help Butcher get an early release from prison after Munroe died?"

"How could I do something like that?"

'If not you, who else from Huntsdale might have done it?"

"No one I can think of."

"What about Chief Earnshaw?"

"Why would he care about Butcher getting an early release?"

Why indeed?

"I was in that car with you when Janos tried to run us off the road. Do you really think I would be involved in that? My God, Nikki! I could have been killed too. The same as the rest of you. I was the arresting officer on Jerry Butcher. I had no contact with him after that. And no knowledge whatsoever about who his cellmate was or if either of them played any kind of role in David Munroe's death. You've got to believe me."

I wanted to believe Billy Weller. I really did. Even after all of this. And everything he was saying did make sense. Well, some sort of crazy sense, I guess. The bottom line was none of it proved that he had anything to do with any of the disappearances or deaths that had been happening in Huntsdale. But then again, what he told me certainly raised questions about him that I still couldn't answer.

"I'm not sure what would have happened with Doctor Grieco," Billy said before we left the diner. "But then her husband got that job in Cleveland and they moved away from Huntsdale. Like I said, I've dated other women. But I've been waiting for someone special to come along. And then... well, then you came to town."

He flashed me that smile again.

A sheepish smile this time.

"I'll be straight with you about everything from now on," Billy told me. "I'll tell you everything. I promise. You have my word on it."

"I'll hold you to that promise, Billy."

"So I can keep working with you on the case?"

"Unless you lie to me again," I said.

Yes, I was going to keep working with Billy Weller.

I could still work with the guy.

But I wasn't sure I could trust him.

In the meantime, though, I wanted to keep him close—so I could keep an eye on him in case he did anything suspicious.

There was a message from Katie Gompers, my high school friend, on my phone when I finished with Weller. One of the two people I'd sent pictures too of Billy Weller, Frank Earnshaw and Michael Franze. Maybe we'd get lucky with this. But instead she got back to me with a "don't recognize any of them" response when I called her back.

"I'm not sure I would remember anyone after all this time," she said. "It was a brief look at the time, and I didn't think much about it since then, after your father told me it wasn't anything significant. Sorry I couldn't be of more help, Nikki. But it was great seeing you again. Let's try to stay in touch."

I said I'd like that too, even though I knew it was one of those things people say to each other without really meaning it.

So I figured this idea was all a waste of time and effort when my phone buzzed again. I looked down at the screen. It was Susan Cabot. I answered it not expecting much more than I got from Katie Gompers.

But I was wrong.

"It's him," she said.

"What?"

"The man who grabbed me outside the store. It's him. He's in one of these pictures you sent me."

"Which one?" I practically yelled at her. "Weller? Earnshaw? Franze? Which one is it, Susan?"

"None of them."

"But you said…"

"He's the other one in the picture."

I took out the pictures I'd sent her and looked at them again. Weller, Earnshaw and Franze. They hadn't been easy to get. Franze was from an old newspaper article about the medical examiner's office; Weller from a picture I'd found on a wall at the Huntsdale station; and Earnshaw on the day he was being sworn in as police chief.

"It's the picture of the police chief," Susan Cabot said. "Not him. The other one in the picture. That's who I remember."

The picture showed Earnshaw with another Huntsdale official at the swearing-in ceremony that day.

The swearing in was carried out by the town's District Attorney.

Tommy Thompson.

FIFTY-EIGHT

"Here's what we've been able to find out about Huntsdale District Attorney Tommy Thompson," Alex said.

She'd been working with our tech and research people at the office back in Washington to build a dossier on the man who I'd always assumed to be just a small-town D.A., but who now could be a mass murderer.

And might be the man who murdered my sister.

"He's been in the D.A.'s office for twenty-two years. It's an elected post but he has gotten elected every four years. Not sure if that's because he's popular or no one else really ever wanted the job. No significant red flags in his record, no controversial overturned convictions or allegations of abuse of power or anything else like that.

"And, of course, he had one big event—one big triumph—that people around here remember him for. The prosecution of David Munroe and his subsequent conviction—for the biggest crime ever in Huntsdale, at least until now: the abduction and murder of your sister, Caitlin Cassidy, Nikki."

We were sitting in Girard's room at the hotel, going over all aspects of the shocking news from Susan Cabot that she recognized Thompson in the picture as the man who had abducted her, then threatened to kill her for a snuff film—before she got away—several years earlier.

I didn't want to meet in the war room or the police station or anywhere else in public because I didn't want Billy Weller involved in this. Or Chief Frank Earnshaw. Or Medical Examiner Michael Franze either. I still wasn't sure I could trust any of them. Even though Tommy Thompson was our new focus now.

Girard was sitting on the bed doing the *New York Times* crossword puzzle while Alex talked. There was an open book on the end table next to him called *The NASA Conspiracies*, which I found out was about how the government was covering up the truth about aliens and flying saucers visiting us in recent years.

Obviously, FBI work was not Girard's top priority these days. But he was still here with us. He hadn't quit to go back to Washington like he threatened. So I was glad about that. Alex and I needed all the help we could get, given our distrust of the local law enforcement people.

Alex went through more details about Thompson, then said: "Here's the interesting part. He's a leading player, some kind of board official, in the Ohio organization of District Attorneys that coordinates all the different D.A. offices throughout the state on a lot of issues. He works closely with prison officials too. Prison officials like the ones at Dagmore. That would give him access to criminals there like Butcher or Janos. Maybe even give him some clout to get them released early—in return for them carrying out favors for him."

"Like trying to kill us and Doreen Trask, or making sure David Munroe had an 'accident' in the shower," I said.

"There's more. As part of this role, he travels a lot for meetings and speeches and appearances."

"Places like Dayton, where Susan Cabot was abducted?"

"Yes. We can't place him specifically there at the time of her incident, but we should be able to find out that information very soon. And get this, he also made a lot of other appearances at other states around the country."

"Maybe San Francisco or Louisville, Kentucky," I suggested.

"We haven't been able to confirm that yet either."

"But it is possible."

"Definitely possible."

"Sounds damn likely to me," Girard grunted as he looked up from his crossword puzzle.

Our next step was to get Les Polk on a conference call back in Washington to fill him in on all of this. He seemed pretty surprised, as I thought he would be.

"Have you tried to talk to Thompson yet about any of this?" Polk asked.

"No. I didn't want to let him find out about any of this until we were ready to make our move to arrest him," I said.

"Also, there's the missing girl. If he still has Natalie Jarvis..." Polk said.

"Right. We don't want to spook him before we can figure out how to get him to lead us to her."

"What about the local authorities? How do they fit into this?"

I told him all about my suspicions regarding the Huntsdale police force.

"I haven't talked about this with anyone," I said. "Except the mayor. She doesn't know about Thompson specifically. That happened after I talked with her. But I raised my concerns about Weller, Earnshaw and Franze. So she knows something is possibly wrong in the Huntsdale government. I think I can trust her. But who knows for sure? My plan would be to arrest Thompson on our own using federal authority and then worry about who we can or can't trust locally after that."

"What about checking out where he lives before you confront him?" Polk said. "If he does have the girl, then somewhere on his property might be the most logical place for him to be holding her."

"And nobody would have ever thought about asking the search teams we had out to go the D.A.'s house, would they?" Alex said.

"Do we have an address for Thompson?" I asked her.

Alex checked the notes she'd compiled on her laptop computer all about Tommy Thompson.

"It's 220 Mountain Avenue. Off of something called State Road. Do you know where that is, Nikki?"

"Yes, I know where it is."

220 Mountain Avenue was right next to Grant Woods.

FIFTY-NINE

Alex and I got more information on our way to check Thompson's place near Grant Woods.

Ray Terlop called us as soon as we pulled our car out of the police station lot for the drive there.

"We have been able to access more information from the Nowhere Men website," Terlop said. "Even though it's been taken down, there are still images and data we've recovered. No question about it, Nikki. You were right. There are snuff videos on there of women apparently being murdered. Not just your sister, like you saw. We've taken some screen grabs and believe we'll be able to match up the faces with other missing girls over the years."

"My God!" Alex said, listening as I had Terlop on speakerphone in the car.

"How many?" I asked.

"Four so far. But we believe there could be more. We're busting our ass trying to get more of this from the deleted site data."

"What else did you find besides the snuff videos?" I asked.

"A lot of names from people on the site. Not their real

names, of course. Those are kept anonymous by the site. But their handles adopted when they went on the Nowhere Men. One of them was Captain Courageous, the name you used to get onto David Munroe's computer. You told us that someone called you that during your online encounter."

"What were the other names?" I asked.

"There were about six of them."

"So there's at least six members of Nowhere Men using the site?" Alex asked.

"At least. Could be more. Probably is. But that's the number of names we've found so far."

"Was one of the handles used 'The Black Knight?'" I asked.

"Yes, that's right. Why?"

"That's the name Susan Cabot, the girl who survived the Nowhere Men, said the man who abducted her told her to call him."

"Why would a grown man call himself The Black Knight?" Terlop muttered.

"I'll ask that question when I see him."

"What?"

"I'm pretty sure we're on our way to The Black Knight's house right now. After that, we'll go see him at his office. The District Attorney's office. Should be an interesting conversation."

We'd left Phil Girard back at the Huntsdale station for now. I wanted him to be there when Billy Weller came in to give Weller something to keep him busy, and not ask too many questions about where Alex and I had gone. It had become harder and harder to keep Billy out of the investigation since I'd found out what I did about him.

The last thing I wanted was for him to discover what we were doing now. I still wasn't sure I could trust the guy. They could all be involved somehow in the Nowhere Men. Weller. Earnshaw. Franze. Along with Thompson. Just like David Munroe had been, right up until the end in prison.

"Phil will ask Weller to do some kind of B.S. assignment to keep him occupied, and then Phil will come out to Thompson's place to join us with what we're doing there," I said to Alex.

"What exactly are we going to be doing there, Nikki?"

"We're going to check Thompson's place out as best we can. See if anything theroke seems wrong. Anything we can use against Thompson when we go to his office afterward to confront him."

"And if there isn't?"

"Then we go to Thompson's office and confront him anyway."

"That's your plan?"

"You got a better one?"

"Nope. That one works for me."

The place where Tommy Thompson lived was big. A Victorian house sat back from the road without any neighbors close by. It looked like there were several acres of land around it. None of the land was farmed or anything, it was just trees and shrubs and foliage, not unlike Grant Woods, which was nearby.

I noticed a separate two-car garage and something that looked like a tool shed alongside the house.

There were several other homes on the road, but they weren't adjoining Thompson. There was plenty of space in between. Still, they were neighbors. I said to Alex that we should try to talk to them. I'd come up with some kind of reason to ask questions about their neighbor, D.A. Tommy Thompson.

Just as we were about to do that, my phone rang.

It was Phil Girard.

"No Billy Weller," he said.

"What do you mean no Billy Weller?"

"Not here."

"What do you mean? Where is he?"

"No one knows."

Damn. Did he get suspicious about us trying to keep him away from us and what we were doing?

"Should I ask Earnshaw about him?" Girard asked.

"No. I don't want him getting suspicious either."

"So what do I do?"

"Come out here and join us. We're going to try to talk to some neighbors first. Then we'll check out Thompson's house as best we can and the area around it."

"What if his family is there? Aren't they going to ask what you're doing? Aren't they going to tell Thompson there are FBI agents walking around the place? How are you going to explain that?"

"I guess we'll figure that out the best we can when it happens."

I gave him directions to meet us outside Tommy Thompson's house.

The closest neighbor was a woman named Ruth Podesta. She lived about a half mile away. She told us she'd lived there for nearly forty years. Raised a family there. Her husband was dead now, and the children grown up and gone. But she still stayed there, she said. It was her home.

Alex and I let her talk about all this for awhile, until we could ask her what we were there for: about her neighbor Tommy Thompson and his house.

The story I'd come up with was that the FBI was still searching the area around Grant Woods for the missing Natalie Jarvis.

"Oh, yes," she said. "I've seen the search teams here. What a terrible thing. It's hard to believe something like that could happen in a quiet little town like Huntsdale."

I wondered if she remembered what had happened to my sister in this quiet, peaceful town. She must have. But she apparently didn't make the connection between my sister and me, even when I showed her my FBI credentials for Nikki Cassidy.

"In addition to the woods around here, we're talking to some of the people who live near here like you in the hopes they might have noticed or seen something unusual."

Ruth Podesta shook her head no. "It's always pretty quiet around here. I rarely see or hear anyone. Certainly not anyone or anything that might be of interest to you."

I pointed to Thompson's house now and pretended I didn't know who lived there.

"What about that neighbor?" I said. "Do you know who lives there? Maybe they saw something."

Podesta laughed. "You people in law enforcement would have been the first to know if that happened. Tommy Thompson, the District Attorney, lives there. He's the face of law enforcement around this town. Tommy must be working with you people. So you would certainly know everything he knows. I'm afraid you're just wasting your time."

"Right."

"But what about his family?" Alex asked. "Isn't it possible they might have seen something in those woods?"

I was hoping she would tell us the family wasn't there now, so that we could get a better look at the property.

But she didn't give us the answer I was expecting.

"Oh, Tommy doesn't have any family. He lives alone."

Alone?

But I'd seen a picture of Tommy Thompson with his family sitting on his desk when I went to the D.A.'s office.

"What happened to Thompson's family?" I asked.

"His wife left years ago. After the tragedy. I guess she couldn't handle it."

"What tragedy?"

"His daughter died. She was hit and killed by a car right here on this road. It was such a horrible thing. She was a beautiful girl. And so young..."

"How old was she?" Alex asked.

"She was only twelve years old."

Twelve years old.

Just like Caitlin.

"What was his daughter's name?" I asked.

"Rose. Her name was Rose."

SIXTY

We started with the house. There was no indication anyone was inside. No lights, no movement we could see through the windows. Which made sense. Tommy Thompson was at work in the D.A.'s office, and the neighbor had said he lived alone.

Still, Alex and I did our best to make sure we were alone on the property.

Then we moved on to the rest of it. The wooded area around the house, leading up to the spot where Grant Woods started, didn't reveal anything significant or noteworthy. I'm not sure what we expected to find. Another body lying out there somewhere? A confession note from Thompson? A big wreath of roses left there for us to find? But there was nothing. Nothing at all.

We checked out the garage. It had room for two cars. Only one car was inside. A gray BMW. There was an open spot next to it, probably for whatever car Thompson drove back and forth to work.

Our next stop was the tool shed. It was really big, almost the size of a guest house. There were no windows to look inside, like at the garage and the house. And the door was locked. With a big padlock and chain.

"Do you think we should break in?" I asked Alex.

"Uh, do we have a warrant?"

"No."

"Then that's breaking and entering."

"Which is against the law."

"Unless there's some indication of a life-threatening situation inside."

"Extenuating circumstances, I believe they call it."

"We don't have anything like that here."

"Well, we do have a missing girl in Natalie Jarvis."

Alex and I decided to go back to the house instead, and check that out further. We looked in the windows and knocked on the door. Nothing there we could see or hear. And we had the same problem we had at the tool shed. We didn't have any authority to break in and search further. Not without a warrant or some indication of probable cause of imminent danger to someone inside.

"We need a search warrant," Alex said.

She suggested calling Polk and telling him where we were and what we needed. Which is what we did. It took a bit of convincing with him, but Polk finally agreed we had enough probable cause for a warrant. He said he'd make a few calls, and then get back to us. When he did, he said he'd found a federal judge from a southern district of Ohio located in a courthouse a few towns over from Huntsdale who had agreed to sign off on a search warrant.

All we had to do was pick up the papers, serve them officially on Thompson at his office and then carry out a complete search of his house, garage, tool shed and anything else on the property.

We agreed that Alex would take the car and drive as quickly

as she could to the courthouse. I could walk back into town, it wasn't very far from Thompson's house, and check in at the police station to make sure Weller or Earnshaw were accounted for and couldn't interfere. Then we'd all meet up there with the papers and go to Thompson's office to confront him. I told Alex I'd call Girard to fill him in on the change of plans. He could meet me in town now too, instead of coming out here.

"Okay, Nikki," she said. "But don't do anything stupid. Don't vary from the game plan. Just go back to town and wait for me to come back with the search warrant authorization papers. The calvary's coming. We're gonna do this!"

"I'll go back to town and wait for you," I said.

Except I didn't do that.

I still had the feeling we were missing something at Thompson's place. Something that couldn't wait until Alex got back with the search warrant.

Once Alex was gone, I turned and went back to Thompson's property. Specifically, to the tool shed with the big padlock and heavy chain on the door. Why do you put such a big lock and chain on a tool shed? Well, to make sure no one steals the tools inside, right? Maybe. Or maybe for another reason.

The tool shed really was a big structure. Much bigger than any tool house I'd ever seen before. It was almost the size of a small house. Like maybe someone else lived there just like Thompson lived in the big house. Except this had a big padlock and a chain that didn't let anyone in. Or out.

I'm not sure what I would have done if I hadn't heard the scream then. It was a girl's scream. And it was coming from inside the tool shed. I ran to the garage, looked frantically for something I could use to break the lock on the tool house door and found a heavy-duty looking metal clipper. I went back to the tool house and used it to snap the chain and padlock off the door.

It was not what I expected inside. There was no girl in danger. No one at all was there. It was just a series of computers on tables and big screens on the walls. I realized exactly what this was now. It wasn't a tool shed. It was a viewing room.

And one of the screens had a video playing on it now.

It was a young girl.

Running through some woods.

Looking back on the screen at someone chasing her.

She was screaming.

All of this had been recorded on video that someone—presumably Tommy Thompson—had been watching for some kind of perverted amusement.

I put my gun away and moved closer to the screen so I could see the screaming girl more clearly.

I was able to make out the features on the face now of the terrified young girl.

It was Natalie Jarvis.

She was still alone in the woods. But clearly being pursued as she continued to look back and scream as she ran. I couldn't tell exactly where it was taking place. But, if it wasn't Grant Woods nearby, it was another wooded area that was very similar. I didn't know how long ago this video was taken. Or if there had been more than one video of her.

But I knew what the final outcome would be, if it hadn't happened already. She would be shot and killed.

I took out my phone and started to punch in Alex's number to tell her what I'd found inside the tool house.

But I never got the chance.

I heard someone coming up behind me.

And then I felt the metal of a gun being pressed into my back.

"Drop the phone," a voice said.

I did.

"Now your weapon."

I took out my .9mm Glock from the holster and dropped it carefully at my feet too with the phone.

Then I turned around to face the person talking.

"Enjoying the little show you just saw?" Tommy Thompson said. "There's another video like that I made with your sister too. But then you already knew that, didn't you?"

SIXTY-ONE

There were two of them. Tommy Thompson and another man. Both of them were holding guns pointed at me. I had no idea who the second man was, but I figured he was probably another ex-con like Janos or Butcher that Thompson used to do his dirty work for him.

"Why?" I asked. "Why, Tommy? Why would you do this?"

"Because I can."

He smiled when he said it.

"Did you kill Caitlin?"

He just smiled again.

"My God, you're the District Attorney. Everyone in this town loves you. You were my father's friend."

"I wasn't his friend."

"He thought you were."

"Your father was the reason for all this," he said, pointing to the computers and screens around us.

"What are you talking about?"

"He wouldn't help me."

"Help you with what?"

"Avenge my Rose's death."

I knew I had to keep him talking. That was my only chance. I'd never had time to tell Girard to meet me and Alex in town instead of coming here to Thompson's house. If I could just play for time with Thompson and his gunman, maybe Girard would show up in time. I wasn't sure if an old agent like Girard, who probably hadn't fired his gun in years, could match up with two armed men. I wished it was Alex I was counting on for help instead of Girard. But she was on her way to the courthouse. Phil Girard was all I had to save me.

"Tell me about your daughter," I said to Tommy Thompson.

"Why should I tell you about Rose? Why should I tell Luke Cassidy's daughter a damn thing about my Rose?"

"Because I think you want to," I said.

And, it turns out, I was right. He did want to talk about his dear daughter Rose. Her death had been the moment that changed his life, shaped it even.

"Rose was such a beautiful young girl," he said now. "Adorable face, adorable eyes, adorable smile. Short brunette hair that was always tousled because she was always too excited about something else she was doing to comb it. Tremendously smart too. She wanted to grow up to be a lawyer, just like her dad. Only twelve years old, but she told me that all the time. I was so happy to have her as my daughter. My Rose. And then... then she died. She died on July nineteenth. Does that date sound familiar?"

"The same date my sister disappeared."

"It seemed appropriate to take away your sister on the same date."

I looked over at the guy with the gun. He was just watching, waiting for Thompson to tell him what he wanted him to do with me. It all seemed so unreal, like something out of a bad dream. But I knew this was real. Too real.

"What happened to Rose?" I asked Thompson. "How did she die?"

"It was a beautiful summer day," he said. "She wanted me to drive her into town to see some of her friends. I said I was too busy. She was very upset. And so she decided to walk there on her own. She ran out of the house, then started down the road into Huntsdale. It wasn't very far, but she never made it. A car hit and killed her right there on the side of the road."

I still didn't know what this had to do with my father.

I asked Thompson.

"Your father refused to arrest the driver. He refused to tell me who it was. He refused to avenge my daughter's death. He refused to make sure justice was meted out for what they did to my beautiful Rose.

"At first after her death, I seethed about that. What made it worse was seeing him so happy with you and your sister. Why should he have such beautiful girls when I had lost mine? So finally I decided I wanted him to feel the same kind of pain that I had earlier, and he had refused to help me.

"Then I discovered something. It was the Nowhere Men. People like me who were angry. People who wanted to hurt other people like we'd been hurt. People who were willing to do anything. And, maybe most of all, people who lusted for the thrill of killing. Taking a life like your sister's just for the thrill of it. And telling each other about what we had done and how exciting it was and how rewarding.

"That's when I decided. I would take away Luke Cassidy's daughter just like mine had been taken from me. It could have been you. But Caitlin was close to Rose's age. I would make her dead, just like Rose was dead. And I would record all of it, especially her final agonizing and terrified moments, on video for all the people on the dark web and the Nowhere Men site to see. To watch over and over again..."

"What about the other girls?" I asked. "Natalie Jarvis? Erica Kent? And who knows how many others. Why?"

"I did all that for Rose. To honor Rose on the anniversary of the day I lost her. Caitlin was first because of your father. But the others... well, I was looking for girls just like my Rose had been."

"Only children?" I said, thinking about how Phil Girard had picked up on that. "No brothers or sisters?"

"Yes. The same as Rose. So that when they were gone, there was nothing for the family to have left. The way it was for me when I lost Rose. You were the only one that was different. You survived after Caitlin. But now..."

Thompson looked over at the other man with the gun.

"Should I kill her now?" the man asked.

"Not yet. First, we want to get some video of her. In the woods, like the others. It's going to all be recorded on video, Nikki. Your terror, your struggles and then your death. You're going to be the star of a viral video all over again—only this one will be for a very select group of viewers."

I wanted to keep him talking. Hoping for Girard to arrive—and do something to stop all this. I had one big question for Thompson. A question I wanted to know the answer to before I died.

"What about my father?" I asked. "How much of this did he know?"

"Too much," Thompson said. "Your father figured it out. All about the dark web and the Nowhere Men site and a lot of other stuff. I'm not sure how, but he did. He even managed to get on the site and learn our secrets. Just like you did. But he died before he could do anything about it."

"If only he hadn't had that heart attack..."

"Oh, right, the heart attack." Thompson laughed. "Well, you see, I helped that along. I had to get rid of him. I just made sure it looked like a heart attack."

"You killed my father?"

"He was getting too close to finding out the truth."

"You killed my sister and my father! And now you're going to kill me!"

"I don't think I have any other choice." He turned to the guy with the gun. "Lawrence, go outside and check to make sure that partner of hers isn't around. The other female agent. Then come back and we'll set up the video equipment to make Ms. Cassidy a star here in our world. We'll get all her last minutes in one of the most memorable snuff films ever. Death of an FBI agent. And the sister of Caitlin and daughter of Luke Cassidy."

The guy nodded and went outside to look around. We waited in silence now. There didn't seem to be much else to say.

Finally, the door of the tool shed opened and someone came in.

It wasn't Lawrence, the guy with the gun though.

And it wasn't Phil Girard either.

It was Billy Weller.

And he had his own gun pointed at Thompson.

"Drop your weapon," Billy Weller said to him.

And then all hell broke loose...

SIXTY-TWO

I can't remember exactly what happened after that. It was a blur. The whole thing probably took place in a matter of minutes—or maybe seconds—but it seemed like forever to me at the time.

This is what I do remember.

Billy Weller standing there at the door with his gun out and yelling at Thompson to put his gun down.

But Thompson didn't do that.

He kept it pointed at me.

And he tried to convince Weller instead that he had it all wrong.

"She tried to kill me, Billy," he said. "She went crazy. Claimed I'd killed her sister and a lot of other wild accusations. You know me, Billy. I'm just defending myself against her, that's all. So stop pointing that gun at me and help me take her into custody. We can sort all the rest of this out later."

"No, don't believe him!" I yelled. "He killed my sister and he abducted Natalie Jarvis and he's probably responsible for a lot of other girls' deaths too. Him and this crazy group or cult on this dark web site who call themselves the Nowhere Men. You have to believe me, Billy. He's the killer we've been looking for."

I know Billy wanted to believe me.

I could see that on his face as he looked at me.

But he had to make a big decision—either believe me or the District Attorney that he and the people of Huntsdale had known and trusted all these years.

And so, Billy Weller hesitated. Which is the worst thing any police officer can do during an armed encounter. Once you draw your weapon, you have to be ready to use it. You have to be prepared to use it immediately before it becomes too late. But Billy just stood there staring at us—at me first, then looking at Thompson with the gun in his hand.

I like to think he would have believed me in the end, but I never found out for sure.

Suddenly there was a gunshot.

And Billy Weller fell to the ground.

Standing behind him was the big guy Thompson had called Lawrence, with his gun now pointed at me.

Would he shoot me next?

Would Thompson be the one to shoot me?

Were they still going to keep me alive long enough to star in a video of my death for one of their sick "snuff films?"

All of these thoughts were running through my mind at that moment. But then there was another gunshot. Not from Thompson and not from his gunman, Lawrence. Lawrence suddenly fell to the ground next to Weller. I looked to where the shot had come from and saw someone else at the door. It was Phil Girard. Goddamn it, Phil Girard!

Thompson saw him too now and swiveled around to point his gun at Girard, instead of me.

Girard was still looking down at the gunman on the ground and wasn't going to be able to react in time, I realized.

So I did.

As soon as Thompson had the gun pointed at Girard instead of me, I charged into him as hard as I could, knocking him to the ground. He still had the gun in his hand though. We wrestled for it and I finally got my hand on it. But I couldn't get it away from him. So I used every bit of strength I could muster to turn his hand so that the gun was pointing at him, not at me or Girard.

During the struggle, the gun went off and Thompson's face exploded in blood right in front of me.

He stopped struggling then.

Tommy Thompson was still alive.

But barely....

Girard got on his phone and called for help while I raced to the side of the wounded Billy Weller. Very quickly after that, I knew the place would be flooded with cops, medical people, state troopers and federal agents as we tried to sort it all out. But right now all I cared about was Weller.

He was still conscious, but barely. The bullet had gone into his back and come out his chest. I feared it might have hit either or both his heart and his lungs. The front of his shirt was covered in blood. I was covered in blood too. But it was Thompson's blood. I leaned down as closely as I could to Billy Weller so he could be sure to hear me.

"There's help coming, Billy. Just hang on until it gets here. Hang on for me, okay, Billy?"

He nodded slightly.

He could hear me.

"I-I wanted to show you that you could-could count on me, Nikki," he said to me now as he struggled to talk. "That you could trust me. I knew that you were keeping me out of whatever you were doing because you weren't sure you could trust me. So I followed you today. I watched you to see what you were doing and to see if maybe you needed my help. And then, when I saw you were in trouble, I... I..."

His voice trailed off.

"Thank you, Billy."

"I wanted to show you I was a good cop."

"You are a good cop."

"I'd do anything to save you."

I leaned down and kissed Billy Weller on the lips.

He smiled at me.

That Billy Weller smile.

The smile I loved so much from that first day I met him at the station.

"You know, Nikki, I really should have asked you to the prom," he said. "Who knows what might have happened if I'd done that?"

Then Billy Weller closed his eyes.

I kissed him again and held him tightly.

I held onto him like that until the paramedics arrived and pronounced him dead.

SIXTY-THREE

We found Natalie Jarvis soon after that. Bound and gagged in the attic of Thompson's house. She was in bad shape, slipping in and out of consciousness, but she was still alive.

She eventually told us a story similar to the other girls we knew about: she'd been held captive for days while they filmed scenes of her. And, yes, she was told that the climactic moment would be a video of her actual murder once they were ready to do that. She said there were other men, more than just Thompson. But she didn't know any of them. He was the only person she recognized.

Natalie said she'd gone with him that day at the movies because she knew him, he was the District Attorney. So when he asked her to step outside the theater to discuss something with her, she had no idea anything was wrong.

The most emotional moment, of course, was the reunion of Natalie and her family. Her mother and father hugging her and laughing and crying with joy. It was a beautiful moment. A moment that made everything I had gone through worth it. I was happy for the Jarvis family.

But, at the same time, I couldn't help but feel a bit jealous that I'd never been able to experience that kind of happiness sometime with my family.

Tommy Thompson survived for a few days after the shootout before lapsing into a coma and dying. But it was enough time for him to fill in some of the holes about the heinous crimes he'd committed in the name of his daughter since she died. I guess he was hoping for some kind of a deal or leniency if he made it alive to jail. Or maybe—like David Munroe—he knew he was dying and felt the need to confess at least some of his sins. Thompson's last words before his own death were: "I'm finally going to be able to be with my Rose again."

Most of what he told us were things I'd pretty much already figured out.

When David Munroe—one of the Nowhere Men—was unexpectedly arrested for Caitlin's murder and Thompson was going to be the prosecutor, he had to make sure Munroe never talked about him or the Nowhere Men site. So he used his clout in the legal system to make sure Munroe was safe and well taken care of in prison—in return for his silence.

But when Munroe got sick and decided to tell the truth—or at least part of it—to me, Thompson made sure Munroe was killed in prison. He used convicts and ex-cons like the guy Lawrence at the end and Butcher and Janos—who tried to kill me and Doreen Trask—by helping them get paroles or reduced sentences.

The biggest question I still had was about my father's death: Thompson confessed on his deathbed that he was with my father that last morning when he got his coffee and donuts. While my father was paying, Thompson slipped something into his coffee. Eye drops. Simple Visine eye drops, he said.

Except, as I found out later, eye drops like that—if taken orally—can be dangerous for a person with a heart condition. It dramatically slows down the heart and can cause a plunge in blood pressure—all of which can be fatal to someone with a bad heart. Which is what happened to my father.

Thompson knew that.

That's how he was able to murder my father.

And no one ever had a clue it was anything other than a heart attack.

The story of Rose Thompson's death turned out to be a lot different than I expected. Tommy Thompson had claimed during our confrontation that he knew who killed his daughter on that road—who was driving the car—and that my father had refused for some reason to arrest that person.

According to Thompson, that is what had fueled his rage for revenge against my father by forcing him to feel the pain of losing a daughter, just like he had.

But, according to the records I had found in the old files for the case, there never was any real suspect in his daughter Rose's death.

Thompson said he got the license plate number of a car he saw speeding away, but the owner of that car had a solid alibi which put him and the car at a location more than a hundred miles away at the time of the accident.

There was a theory back then that Thompson himself might have accidentally killed his daughter. That he tried to go after her in his car when she started walking into town and tragically didn't see her until too late on the side of the road.

I found out Thompson's wife left him soon after that, and he was clearly in severe distress for a long time. Maybe he had simply imagined the other car and license plate to avoid dealing with his own inner guilt. And at some point he had actually begun believing his own imaginary story.

Grief does strange things like that to a person.

I only had to look at my own mother to see that.

From what the FBI in Washington were able to determine, the Nowhere Men website had at least a half dozen other people who regularly used to access it, besides Thompson and Munroe.

They were still out there, which was a scary thought.

The Nowhere Men website had been shut down after I got on it, but it wouldn't take much for them to create a new website on the dark web where it was difficult to uncover secret places of evil people and evil deeds like this. And teams were still searching for more bodies in Grant Woods next to Thompson's house.

But we knew about them now—we knew about the Nowhere Men—and would be on the alert to hopefully track the rest down in the future.

Also, the FBI's tech experts were able to access more of the "snuff films" from the Nowhere Men site and match them up with dead or missing young girls from past unsolved cases.

That at least gave the families some kind of closure to deal with their grief.

Law enforcement wasn't perfect.

We can only do so much.

But we got Natalie Jarvis home safe.

And we made sure a monster like Tommy Thompson could never hurt any other young girl.

The funeral of Billy Weller was pretty emotional. The entire town turned out to honor him in death, including Mayor Stacy Harris and Chief Frank Earnshaw. Earnshaw delivered an emotional eulogy—I didn't think he had it in him—about Billy's dedication and devotion and determination to be the best police officer he could.

He said that a picture of Billy Weller would hang prominently at the entrance to the station house with the words: "Huntsdale's Finest—He gave his life in duty for this town. We will never forget." There was a picture of Billy now hanging too above his casket. He was smiling in the picture. That infectious, friendly smile Billy Weller always had.

Even Karin Grieco was there. She came back from Cleveland to say her goodbyes to Billy. She was crying and very emotional, not what you would expect from a professional therapist. Maybe Billy had gotten to her too, just like he did with me. Maybe there was a part of her that had wanted to leave her husband and family to be with Billy. Just like me with Greg. Probably not, but who knows? Billy had that effect on people.

Me, I was crying too. The man had helped save my life, I'd kissed him seconds before he died and... well, there were so many "ifs" about me and Billy Weller. If I'd paid any attention to him in high school, if I'd left Greg earlier and started up a relationship with Billy, if...

I'd never know the answers to any of that.

Doreen Trask is due to have David Munroe's baby this fall, she told me. She didn't understand why Munroe had gotten involved with a group like the Nowhere Men, she still believed he had been basically a good man. I didn't agree with her. But I did know now he was telling the truth when he said he wasn't the one who murdered my sister. It had been Thompson all along.

And he did give me the clue that I needed to discover what Tommy Thompson had done and stop him before he did it again. So there was that.

At some point, Doreen Trask startled me by asking if I would be the godmother of her kid. The godmother of little

David Munroe Jr. She said she thought it might create some kind of closure for all of us. I wasn't sure how to respond.

I'd hated David Munroe for a long time, and I still did. So I wanted to hate his unborn son too. But it's difficult to hate someone who hasn't even been born into this world yet. Even David Munroe's baby didn't deserve that. I told her I'd get back to her.

Phil Girard did a lot of victory laps and got plenty of acclaim afterward for his performance to save the day—not to mention my life—in Huntsdale. All of it was well deserved. "The old guy can still dial it up and come through in the clutch when you need him," he said. I told him he was right about that, and I was sure glad he had stayed around and not gone back to Washington.

He smiled, then went back to the crossword puzzle he was working on at his desk.

You never know about some people.

You think you've got them figured out.

And then they surprise the hell out of you, like Phil Girard did.

Alex was disappointed she wasn't there at the end, but she knew she played a key role in the cracking of the case, too. She was also happy when the *New York Times* did a feature on both of us with a headline that said: WOMEN OF THE FBI: HOW THESE TWO FEMALE AGENTS GOT THEIR MAN.

I got a lot more publicity too. There was a video of me, still covered with blood, from Tommy Thompson and Billy Weller, leaving Thompson's place with Natalie Jarvis after rescuing her from inside. It quickly trended on social media too and I found out I had gone viral again. Not my choice, and I didn't think Les Polk would be too happy about it.

But hey, there are worse things than being famous for fifteen minutes on Twitter because you did something good.

There was one other good thing that came out of all this. I was able to reconnect with my mother. Well, sort of. My brush with death at the Thompson place shootout had been a shock to her. I guess it made her realize that I was the only thing she had left of our family, and she had come very close to losing me that day.

We talked—really talked, as mother and daughter—during those days afterwards.

About my job with the FBI.

About me calling off my wedding plans with Greg.

And even about Caitlin.

I think she was grateful that I had finally made the right man pay for what happened to take Caitlin away from us fifteen years ago.

And I believe it made her feel better in some way to learn that my father had not died of a "broken heart" over Caitlin—that he had a heart condition which would have killed him very soon anyway.

And even though she never came right out and said it, I suppose she was happy too that it was me, her daughter, who had shot and killed Tommy Thompson, the man she now knew was responsible for Caitlin and my father.

But, at the same time, I realized this had opened up old wounds for her. Horrible memories that maybe she thought she had put behind her, but now were part of her life all over again years later.

Maybe she would still blame me on some level for that.

One way or another, I knew our relationship was always going to be a difficult one.

But I was going to try to be there for her, no matter how challenging that might be.

I'd been wrong about Billy Weller being involved with the Nowhere Men. I'd been wrong about Chief Frank Earnshaw too. And I was wrong about Medical Examiner Michael Franze.

I went to his office to tell him that. He was as shocked as anyone about Tommy Thompson. He said he was sorry he wasn't more helpful and friendly to me that last time I was there.

"You see, your father and I were very close friends," Franze said. "But I'd never seen him like that after your sister's murder. He was in a terrible state. And I believe there was something more upsetting even than just your sister's death, as terrible as that was. I believe there was something he discovered in his investigation of Caitlin's murder that was the reason."

"I think he found out about Tommy Thompson," I said.

"How do you know?"

"Well, Thompson told me. He said that's why he killed my father with those eye drops he put in his coffee. That never showed up after my father's death?"

"No. But something common and seemingly harmless like Thompson told you about might not show up. And there was no real autopsy ever done on your father. No reason for one. I mean we knew he had heart disease, and there was no reason to think it was anything other than a death by natural causes."

"Okay, my father had found out about Thompson. He'd found out about the Nowhere Men. And he even went on the website looking for them. What else did he find out? What else was on those missing papers from his official report on the case?"

Franze shook his head.

"I don't know."

"You were his friend."

"That's why I'm telling you the truth now. I really don't know. All I do know is that your father came to me and said he had removed those pages. He said no one could ever see them.

He wouldn't tell me why. But he made me promise—vow to him as a friend—not to ever talk about deleting those pages with anyone. I never have either. I've kept that vow to your father. Until now. After everything that's happened, I guess you have a right to know about it now, Nikki."

"And you never found out what my father removed from the report?"

"I have no idea. I think he would have told me, sooner or later. But he died before he could do that."

SIXTY-FOUR

I was back at the cemetery where Caitlin and my father were buried.

Standing over my father's grave. And thinking about the detective game we used to play on the front porch of our house when I was growing up. The one where he would go over the evidence in a baffling case and challenge me to figure it out. How I almost always would need his help for me to solve the crime.

Well, I'd solved this case on my own.

Or did I?

My father had taken a lot of secrets to the grave with him.

He knew about Tommy Thompson.

He knew about the Nowhere Men site.

What other secrets had been in those pages he deleted from the official police report on my sister's case?

I looked down at my father's grave.

"Am I missing something, Dad?" I said to the tombstone with his name on it. "Is there more to all this that I don't know? What were you hiding about Caitlin at the end? Give me a clue.

Just like you used to when I was a little girl playing police games with you on the front porch."

I stood there for a long time and waited.

But I didn't hear anything.

Except a wind blowing through the trees next to me.

At first, I thought that might be some kind of sign from my father.

A message from beyond the grave.

But then the wind stopped, so I said goodbye to my father and to Caitlin and walked back to my car.

It was only the wind.

Nothing but the wind.

Just my imagination.

It was all just my imagination.

A LETTER FROM DANA

I want to say a huge thank you for choosing to read *The Nowhere Girls*. If you did enjoy it, and want to keep up to date with all my latest releases, just sign up at the following link. Your email address will never be shared and you can unsubscribe at any time.

www.bookouture.com/dana-perry

FBI Agent Nikki Cassidy is a new character for me. Although she has won national acclaim for high-profile arrests, she is still haunted by the one case she's never been able to solve —the abduction and murder of her own twelve-year-old sister when Nikki was a teenager. So we see how obsessed she is about returning to her hometown now as an FBI agent to finally get some answers. But, when more girls go missing and are murdered just like her sister, Nikki must confront the ultimate evil that this town has kept secret for so long.

The setting for this book is different too. I like to write about locations I know first-hand. My first two books were about New York City, where I have lived for many years. The next two were based on the island of Martha's Vineyard off of Cape Cod, where I regularly vacation. And now... well, I'm from Ohio and I went to college there in a small town like where this book is set. Nikki's hometown of Huntsdale is fictional, and the people and events aren't real. But I was certainly inspired by some of my real-life experiences in small Ohio towns to write this story about an FBI agent from Washington returning home to exorcise her own demons and solve the biggest case of her career.

I like Nikki Cassidy. I hope you did too. And there will be more Nikki Cassidy stories coming soon.

Meanwhile, if you did enjoy *The Nowhere Girls*, I would be very grateful if you could write a review. I'd love to hear what you think, and it makes such a difference helping new readers to discover one of my books for the first time

I love hearing from my readers—you can get in touch on my Facebook page, through X, Goodreads or my website.

Thanks,

Dana

www.rgbelsky.com

 facebook.com/DanaPerryAuthor
x.com/DanaPerryAuthor

PUBLISHING TEAM

Turning a manuscript into a book requires the efforts of many people. The publishing team at Bookouture would like to acknowledge everyone who contributed to this publication.

Audio
Alba Proko
Sinead O'Connor
Melissa Tran

Commercial
Lauren Morrissette
Jil Thielen
Imogen Allport

Data and analysis
Mark Alder
Mohamed Bussuri

Cover design
Ghost

Editorial
Helen Jenner
Ria Clare

Milton Keynes UK
Ingram Content Group UK Ltd.
UKHW012011280324
440101UK00004B/359